The Marshal and the Sinister Still

A NELSON LANE FRONTIER MYSTERY

The Marshal and the Sinister Still

C. M. Wendelboe

FIVE STAR
A part of Gale, Cengage Learning

GALE
CENGAGE Learning

Farmington Hills, Mich • San Francisco • New York • Waterville, Maine
Meriden, Conn • Mason, Ohio • Chicago

GALE
CENGAGE Learning

Five Star Publishing, a part of Gale, a Cengage Company

LIBRARY OF CONGRESS CATALOGING-IN-PUBLICATION DATA

Names: Wendelboe, C. M., author.
Title: The marshal and the sinister still / C. M. Wendelboe.
Description: First edition. | Waterville : Five Star, a part of Gale, Cengage Learning, 2019. | Series: A Nelson Lane frontier mystery #2
Identifiers: LCCN 2018025276 (print) | LCCN 2018026011 (ebook) | ISBN 9781432849528 (ebook) | ISBN 9781432849511 (ebook) | ISBN 9781432849504 (hardcover)
Subjects: | GSAFD: Mystery fiction. | Western stories.
Classification: LCC PS3623.E53 (ebook) | LCC PS3623.E53 M374 2019 (print) | DDC 813/.6—dc23
LC record available at https://lccn.loc.gov/2018025276

First Edition. First Printing: January 2019
Find us on Facebook—https://www.facebook.com/FiveStarCengage
Visit our website—http://www.gale.cengage.com/fivestar/
Contact Five Star Publishing at FiveStar@cengage.com

Printed in Mexico
1 2 3 4 5 6 7 23 22 21 20 19

For Rick Cunningham and Tom Walker

ACKNOWLEDGMENTS

I wish to thank the Wyoming State Library and the Hot Springs (Thermopolis, Wyoming) Museum for access to their fine research materials; many friends in and around the Wind River Indian Reservation; and my editors Tiffany Schofield and Alice Duncan. And for my wife, Heather, who puts up with all my 'puter illiteracy and always comes through to fix my mistakes and give me encouragement.

Chapter 1

When the phone rang, I suspected I'd made a mistake returning to my office to pick up my creel and fly rod. I hesitated for the longest moment, looking over the new batch of flies I'd tied this last week, before I closed the lid and picked up the receiver.

"We need you over here," Yancy Stands Close sputtered into the phone. "Darla Lone Tree's missing."

"Thought the Lone Trees still lived on the reservation."

The Wind River tribal policeman held his answer like a trained actor. "They do. Got a ranch the other side of Ethete."

I felt a headache coming on, as I usually did when Yancy called about some perceived emergency. "Slow down and tell me just why a US marshal ought to be traipsing over to the rez looking for a missing person."

"Will Lone Tree," Yancy answered, as if that were the only explanation necessary. I opened the top of the creel and took out the small Bakelite box containing the fly assortment as I thought about Will. William Tell Lone Tree had been the bane of Wind River tribal policemen in his drinking days. He'd never met a policeman he liked, nor one he hadn't fought with and beaten. In his drinking days.

"I'm listening," I said and set the box back into the creel. A hook jabbed my thumb, and blood dripped from my finger onto the floor. The county was gracious enough to let me have an office in the courthouse. Just not gracious enough to forgive staining their beat-to-hell hardwood floors. "You got one minute to make your case," I told Yancy, "then I'm out of here and on my way to a nice little mountain stream I hear is running cutthroat trout right now."

"Okay," Yancy said. "Okay." He paused for a moment before making his plea. "Will's daughter, Darla, never came home. And Will's turning the reservation upside down looking for her."

"How old's Darla?"

"Seventeen."

"Has she ever run away from home before?"

"She didn't run away," Yancy answered.

"How do you know?"

"Will said so," Yancy said with as much conviction as a drummer pedaling prophylactics at a nunnery.

"And he's never lied to you?" I asked as I rooted through my cluttered desk drawers until I found a roll of black tape. I tore off some and pasted it around my bloody finger. "You haven't said one thing that convinces me a federal marshal ought to look for a missing person."

"Will specifically asked for you," Yancy blurted out. "He won't tell me squat. Says us damn Shoshones never did anything for him. I told him the damn Arapaho never did anything for us, neither."

I stood and grabbed my fly rod, so inviting in my hand: the heft, the familiar feel. "He'll tell you if he wants to find his daughter."

"Damn it, Nels, we got to find her. She might be out here hurt somewhere."

I slipped my arm through the handle of my creel. A mountain brook was calling my name, and I dropped an apple in the creel for later. "You say Darla's seventeen?" I asked. My second mistake that day.

"She is," Yancy answered. "Not much older than your Polly."

Now it was my turn to curse. Not at Will, but at Yancy for hitting below the belt and bringing my daughter up. In a few years Polly would be as old as Darla. And if she went missing, I'd want someone—even an aging US marshal—out looking for her.

I set my creel back onto the floor and hung my fly rod across the pegs on the wall in back of my desk. I needed all hands free while I tried one last time to talk my way out of a long drive. "Do you know how far it is from Bison to Ft. Washakie?"

"Little over two hundred miles," Yancy answered.

"Then call Maris."

"I tried," Yancy said. Maris Red Hat—the Southern Cheyenne I'd worked with on a fugitive case while she was a deputy sheriff in Oklahoma—was my newest hire. I had gotten grief over hiring a woman as a deputy US marshal and shrugged it off. When she had lost a rigged sheriff's election in El Reno, she was out of a job. And I was out a deputy, since my last one quit to travel the country selling women's brassieres and corsets. Maris seemed like a good deal to me. "She drove up to Cody to serve some eviction papers at a ranch up thataway."

"Again?"

" 'Fraid so," Yancy said.

It seemed to me nowadays that we marshals served far more foreclosures and evictions than we investigated crimes. *Damned Depression.* "Leave criminal work to the Bureau of Investigations," Senator Kendrick told me one day when we were out putting the sneak on a herd of pronghorns during season. "J. Edgar Hoover is trying to expand his organization, and the only way to do that is to leave the real police work to them."

I'd disagreed with the senator, which accounted for him missing a fifteen-inch buck. Or so he claimed. "I've seen very few Bureau agents who travelled out in the middle of nowhere," I told him as I dropped the buck for him. "It gives them pretty boys little glory to come out here to Wyoming. Hell, they might get lost."

"When can you get here?" Yancy pressed, knowing that—when he played dirty and brought up my daughter—I had little choice but to go.

"By the time I pack, it'll take me until nightfall to get there." Even with the motor just rebuilt, it would take me a while to get through the Big Horns. Yancy knew the rigors of driving roads that changed two thousand feet within a mile. "And Yancy"—I paused for effect—"you better have a decent place for me to sleep, and some victuals if I'm driving that far."

"I'd expect no less if it were me," Yancy said and hung up before I could talk myself out of it.

I looked a last time at my fly rod and suspected that it would be some time before I held it again.

I started down the other side of the Powder River Pass, and the new Ford picked up speed too fast for my liking. Soon, I'd have to grab lower gears so I could make it down Ten Sleep Canyon without burning up my brakes. The old surplus army ambulance I drove this spring never made it without some problems. I always had to pull to the side of the road to wait for the brakes to cool, and I'd wanted to buy something else to replace the old agony wagon. The government's five cents a mile just never seemed to cover the maintenance. So, when a Burlington Railroad freight car derailed outside Gillette, the load of grain waffled the old Dodge I'd parked beside a diner next to the tracks. The railroad felt obligated to pay me for my truck. Not compensation for a new truck. Just enough so I could buy another beater like the one they wrecked.

The thousand-foot drop-offs made my stomach queasy every time I drove this road. Today was no exception, and I concentrated on making sure this truck lasted as long as the Dodge. I held my breath as I downshifted into second to make a sharp hairpin loop, then it was nearly straight down again. But it was a whole lot safer than the ambulance. I'd picked this delivery up for a song when two pistons burned up on the previous owner. McColley's Funeral Home in Sheridan bought the delivery to convert into a hearse. McColley had beefed up the suspension to handle heavy coffins, and he slapped two Stromberg carbs on it to give it more power to motor to back-country plots with the dearly departed riding in back.

The road took a marked ascent, and I was grateful for the power as I grabbed first. When McColley said the Ford vapor-locked on him in the summer, and the fuel pump froze up on him this spring, I saw an opening. "Good riddance," he said after I made my offer. "I'm buying a Lincoln." In less than a weekend I'd replaced the burnt pistons and isolated the fuel pump to prevent vapor-lock. I could live with the high oil consumption, but at least when I shifted, it was through synchronized gears. Which Dodge didn't have in 1922. Ford brochures claimed eighty miles an hour with the new V-8. As the road once again took a steep downward attitude, the Ford picked up speed.

I never wanted to test Ford's claim, so I doubled-clutched into second when I smelled the odor of hot brakes and made the switchback coming out of Ten Sleep Canyon at a crawl. By the time I rolled into the sleepy little mountain town of Ten Sleep, the odor was gone, and I pulled into the Esso Station along Highway 16.

I pried the seat cushion out of my kiester and stepped outside to stretch. A stooped old man half again my age limped out of the station buckling the straps of his bib overalls. He grabbed the gasoline nozzle.

"Three gallons should do," I said.

He began to pump the fuel and tapped the fender. "I bet you

need oil for this beauty," he said through a mouth devoid of teeth. "They usually do."

"You got a good eye," I said. "Top off the oil, too."

I took off my Stetson and wiped the band with my bandana before I stepped inside the station. The old man held onto the oil rack as he painfully bent and filled an oil jar, and I felt sorry for him, having to work at his age. But I felt even sorrier for the quarter of the population of Wyoming who didn't have *any* job in this damned Depression. Those were the ones I pitied, even though those were also the ones I had to foreclose on.

A woman—she could have been the old man's twin, and I imagined them sharing teeth—sat behind a glass display case full of used guns, hunting knives, and boxes of ammunition. A Mahjongg board was being used as a coaster for her chipped coffee cup, and she eyed me suspiciously as tobacco juice dribbled down one side of her mouth. "You here for the hunting?"

I opened the top of the pickle barrel beside a pot-bellied stove and speared the biggest dill I saw. "I didn't realize it was hunting season just yet. Not much for hunting hereabouts in the summer."

Her smile faded. "There's always something to hunt around here when you're hungry." She got off her stool and lumbered around the corner of the glass display. She looked up at me and cocked an eye. Or was it two eyes? I couldn't tell through her Coke-bottle spectacles. "Sheriff Darcy ain't sent you here by any chance."

I dipped a ladle into a stone water container on the counter and took a long sip before trickling some down the back of my neck. "Why is that?"

"He likes to stick his nose into Washakie County business."

I assured her Darcy had not sent me. Milo Darcy had been the sheriff in neighboring Hot Springs County for the past eight years. I'd spoken with Milo a time or two. Now and again I came into his county hunting fugitives, much to his displeasure, and I kept away from him as much as I could. But Milo kept his job—it was rumored—because he did favors for people. All sorts of favors. And they, in turn, did favors for him. He always drove the newest car one could buy, and his house in the mountains outside Thermopolis would put the governor's mansion to shame. A lot came from his wife's old money, it was said, and Milo went out of his way to flaunt his good fortune.

"If you ain't here hunting, what the hell you doin' in these parts?" the old woman said just as the duffer came in from pumping me gas and oil. " 'Cause most folks just pass on by rather than stop."

I pulled my vest back to reveal my badge. She stiffened as she eyed the corner behind the door where a shotgun stood propped against the wall. "We don't cotton to revenuers—"

"I'm not a revenuer," I told her. "And, like you said, I'm just passing through."

Even after she wrote me out a receipt I could turn into the government for reimbursement, the old woman continued eying me like I was fixing to haul her in. But right now, the only thing I wanted was to get to Wind River before nightfall. I really didn't want to do any of that hunting she talked about when the deer came out onto the roads at night. I'd paid too much for the Ford to sport a mulie as a hood ornament.

Yancy sat at the Ethete Store in his Chevy truck, headlight on, picking his fingernails with a knife as I drove up. He set his knife on the dash and hopped out to meet me even before I rolled to a stop. "Thank God you're here, Nels."

Yancy usually dressed like he was headed for a barn dance, which he often was when he got the chance. It's where the ladies were. But even the darkness couldn't hide the grime on his shirt and denims. "I am *so* glad to see you." He shook my hand like he was priming a water pump.

I took possession of my hand before he dislocated it. "You look like you've been busy."

He took out a pouch of Bull Durham and papers and began rolling a smoke. The wind blew tobacco into his eyes, and by the time he'd licked the paper, his cigarette wasn't much bigger around than a pencil lead. He never was adept at rolling a smoke. "I been putting out fires is what I been doing." He sucked in air, and the paper flared up once before dying out. He waved his hand around as if it encompassed the entire Wind River Reservation where the Arapaho and Shoshone co-existed. "Will Lone Tree's been beating hell out of whoever he comes across that he thinks might know where Darla is hiding."

"Then I'd better pay him a visit. I'll follow you."

Yancy batted sparks that had dropped onto his shirt front. "Not that easy. His sister told me Will drove to Crowheart to talk with one of Darla's friends. He'll most likely stay there until morning."

I drew a match across my dashboard and held it to my Waltham. "Just as well. We can hunt him up in the morning. It's late. I've had a long day, and I'm starved."

"Nels." Yancy seemed to back away from the Ford just a mite. "I got a place lined up for you, but it's not much."

"Any place will do as long as I can get some shut eye."

Yancy smiled wide. "In that case, I think you'll be plumb happy with your accommodations."

CHAPTER 2

"You have got to be shitting me! A teepee?"

Yancy forced a smile. "I had to come up with some place to stay on short notice last week."

"I thought you were renting a room from the widow Eagle Plume?"

"I got . . . a little too friendly with her, and she had to kick me out of the house real sudden like."

"I don't understand," I said. "I thought she *wanted* you to get friendly. Last we spoke, you two were thinking about walking down the aisle to wedded bliss."

"Me too." Yancy pulled the canvas flap aside. I tucked my bedroll under my arm and ducked and wiggled through the doorway of the teepee as I followed him inside. Yancy grabbed a lantern hanging by a nail to one of the poles and struck a match to it. "Until old man Eagle Plume came home one night. Seems like he wasn't actually dead like she claimed but spending the last four years in the state penitentiary in Rawlins."

"Bet that was a shock. What was he in for?"

Yancy shrugged. "He wasn't an Arapaho, he was a Slap-a-ho."

"How's that?"

"Seemed like he liked to rough up his ho—that being the former-widow Eagle Plume. Anyway, the damned parole board let him out early, and I had to vacate the house, so to speak, on the run." He swung the lantern like a railroad brakeman. "So, this is the best I can do until I find another place."

He hung the lantern back on the nail and stood waiting for my reaction to his new place. He had made it his home, as much as a forty-year-old bachelor could. He had strung a rope across one part of the teepee for a clothesline, where his signature white shirt hung drying beside a pair of patched faded denims. A pair of underwear with more holes than my socks dripped water beside the jeans. A single army cot sat nestled between a milk crate Yancy used for a clothes dresser, and gear he might need for work: a Winchester rifle in a scabbard; snowshoes affixed to the side of a pack for when the weather turned sour this fall. I hoped he had a place to stay before then.

In the center of the teepee a fire burned and spat tree sap under a Dutch oven suspended over the fire. Next to the pot hung a tin coffee pot, and I feared it contained Yancy's coffee. "I see only one cot," I said as I looked around the teepee.

"You got a good grasp of things, Nels. I only have the one. I would have begged another someplace, but—no offense—you're a little too big for a cot anyway. You'd just break it."

"At least there's room enough to spread out my bedroll," I said and dropped it on the ground opposite Yancy's cot. "Now where's those victuals you promised." I nodded to the Dutch oven.

Yancy grinned a perfect set of pearlies. "My famous antelope stew," he said proudly. "Have a seat, and I'll dish it up."

I sat on the ground in front of the fire, thinking of the last time I ate antelope stew. Growing up on a ranch, we'd butcher a steer every year and only occasionally ate the wayward deer or antelope dumb enough to wander through the yard. I had hunted them a time or two when I came back from the war, because Helen liked wild game, but hadn't since she died ten years ago. Still, prepared properly, it could be tasty.

I accepted the bowl of stew from Yancy and scooted toward

the poles so I could rest my back against one. My spoon found a piece of parsnip and chunk of cabbage, and I let it linger in my mouth a moment before swallowing. "What do we know about Darla Lone Tree?"

Yancy's spoon paused mid-mouth. "Will's sister, Josephine, tells me Darla's one of the new generation of Shoshone. She cut her hair short in one of those goofy flapper styles, because that what white women been doin'. And because it pisses her dad off."

Yancy blew on the stew. "She dyed her hair red for the same reason and uses more makeup than Joan Blondell. Josephine says every time she does stuff like that, it drives Will nuts. And pleases the hell out of Darla."

I spooned a chunk of potato, and another shard of cabbage, and washed it down with Yancy's bitter coffee. "And Will claimed she never ran away before?"

"Never. She's stayed out overnight a time or two but never ran away."

"Do you believe him?"

"I believe his sister," Yancy said. He ladled more stew into his bowl, but I waved seconds away. I was hungry, just not *that* hungry. "Josephine said Darla never got a chance to run away. She said Will keeps too tight a rein on the girl."

I moved my spoon around the bottom of the bowl, and held it to the lantern. Perhaps it was the poor kerosene Yancy was using, but I could not find a single piece of meat. "I thought you said this was your famous antelope stew?"

"It would have been," he said as he finished his bowl, "but I missed the shot yesterday. But I promise you"—he stabbed the air with his spoon—"before you leave the rez, I'll make sure you get some meat in that big belly of yours."

I awoke the next morning when Yancy ducked through the door

wearing the clean white shirt and the jeans I'd seen hanging on his clothesline last night. Newly washed clothes dripped water where he had hung them this morning. His stag-handled revolver was strapped to his belt, and his medicine bundle—a small, rawhide lizard—hung from his neck by a leather thong. "Good morning," he said too cheerily for my taste. "Fresh coffee waiting."

I eyed the pot and shook my head. "I'm good."

"Then I'm betting that if we get to Will's house early enough, Josephine will feed us."

I sat up and pulled on my boots. "You got this panhandling thing down pat."

Yancy shrugged. "What's an unmarried guy to do when the love of his life kicks him out hungry?"

"Yancy," I said as I grabbed onto a teepee pole to stand, "every woman you meet is the love of your life."

"Well, this morning it's Josephine. Let's get going."

I stood erect and stretched. Despite sleeping on the ground, I felt refreshed. The teepee had stayed warm. Almost cozy and comfortable, if one discounted Yancy's snoring.

"We'll take your new truck," he said as he snuffed the fire out. "I've never ridden in anything fancy like that."

"You'll be disappointed," I told him. "There's nothing fancy about it. It's just newer than the old agony wagon." I opened up my rucksack and took my razor and shaving mug out. "Where'd you wash your clothes?"

"Why?"

"I need to knock the whiskers off. Might as well be the same place you washed."

Yancy grinned sheepishly. "Hundred yards north is a tribute of the Popo Agie. That's where I washed my grubbies this morning." He poured the last of the coffee over the coals. "But if you're shaving and brushing your teeth, you better do it upstream from that big red rock I squatted over this morning."

I steered the panel around an emaciated steer shuffling across the road. The truck kicked up fine dust that swirled around us, and Yancy patted dust off his shirt. "When did you say Maris was coming back to Riverton?"

When I hired her, I stationed her in Riverton, a small off-reservation town centrally located to respond to calls on this side of the state. With only two deputies in Wyoming to help me, I needed someone willing to live in Riverton who could swing over to Casper or Rock Springs if needed. But, most importantly, I needed her in Riverton because it was close to the Arapaho-Shoshone reservation. Lot of good that did me now, with her serving foreclosures up north around Cody. "She's supposed to come home tomorrow."

"Maybe she'll want to go into Lander when she comes home and grab supper."

"Maybe," I said. But I doubted it. When I invited Maris and her uncle Byron to come up for a visit after she lost the election, she and Yancy hit it off immediately. They had one major thing in common—they both liked seeing folks of the opposite sex naked. But when she moved here, her fling with Yancy lasted all of two weeks before she moved on. Given her propensity to bed as many men as possible in the years she had left on this earth, I figured Yancy did okay keeping her interested for a couple weeks.

Yancy directed me to take a fork in the road headed northwest. "Will's place is along Sage Creek at the base of Juniper Butte. He runs about twenty head of cows and a few hogs." That was twenty head of cows and some hogs more than most folks hereabouts had. The reservation had been particularly hard hit by this Depression, and Yancy told me fully half the men on Wind River were out of jobs. That would explain the lack of deer and antelope I was used to seeing on the rez—those men had to eat something.

We crossed a dry creek bed that ran across the road, and we continued along the two-track for another mile before we popped over a hill that overlooked Will's spread situated on the floor of a shallow valley. Cows grazed on drought-wilted grass in a scrub field to one side of the ranch house, and hogs squealed and ran out of the way of the truck when we pulled up to the house.

Even before I stopped the panel in front of a hitching post beside the front porch, a small woman emerged and strode out to the truck. She would come up to my chest—if she stood on the milking stool propped against a fence—and her braided gray hair bounced as she stomped toward us. She stood with her hands on her hips as she eyed me unfolding myself from the Ford.

"That the marshal you said was happy to come here and talk with Will?" she asked Yancy as if I weren't there.

"That's him, grandmother," Yancy said with the title of respect to one of the elders.

She turned on her heels and walked up to me. "I hope you can talk some sense into that brother of mine. He has about gone off his rocker," she tapped the side of her head, "looking for Darla."

"I'll do what I can."

She turned and headed for the house. "Then come inside, and we can jaw over breakfast."

"Told you." Yancy nudged me and led the way to the breakfast table.

We entered the one-story ranch house, and I noticed it had more amenities than most hereabouts. We passed through a neat washroom, folded flour sack towels hanging on antler pegs above a double sink. Beside the sink clodhoppers half again as big as my boots and caked with dirt and manure sat on a rag rug. We passed through the kitchen on our way to the dining room, and the odor of cooking meat and hot bacon grease drifted past my nose as I trailed Yancy.

William Tell Lone Tree sat at a rough-hewn oak table staring down at a mug of coffee. He looked up, and it took a moment for his red-rimmed eyes to focus on me. He stood to his full height, and I instantly recalled why I hadn't wanted to fight him that day after the rodeo when I was a kid. Even back then, he towered over me, and I was lucky to get the first hard shot in to start the party. Now, he still towered over me—which was no small feat—and had me by thirty pounds. Which was even more amazing. Like me, he had wintered well. Unlike his scrawny livestock.

He walked around the table and stopped, looking down at me. His stubble hadn't been touched in days, and his sweat-stained shirt was torn at the sleeve. As if he'd spent the last few days looking for his daughter.

He thrust out his hand, and I shook it. His grip was firm, as I expected of a man his size, and his rough calluses showed me Will was used to hard work. When he wasn't gallivanting around threatening people to find his daughter anyways. "Been a while, Nels."

"Wind River Rodeo. Nineteen-seventeen," I answered. "Year before Dad died."

"And a year before you went into the Marines," Will said.

"You got a good memory."

Will smiled for the briefest second as he rubbed the mis-shapen nose I'd given him in back of the bull chutes that day. "Let's say I waited for the next year so I could stomp a mud hole in your butt, but you were off to war by then."

"Hope you're over it," I said.

"I got over it," Will said, and turned his attention to Yancy.

"Unlike the damned Shoshones. I'll never get over them—"

"Let it be, Will Lone Tree," Josephine said as she stepped between Yancy and her brother. She craned her head up to look him in the eye. "He is here with the marshal to help you."

Will turned back to the table, mumbling something about how one can't trust a Shoshone, and sat at the table

"Sit," Josephine said. "I will get breakfast."

I pulled up a chair across from Will, while Yancy wisely took a seat at the end of the table out of the reach of Will's long arms.

"I am glad you came, Nels," Will said.

I nodded to Yancy. "You can thank him for that."

Will guffawed. "First time I ever had anything to thank a Shoshone for."

"I said that is enough." Josephine carried a plate of flapjacks and set it in the middle of the table beside a jar of molasses syrup.

"But he is just like the rest of the tribal policemen—never lifted a finger to help before—"

"Leave it be." She disappeared into the kitchen and returned within moments with a platter of bacon. She handed out utensils and motioned to the food. "Dig in while we visit."

Will looked at the food and scooted his chair back. "Got to see a man about a horse." And he slammed the back door in leaving for the outhouse.

Josephine sat at the table warming her hands around a hot mug of coffee and looking after her brother. "Sorry, Yancy. Since Marcella died, he never had any use for tribal police. Especially you Shoshone."

But then *most* Arapaho had little use for a Shoshone, and vice versa. When some genius working for the government decided to throw two tribes together to live on the same reservation, they couldn't have done any worse than to throw mortal enemies—the Shoshone and the Arapaho—onto the same land.

I put two flapjacks on my plate, then—so as not to offend the cook—put another to join the bacon strips already there. "Was Marcella another of Will's children?" I asked.

"Marcella was his wife," Josephine answered.

"Found froze in a snow bank a couple years before I started," Yancy said between mouthfuls of food.

Josephine stood and grabbed the coffeepot warming on the Franklin. She refilled our mugs and sat back down. "Will used to drink a lot back in his hell-raising days. Him and Marcella both."

"I remember when we were younger travelling the rodeo circuit I saw him many times," I said. "And most of the times he was schnockered-up."

"That is how Will and Marcella met." Josephine forced a laugh. "How many relationships here on the reservation start over a bottle. But Will gave up drinking when Darla was"—she looked at the ceiling—"ten or eleven."

I sipped the coffee between bites. It was strong, something I hoped Yancy would learn from her.

"But Marcella did not stop when Will did," Josephine continued. "She thought of nothing else besides getting that next drink." She held up her hand. "But do not expect me to tell you who supplied her with her booze. No offense, Marshal, but we do not like revenuers coming on to the reservation."

"I wasn't going to ask." During my drinking days, and for much of my lawman career, I bought illegal hooch from my own source. Even once I got clean and sober, I never thought about busting the moonshiners. I left that to government agents.

Will came back into the house and made a stop at the coffee pot. I could tell he had been crying, and he turned and swiped a hand across his eyes when he thought I wasn't looking. "Can you find my girl for me?"

"I'll try." I took out a piece of paper and pencil stub from my pocket and laid the paper flat on the table. "Yancy said Darla went missing four days ago."

Will nodded.

"Why did you not call the tribal police that first day?"

Will pointed to Yancy, who had speared another piece of bacon. "The night Marcella failed to come home from drinking with friends, I called the police then. They could do nothing, they said. She will come home on her own, they said. They never even looked for her, even though it was snowing out." He downed his coffee and brushed a napkin across his chin. "That morning they sure found her—froze to death in a snow bank as she was walking home. I was afraid they'd no nothing again with Darla." He leaned across the table. "I am afraid she is headed on the path her mother took."

"I do not know how," Josephine said, "as close a watch as you keep on that girl."

"If I did not, she would wind up just like her mother."

Will's voice had risen, and Josephine held up her hand. "Do not raise your voice with me Will Lone Tree. Just tell the marshal what you know."

Will looked into his coffee cup and took a deep breath before beginning. "Four days ago Darla was going to spend the day with her friend Wanda Bent. She lives next to St. Stevens. But Darla never showed." He sipped the last of his coffee and set the cup down. "I have been looking for her—"

"You mean you have been terrorizing folks on the reservation looking for her." Josephine shook her head and turned her back on her brother. "Darla is a good girl, Marshal—don't get me wrong. But she is night and day different from her friend. Wanda and her aunt, who is raising her, live the traditional life. Keep to themselves. Kick up no dust. But Darla's always had a wild streak in her. Like her mother."

"And she drinks now," Will blurted out. "That is why I

thought Wanda would be a good influence on Darla. Wanda does not drink."

Yancy finished his second plate of bacon and flapjacks and sat back, dabbing his mouth with a napkin. "Perhaps the one she bought the booze from knows something." He held up his hand and turned to Josephine. "I know you don't want to say who she buys her hooch from, but it may be the best shot we have of finding her."

Josephine shrugged. "I think it is that Italian man who moved by Thermopolis two years ago. He supplies many of our people."

"Do not waste your time talking with him," Will said.

"You know something you're not telling us?" I asked him.

Will stood, and his chair creaked. He started to pace in front of the table, gathering his words carefully. "The first time I realized Darla had started to drink was last fall. I traded a yearling calf to a hunting guide if he would take Darla on an elk hunt. I thought if she got a taste of the old ways—"

"And you had her dress out that whole bull elk," Josephine said, shaking her head. "Imagine a young girl doing that."

"It is the way we did it in the old time," Will said.

"I am older than you," Josephine said, "and I never have had to dress out an elk. Or pack it down a mountain alone like you made her do."

"Why do you think that's when Darla started drinking?" I said quickly.

"When a man is addicted to the booze like I was," Will began slowly, "he can tell when another man has been drinking. You know what I mean, Nels."

I knew just what Will talked about. Since I went on the wagon years ago, I could tell all the way across a room if a person has been drinking, even without the telltale smell. I just *knew* by the way in which their eyes looked, or the way in which they fought to maintain their balance, or a dozen other little tells a person can't hide. Will knew I had once been a boozer. Did he know I drank at the same time I was enforcing criminal laws? If he did, he gave no indication.

"If I knew that guide was gonna' get Darla started on booze, I would have never agreed to let her hunt with him."

Josephine used the arms of the chair to stand and walked to a radio in one corner of the dining room. She grabbed a photo propped against a whitened buffalo thigh bone atop the Philco and handed me the picture frame. "That was taken this spring," she told me, tracing Darla's form with a finger. "At that carnival in Lander. Take it with you. Maybe someone seen her."

I took the photo out of the frame and put it inside my vest pocket. "I'll pay her supplier a visit. Not to arrest him, just to find out when she was there last. Give me a name."

"Axle Denny," Will said and began writing down directions to his place. But Will needn't have wasted pencil lead. I knew just where Axle lived—out of the way with few neighbors around to see who came and went. I'd been there many times during my drinking days. Picking up my own month's supply of bathtub gin.

Chapter 3

"You going to be all right meeting up with Axle Denny?" Yancy asked after we'd been back in my truck for a few miles. "After all, it's been four years since you talked with him."

"Four years, seven months, and a day," I answered as I downshifted to pull a steep hill. "Been that long since I last bought booze from him." Yancy had broached the subject of my addiction years ago when he first hired on with the tribal police. He'd heard it through the moccasin telegraph that I'd once been an alkie, and it caused him concern that I wouldn't be able to assist reservation police like I should. "I'll be all right if I don't go off on Axle. What the hell's he thinking, getting a young girl started on the booze?"

"If he *is* the one." Yancy took out his makin's and started rolling a smoke. I turned my head away from the loose tobacco blowing over his shirt front as he tapped tobacco in the paper. I'd have given him a factory cigarette if he'd just asked. "I'm thinking that other person Josephine talked about—that Italian guy—would be good for it, too. Word is that old Gustavo Napoli had to flee Chicago right ahead of Capone's enforcers. Seems like Capone didn't cotton to Gustavo cutting into his business."

"If this Napoli character were that much a threat to Capone," I said as I grabbed a lower gear, "he wouldn't be on this side of the grass." I stopped to allow a mulie doe to cross the road. She only glanced at us. If this were hunting season, she'd be nowhere to be found.

"I don't know—I've been hearing whispers that Gustavo's been selling to whoever from the rez wants a jar of his shine."

"If he's such a big operator, how would a young girl like Darla get close to him?"

"Beats me," Yancy said. "That's why I called you—to figure out these things. I just put theories out there for you to prove. You might say I'm the thinking part of our team, and you're the proving part."

"Or I might not say that."

While the truck was stopped, I took the opportunity to do dust control and stepped outside. After I checked the wind, I said over my shoulder to Yancy, still in the car, "I'm betting Axle sold Darla the booze. He'll sell liquor to anyone. You'd be surprised at the people I saw coming and going from his place the times I drove there to buy mine."

I buttoned my denims and hopped back in the car. "But I'll be all right."

"I'll go along with you, if you need me to, even though Axle's ranch isn't on the reservation," Yancy said. "But as I recall from the one time I met him in Lander, he doesn't like us Indians."

I laughed. "Axle Denny doesn't like anyone. I was surprised he took Will and Darla on that elk hunt."

"A fresh beef would look mighty good after all you've been eating is deer and antelope and the occasional elk."

"At least he'd have meat to put in *his* stew."

We spent the next half hour talking about Yancy's favorite subject—Maris. Try as I might, I couldn't convince him that she was interested in most men she met. All sorts of men. And the two weeks she and Yancy were an item was about all she could take of one suitor. Even one as smooth and debonair as Yancy thought he was.

I drove across the field to his teepee and let him out. "Maybe you ought to ask if you can stay at the tribal office until you get back on your feet."

"I'm like a cat." He grinned. "I always land on my feet."

"Then land your way into the telegraph office and send this." I jotted Maris's room number at the Irma Hotel in Cody where she was staying. "Tell her to get down here and meet me in Thermopolis."

"You getting frisky?"

"At my age? Not hardly. I'm just going to turn this missing-person case over to her. That trout stream is still calling my name."

I drove the road paralleling the Wind River, five-hundred foot cliffs keeping watch on both sides of the road. I was as much in awe today as I was when I drove through these canyons with my father on our way to a fishing spot. I looked over and saw the river flowing considerably slower than it had in years past because of this drought. When Dad and I steered a makeshift raft down the rapids when I was twelve, the river was high. The current strong. The rapids frightening, giving me more nightmares than I'd ever had. Until I went over to France during the war.

I slowed, taking my time driving to Thermopolis, enjoying the beauty of this part of the reservation. When I pulled into town, it was noon, and my gullet told me it was time for lunch.

I drove through town and fell in behind a tour bus with *YELLOWSTONE PARK* pasted on the side. A faded picture of a grizzly bear battling a buffalo adorned one side. Asian tourists piled out of the bus: at least someone had enough money for a vacation. Guess the Depression hadn't hit them like it did here in America.

I pulled to the curb between two diners, a sign that directed people to the state bath house in front of the cafés. Dad and I had soaked the aches of a hunting trek away in the mineral hot springs whenever we made it down here, and I dearly wished I had time for a soak right now. But I wanted to notify Sheriff Darcy about working in his county. Besides, my stomach had other ideas than soaking in the pools.

I looked over the two diners, and it didn't take me long to decide where to eat. The Asians had poured into Delmonico's, and local cars were parked two deep in front. I'd never get any service. Besides, the diner next to it was named Mom's. How could a person ever go wrong eating at Mom's? Perhaps I recalled my mother's cooking, or Helen's when she was alive. Maybe I was thinking back to the fine breakfast I had in Josephine's kitchen this morning. Later, I'd try to figure out just what the hell I *was* thinking picking Mom's.

There were empty spaces in front of Mom's, and I stopped. I climbed out and had arched my back, stretching, when two women tourists ran up to me. I had little experience with Asians, but one explained in broken English they were from Japan. They were excited to meet a real, living wild-West marshal and asked to take my picture with each of them. *Dozo.*

They directed me to stand beside the bronze statue of a mountain man in front of Mom's, and, in turn, each sidled up next to me and made sure my vest was pulled back to show my badge for the photo. They thanked me and bowed more times than I could count, and I thought how they created an instant celebrity in me. Like Douglas Fairbanks. Or Edward G. Robinson. Except not quite so handsome.

Feeling pretty good about my recent notoriety, I stepped into Mom's. A cow bell over the door announced my entrance, and I took a booth. Including me, there was one customer in the café, and I grabbed a menu that looked as if it had just been printed. Or at least had no one else open it.

A woman emerged from the kitchen—early seventies by her looks—and she stopped as if surprised that a customer had entered her place. She cocked her straw cloche hat sporting a feathered headband and hitched up her skirt with the dropped waistline. She must have some success in the diner business if she could afford as much Ingram's rouge and Nadine Face Powder as she had pasted on. And her lips were painted a bright red that created a rosebud pout—the bee-stung lips the ladies wore in the cities. In short, she looked like an old prostitute with one foot on a banana peel.

She shook off her surprise and sauntered over to the booth. "Howdy," she said, waving a cigarillo around. "You must be *real* hungry."

"How'd you guess?"

"Because you're here instead of Delmonico's," she said and exaggerated a look over me. "And because you look like someone used to eating."

"Only if it's good."

She shrugged. "You'll be the judge." She held out her hand. "I own this joint. Lucille. But folks hereabouts call me Mom."

"Bet your kids suggested you call the place Mom's."

Lucille tilted her head back and laughed, cigarillo ashes dropping onto the floor. "Never had kids. Too busy marrying and divorcing men. Four of them." She paused and looked at the ceiling fan. "Make that five. But what do they call you, besides Too Big To Fit In A Booth?"

"Nelson," I answered.

She dropped her cigarette butt onto the floor, snubbed it out with the toe of her shoe, and stuck another between those luscious red lips. "What do you want to take a chance on, Nelson?"

I replaced the menu in the arms of the little Negro statue beside matching salt and pepper shakers. "The pot roast with carrots and mashed taters."

"And apple pie for dessert, I'd wager?"

"How can I refuse."

She smiled and had turned to leave when I stopped her. "You gonna' write my order down?"

"With this?" she grabbed a pencil stub from behind her ear. "No more customers than I get, I can remember your order. Besides, this is for digging." She used the pencil end to root around in her ear. "Be back with coffee."

While I waited for my meal, I walked to the pay phone hanging on the far wall beside a Rockola juke box with the front smashed in. I dropped a nickel into the phone's coin slot and tapped the switchbox. Within seconds, an operator came on, and I asked her to connect me to the Hot Springs county sheriff. When I was connected to the sheriff's office, a woman asked what I wanted. I introduced myself and told her I needed to meet with Sheriff Darcy. "I'll buy him coffee at Mom's Diner."

"Mom's?"

"Mom's," I answered. "Next to Delmonico's."

"I know where it is," she snapped. "I'll give Milo . . . Sheriff Darcy the message."

By the time I returned to my booth, Lucille had just emerged from the kitchen cradling plates in her arms. Her cigarillo bobbed between her lips, and the ashes threatened to fall into my food. "Bon appetite," she said as she set the plates on the table. A pork chop with crusted breading shared the plate beside wrinkled peas and a baked potato that could have been used as a door stop. "Cherry pie whenever you're ready."

She had started walking away when I called her back. "I ordered pot roast and mashed potatoes."

Lucille glared at me. "You questioning my memory?" She tapped her temple, and her ash fell on her ear. " 'Cause I ain't never got an order wrong."

She stood with her hands on her hips like my mother used to do when she was about to let loose with a nasty scolding. I thought it prudent to let it be. The last thing I needed was a fight with an old lady. "At least bring me a cup of coffee."

She turned to the counter, snatched a cup from a stack, and blew dust off it before pouring. She topped her own cup off and returned to the booth. She took off her hat and cupped her hand around her mug as she sat across from me. "Nelson, you say?"

I nodded and began sawing away at the pork chop.

"What brings you here, Nelson?"

I pulled my vest back to show my badge.

"You a revenuer?" Her tone turned hard.

"US marshal," I answered. When the knife she gave me failed to cut through the tough gristle, I dug my pocket knife out and completed the deed. "Not my job to look for moonshiners."

"Then why *are* you here?"

"Looking for a girl missing from the reservation."

Lucille settled back down and stuck a fresh cigarillo between her ruby lips. She struck a match on the side of the table and lit up. "Lots of girls come through who are running away from something. Most just running toward something better. Some from the rez. What's this one you're hunting running from?"

I held up my hand while I struggled to swallow the meat. Lucille had brought up an interesting question: just what *was* Darla running from? When I talked with Will and Josephine at their house, I'd thought it obvious—she was running from a father who had grown too strict for a young lady. Now I wasn't so sure. "I can't say for certain. Don't really know if she's even a runaway." I took Darla's photo out of my pocket and handed it to Lucille. She turned away and donned spectacles before handing me the picture back. "I seen her in here once"—she paused as she recalled—"with some guy 'bout your age."

"Recently?"

"Couple months ago."

A young girl with somebody my age could have been Will or

some other elder from the reservation. "What'd he look like?"

An ash dropped into her coffee, but she paid it no mind. "He was dressed good enough. Nothing fancy." She leaned across the table. "Now *she* was dressed like she was trolling downtown Billings looking for customers. Know what I mean?"

I vaguely did. I'd lived a pretty bland life—sexually speaking—having married Helen right out of the military hospital at Portsmouth. Since she died, I'd never had the urge to be with another woman. Someday I would, I knew, but I sure wouldn't be paying good money for it. I knew a few ranchers who sneaked away on business trips to Billings, telling their wives they were going there to look at cattle to buy. And most wound up with fifty dollars less in their denims in the morning.

A car pulled to the curb, and Lucille got up. She went to the window and cupped her hand to the glass. "Thought it odd I get two customers in a day, but it's just that blowhard."

That blowhard got out of his car marked with *HOT SPRINGS COUNTY SHERIFF* above a star on the door.

By the time Milo Darcy walked into the diner, Lucille had disappeared into the kitchen. He took off his Stetson and hung it on the elk antler coat rack, and walked to the counter. "Helping myself to a cup of whatever the hell this is, Lucille," he called out as he grabbed a cup and filled it. He dropped a nickel on the counter and said loud enough for Lucille to hear, "I put money on the counter so the old gal won't accuse me of stealing again."

He strode over to my booth, grabbing a clean checkered napkin from a table in passing. He sat in the booth across from me and propped his feet up on a chair. "Old Lucille accused me of stiffing this joint out of a meal last summer," he said as he wiped dust from his boots with the napkin. "But I didn't stiff her. I was just mad that she brought nothing that I had ordered." He nodded to my half-eaten meal. "That happen to you?"

I coaxed another chunk of overcooked pork chop down my throat. "Everything was just as I ordered it." I'd talked with many folks hereabouts through the years that swore that Milo was an A-one horse's patoot, and I wasn't going to give him any satisfaction. "The meal's plumb tender and tasty."

He frowned at the kitchen door as if expecting Lucille to come out and confront him. He finished his coffee and scrunched his nose up. "How's your coffee?"

Tastes like mop water, I wanted to tell him. But didn't.

"Now what does a federal marshal want with a lowly local sheriff?"

"Missing person," I answered. I handed Milo Darla's picture. He barely glanced at it before handing it back. "Since when do US marshals take missing-person reports?"

"It's a favor for a friend."

Milo laughed as he took a pack of Mail Pouch out of his vest pocket and stuffed tobacco in his cheek. "At least you marshals have time to piss with the piddly stuff like that."

Milo was already getting under my skin, and I felt like shoving his pearl-handled Colt up his kiester. "I only called you as a professional courtesy, since I have to look in your county."

He picked up the photo and looked at it again. "You have a line on this Indian girl?"

"Her father thinks she might have stopped and bought booze from the man who'd been selling it to her. Thinks he might know something about her whereabouts."

"Got a name on this feller?"

"Axle Denny."

Milo whistled. "Axle's a hard customer. If you're planning on going to his place and talking with him, I'd better tag along."

"Suit yourself," I said and called for Lucille. When she poked her head out of the kitchen, I said, "Give Sheriff Darcy the noon special. I know he'll like something tasty to start our trip with."

Chapter 4

Milo insisted I ride in his new Buick to Axle's place. "So you know how the other half lives," he said, bragging about his car. But I knew it was just as much about padding his mileage for the taxpayers of Hot Springs County. Which I suspected he did often.

"You ever have any dealings with Axle?" Milo asked. He'd flipped open a pocket knife and was busy picking gristly pork chop out of his teeth as he steered.

"Never met the man," I lied. Yancy and—it would seem—half the reservation knew I was once a boozer. But Milo didn't need to know that. "But I heard he can be a mite unpleasant."

"Unpleasant, hell!" He slowed to allow a skinny porcupine to waddle across the road. Even porcupines were lacking in this damned Depression. "Axle is mean as hell would be a better description. The last time I dealt with him, he kicked the shit out of two hunters he had caught on land he claimed belonged to him. It was all I could do to rap my flat sap alongside his head."

"Was it his land?"

"Said it was," Milo answered. "But you know how them Bohunks lie."

We turned off the hard-packed gravel of Highway 20 onto a dirt road. The big Buick kicked up as much dust as a dust devil, and we quickly rolled the windows up. "Another fifteen miles," Milo said.

But I already knew that, though I'd never say it. "I heard you had a tough re-election this time around," I said, as much to gouge the arrogant bastard as get my mind off meeting Axle again after all these years. Would he say anything to Milo about our past . . . business dealings? I doubted it, but his reaction to my being in his house once again might tell Milo as much as if I'd spilled my guts. "I heard it was a nasty election."

"Not as hard as the newspapers told it." Milo downshifted to crawl up a steep grade. "That little prick Erik Esterling tried pulling some dirty tricks—accusing me of womanizing. Hell's bells, that damned near cost me my marriage when the little lady heard it." *And damned near cost you your sugar tit,* I thought. Milo had married spinster Roberta Rains, sole heir to the man who once held controlling interest in a string of oil wells up by Hamilton Dome before he drowned fishing in a reservoir in South Dakota. And now it was all Roberta's. Milo didn't need the sheriff's job, or to pad his mileage whenever he got the chance. He just liked the power. And—it was rumored as far away as Bison—Milo enjoyed the time spent away from his wife. "You might say I was saved at the eleventh hour when Esterling dropped out."

"Why'd he drop out of the race?"

"Money," Milo answered. "The sheriff's job only pays two thousand a year, plus what you get for housing prisoners and mileage. Few men can live on that wage with a family. He went freighting, driving for some company delivering grain that pays more. Like there's very much grain to haul nowadays."

Milo was right: there wasn't much grain to peddle, let alone haul for someone else. The drought, plus the bottom falling out of everything—including crops—would put a damper on Esterling's driving.

"Erik was my deputy for a couple years." Milo cracked his window far enough to spit a string of tobacco juice that dripped on down the side of his window before rolling it up. "Thought he could do better. Had some notions about modern ways of enforcing the law. And when we had one too many disagreements, he tossed his badge on my desk and threatened to run in the fall." Milo chuckled. "Even if he had stayed with it until the election, he would have lost."

I wondered what kind of man Esterling was. Two thousand dollars would be a God-send to most men rearing a family in these times. I just couldn't imagine him making more than that driving truck, when a field hand is making five hundred dollars, a mill worker—when there's work to be had—twice that. Erik Esterling must be one lucky man to have landed a lucrative truck-driving job.

"We are getting close to Axle's," Milo said.

My gut tightened as we neared the North Fork of Mud Creek at the base of the Owl Creek Mountains. We drove on the flats, slowly ascending to higher ground as we made our way to Axle's place. I knew, from being at his cabin enough times, that he commanded an excellent view of anyone approaching. I also knew he'd be taking a bead on Milo's car right about now in case we were revenuers. I recalled his hunting rifles equipped with scopes bigger than my binoculars hanging on his wall, and I thought about the wisdom of climbing into a car with a big star pasted on the door. If Axle started shooting, the .45 automatic on my hip would be no more effective than Milo's fancy thumb buster.

We turned onto Axle's driveway lined with thick sage brush—if you called the narrow passage on the dirt road a driveway—and Milo fought the wheel to keep on top of the deep ruts. His Buick would drop all the way to the axles if he wasn't careful, and I wished we'd driven my Ford panel instead.

We drove higher along the road, passing a small herd of antelope grazing to one side, and a lone spike mulie buck in velvet on the other. Quick movement caught my eye, and I turned my head just in time to see a running coyote disappear into a gully.

Around the next curve in the road I knew we'd come onto Axle's cabin, and I scooted down further in the seat. Milo pointed to the house as it came into our view. "Bet you're wondering how a man who has a seasonal guide business can afford such a nice place."

"Like how can a sheriff afford a new Buick?"

Milo glared at me.

"But no, I never wondered. This is my first time here."

"Well, I can tell you that he does a pretty good moonshining business. Been hearing about it for years." Milo cracked his window and spat his tobacco out. "Like the rumors I've heard for last couple years about the two revenuers who came sneaking around Axle's place and never checked back in with their Casper office. Speculation was that they're buried out here someplace, as familiar as Axle Denny is with this land."

"Anybody come looking for them?"

"Couple suits from Denver, but they seemed more put off for having to come all the way out here to the sticks than concerned for finding one of theirs."

I'd heard the same stories over the past couple years. As big an SOB as Axle is, I doubted he'd murder two federal agents. Rough them up and threaten them, perhaps, but murder? "He's in your county. You could bust his operation."

"He's in *your* state." Milo grinned as he slowed his approach to the house. "But he's not bothering me. Unless he actually kills someone, I got no reason to hassle him. Besides"—he downshifted—"folks hereabouts aren't complaining about him. And they're voters." Milo laughed. "Best I could do is to warn him that revenue agents are looking for him every time I see him in town. Makes his stay in Thermop a whole lot shorter."

I tried making myself smaller in the seat as my hand rested on my pistol. "And when was the last time you saw him?"

"Four, five days ago," Milo answered. He pulled in front of the house and turned the car off. "He came into town to buy some grain for his horses. Make a few deliveries, too, I'd wager." He held up his hand. "But Axle's business is none of mine."

"You're here with me."

Milo opened the door and dust swirled around his new Stetson. "Maybe I just wanted to be here when he kills you so I got something to investigate."

"Thanks for the support," I told him. "If I knew you were tagging along for the entertainment, I'd have brought you some popcorn to watch the gun fight."

I unfolded myself from the car and looked about. Milo had stopped in front of the well-worn hitching rail. Horse hair imbedded in the weathered wood flapped in the breeze, showing where hunters had tied their mounts, beside deep ruts where others had parked their hunting trucks. Every time I'd bought booze from Axle, he had come out the door cradling his Winchester in one arm and his Colt slung low to greet me. He had never trusted me any more than I did him. He'd always been short, gruff, and came across as if he liked no lawmen, not just federal marshals. But that was all right—I'd always been there for a simple business exchange. And he knew we would both be harmed if I ever arrested him for moonshining or told about his operation. Like Milo said adeptly—Axle never did any harm to me.

What bothered me today was that Axle *didn't* come out of his house when we drove up. The hair on my neck stood at attention, and I imagined Axle drawing a bead on us with his rifle. I casually brushed my hand over my holster and unsnapped my strap as I walked beside Milo to the front door. He hummed to himself, and his holster remained secured. As we approached the door, Milo strode right up and stood in front as he banged on it. If I suspected Axle had killed a couple revenuers, like Milo thought, I'd have been a lot more careful.

Milo was taking Axle Denny way too lightly as he stood in front of the door and banged away. I stood to one side of the heavy oak door and held my palm against the side of the house but detected no movement inside.

"Looks like no one's home," Milo said and turned to leave.

I walked to the far end of the porch in front of the house and brushed fine Wyoming dust off a window pane. I cupped my hand to the glass but saw no one inside. "Axle works as a hunting guide," I said.

"Of course he does. So, what's your point?"

"The point is this isn't hunting season, and he doesn't raise any livestock. So, where is he?" I pointed to a beat-to-hell Model AA truck with a dented box parked in front of the horse barn. Dried blood caked the side, and Axle had screwed a set of elk antlers to the hood. That was Axle—all class. "He ought to be here."

Milo shrugged and patted dust off his hat before climbing into his car. "Maybe he found himself a job."

"And maybe you're just a little bit too afraid of Axle to go looking for him."

Milo climbed back out. "What's that supposed to mean?"

I'd run into dozens of Milo Darcys over the years. They puffed up their chests like a prairie chicken and talked a good fight as they went around town bragging about their exploits. But when the time came to actually back up their rhetoric, they shrank. Or turned tail outright and ran. I wasn't about to let Milo off the hook easily.

"We haven't checked the barn." I walked toward the barn, my hand close to my pistol. "You coming?" I said over my shoulder. "Or are you going to sit in your fancy new car your wife bought for you?"

Milo slammed the door and stomped after me. "If I get my ass shot off looking for some damned runaway Indian girl, I'll come back and haunt you forever, Nelson Lane."

"Fair enough," I answered.

CHAPTER 5

When I reached the barn, I paused and put my ear to the door before opening it.

Silence. Which was good news. At least I didn't hear the sound of a gun cocking.

I cracked the door an inch and peeked inside, but it was too dark, and I prepared to enter. I positioned myself to one side of the swinging door in case Axle decided to ventilate this federal marshal. I was drawing my .45 when Milo brushed past me.

"If we're going to look for him, let's look."

He grabbed onto the door handle when I stopped him. "Maybe we ought to slow down. Remember those two prohibition agents—"

He jerked his arm away and flung the door wide. "Let's see if he's inside, unless *you're* too chickenshit."

Milo practically ran inside the barn. I had stopped long enough for my eyes to adjust to the darkness when I heard, "We found Axle."

Even before my eyes saw him, the odor of decaying and putrefying flesh reached me a moment before the sound of buzzing flies did. I holstered as I walked closer to Axle. He hung from an overhead rafter by a piece of hemp rope. He swayed ever so slightly with the wind passing through the barn, and a milk stool lay overturned on the floor directly beneath him. His tongue protruded from his swollen and blackened mouth, and his eyes were hard and fixed, lifeless, upon something on the wall. I opened the barn door to allow the smell out and the light in before I took my bandana from my neck and tied it over my nose and mouth.

"Guess I won't have to kick his ass anymore." Milo grabbed the milk stool and flipped open a pocket knife to cut the body down.

"Hold off a minute," I said. "I want to look things over."

"This your crime scene or mine?"

"Yours, of course," I answered. "But give me a minute to look at things first. It's not like Axle's going to come alive and slip out of that rope."

"And waste more of my time?" Milo bitched. "But what the hell, it's all in the spirit of cooperation between agencies."

A sorrel gelding hung its head over a stall next to a small pack mule and whinnied a greeting at me. Rigging used by hunters straddled both stalls: saddle for the horse, pack frame for the mule. They eyed me as I walked slowly around the corpse, looking at Axle from different angles while Milo looked at the floor, the stalls, anywhere except at the body.

He opened an empty stall door and whistled. "Hello," he said. "Come look at this."

I walked into the stall and stood beside Milo. Axle had set up his cooker in the stall, and mason jars lined one wall waiting to be filled. Wood was piled along the opposite wall, and cold wood lay in the firebox.

A rock held a piece of paper to the top of the cooker, and Milo grabbed it. "Pretty cut and dried," he said and handed it to me. I read the note slowly, as the English was poor, the grammar non-existent, the cursive sloppy. In Axle's suicide note, he regretted selling booze to young kids, especially reservation youngsters. He couldn't live with himself. The note was dated four days ago.

"Guess he did the right thing after all," Milo said.

"But why now?" I asked. "If he sold booze to kids for years, why would he have a case of guilt now?"

"Maybe that runaway girl you're looking for has something to do with this." Milo opened the spout of the cooker just long enough to wet his finger. He tasted it, and his nose scrunched up.

He passed it under my nose, and I turned away. No sense dredging up old friends. "If he gave that girl this coffin varnish, maybe she didn't make it off his property. Wouldn't be the first time someone died of alcohol poisoning from crap like this. Might be she's buried on his place somewheres."

Milo walked back to the corpse and grabbed the stool. He set it upright and looked away from Axle. "You want to hold onto him so's he don't fall down?" he said, his voice wavering. Like he'd never seen a blackened, bloated corpse in the summer. "I don't want him exploding. Be hard to haul back to town, and"—he nodded to Axle—"as you can see, he's getting close as it is."

While Milo stood on the stool with his knife poised, I held on to Axle, careful not to get too high on his midsection where he might, indeed, explode if we weren't careful. Milo cut the rope, and I eased Axle to the floor of the barn.

"I'll grab a blanket," Milo said. "No use messing up my nice Buick for the likes of him."

Milo disappeared through the barn door, and I sat on the milking stool and looked the body over. The entire scene screamed suicide:—from the note explaining that guilt drove him to step off the stool, to the condition of Axle, to the manner in which he chose to kill himself—there seemed little doubt that Axle's dangle of death was by his own hand. Had Milo's constant mention of revenue agents looking for him worn on Axle so badly he had taken his own life, thinking they were close to making a case?

Yet something here stank as much as the body, and I struggled to think what it was.

I finally realized just what stuck in my craw. If there ever was a hard man, it was Axle Denny. He wouldn't have lost a minute of sleep over selling booze to Indian kids, or any other kids, any more than he would have worried about revenuers looking to arrest him. His conscience—if he even had one when he was alive—certainly wouldn't have driven him to kill himself.

I stood and walked upwind of Axle, toward the horse stalls. Axle's liquor still hadn't been fired in days, the coals cold. But that might be normal if his business was slowing down for some reason. I'd ask around about that later, not that I wanted to make it easier for Milo Darcy and his investigation. He had signed off too easily on the suicide angle. He had taken the easy route. Perhaps I could make his life a little more difficult, especially since I was having doubts as to Axle's death being a suicide.

The sorrel whinnied again, and I walked to the stall. I held his head and stroked the bridge of his nose. I saw there was no hay in the stall, and I grabbed a pitchfork leaning against one wall and tossed some over into the stall. He started eating right off, and I did the same for the mule.

They were darned sure hungry, and I looked over the railing. The grain bins were empty for both animals, and their water troughs were dry.

I snatched a pail from a peg and walked to a pump beside the barn door. I held the pail under the spout and pumped, but the leathers had dried out and no water came up.

I looked around for a tin of water that Axle might have used and found it hanging on the barn floor beside the pump. I poured some down the spout and waited for a few moments for the water to swell the leather gaskets, then gave the handle a pump. Water gurgled below, then finally came up and filled the pail. I filled the water trough just as Milo came back to the barn carrying a blanket. He laid it out beside Axle and stepped back. "Want to grab his feet or his head?"

"Neither just yet."

Milo looked up at me. "Now what the hell?"

"You know much about horse flesh?"

Milo stood and glared at me. "That's almost an insult. I've been rigging a saddle all my life. Got many a head at the ranch. Fine stock, too. And Roberts raises Appaloosas."

"No offense." I held up my hand, and it occurred to me how little I knew about other lawmen in my state. "What would you do with your critters if you and the missus went on an extended vacation—someplace simple for you folks, like France, maybe South America for the winter?"—

"That's a dumb question—we have hired hands who'd take care of them—"

"How about if you were a common man, like Axle here? What kind of arrangements would you make for them?"

Milo folded one corner of the blanket over the corpse. "What the hell you getting at?"

I motioned to Axle's horse and mule making short work of the hay I'd just given them. "And look at the way they're curried. Axle might not have been rich in horseflesh, but what he had he took care of. They've been recently shod, and their coats are tight."

"What *are* you rambling on about?"

I shook out a Chesterfield and lit it, careful not to drop the match on the floor of the barn. "Axle obviously thought a lot of his stock. If he were going on a long vacation, don't you think he'd make arrangements to have someone take care of them?"

"But he didn't go on vacation," Milo laughed and cinched his bandana tighter around his nose. "He went to hell. Dead. Worm food. *Finito.*"

"For the sake of argument, let's say Axle knew beforehand—even minutes before—that he intended hanging himself. Don't you think he'd put enough hay and water, maybe some of that grain he just bought in town when you saw him, for his critters to last in case he wasn't discovered any time soon?"

"That don't prove nothing—"

"And just now, when I tried pumping water for them, the leathers had dried out enough I couldn't get a drop of water to come up. I had to prime the pump. With this hot weather, I can get two, sometimes three days at the most before my pump dries to the point where I need to prime it. Axle hadn't given his horses water for four days. Maybe more."

"That still don't prove nothing."

"Damned double negatives."

"What?"

"Nothing," I said. Fighting down the English major in me. "And Axle's gun is still strapped to his belt."

"Oh, this one I gotta' hear," Milo said, stuffing his cheek with Mail Pouch.

"As much as he hated the law," I began, "Axle would know we'd eventually get around to finding him. He would shoot himself, knowing it would be such a big mess for us to investigate, it'd be his revenge from the grave. Especially as hot as it's been lately."

"That's as much speculation as I can handle for one day," Milo said. "I'm going with the suicide note, not some cockamamie theory—"

"Is this a cockamamie theory?" I said as I squatted beside the body. I ran my finger over a dark mark encircling his neck going straight across his throat. "In suicides—and this is just a dumb paper-server talking here—the rope is at a sharp upward angle where the body pulls on the rope while it's hanging."

"Did you see the same body hanging with the rope across his

neck like I did?"

"I saw a body hanging with the weight of a two-hundred-pound man. This"—I pointed to Axle's neck again—"goes straight across his throat." I paused long enough that Shakespeare would be proud of me. "Whoever strangled Axle did so from behind *before* they hung him from those rafters." I stood and stretched. "Someone staged this little party. Now grab your *murder victim* and let's get him to your car."

CHAPTER 6

We tied a rope around the corpse. Then—as Axle was bloating even more as we carried him—we grabbed a horse blanket from the barn and wrapped him again. In case he exploded in this heat, Milo's new Buick wouldn't get messed up so badly. Or should I say, his wife's new Buick.

Milo pulled his car close to the barn. When we finished loading the dearly departed—for with as many customers as I recalled Axle having, many folks would mourn his passing—I bent to the pump and stoked the handle. I washed my hands with a bar of lye soap hanging beside the pump and handed it off to Milo. I pumped water for him, and we dried our hands on a flour sack stuck on a nail.

We walked back to the car, and Milo had climbed in when he noticed I hadn't. "Now what?"

Denise Denny had been married to Axle for longer than I bought my hooch from him. But the last thing I wanted Milo to know is that I knew the family. "Axle married?"

"Sure. Nice lady, too."

"Don't you think we ought to talk with her?"

"She ain't here," Milo said immediately.

"Oh? You one of those fortune tellers like they have at those goofy travelling circuses?"

"Don't need to be," Milo said as he settled behind the wheel. "I had my own runaway case from Worland dropped in my lap last month. Somebody said they saw the girl with Denise in

Thermopolis, and I drove out here to talk with her. She was packing her bags."

"Leaving Axle?"

"Naw." Milo opened his bag of tobacco and stuffed his cheek. Some ran down onto his white shirt, staining it brown. Like the trout that I should be out catching. "Denise said Axle's business had slowed lately, though she never admitted he cooked moonshine. And I didn't ask. She said she landed a job in Billings plucking chickens at a cannery. I asked if she'd seen the girl from Worland, and she said only once while shopping in town."

"Believe her?"

"About the girl or the job?"

"Both."

Milo put the Buick in neutral while he pondered that—I think, though his expression never changed. Like he was incapable of free thought. "I don't believe she knew anything about the girl. But I think she lied about the job. Rumor was that Denise had a roving eye for the men. Just my guess—Denise ran off with another man, but I can't prove it."

But it did prove my theory right about Milo's free thinking. At five-foot-three and tipping the scales at one-seventy-five if she were an ounce, I couldn't imagine Denise the kind of woman who would attract too many men. But to each his own.

"I'd hate to be the man who takes away Axle's wife," I said. "With Axle after me."

Milo chuckled and looked at the bundle of blankets lying across his backseat. "Guess the lucky feller won't have to worry about that now."

Milo started the car, but I wasn't done here yet, and I headed for the house.

"Now where you going?" Milo called out.

"I'm going to the house. Maybe there's something inside that tells us what happened here."

Milo shut the car off and ran after me. "I don't see what good—"

"If Denise wasn't here, it'd be logical to figure the killers would break into the victim's house. I'm going in and look things over."

Milo grabbed my arm to slow me down. It didn't work. "We can't go breaking into another man's home. That's illegal."

"Like Axle is going to rise up and press charges." I chuckled.

"But Denise might."

I stopped and flicked his shiny, silver sheriff's star. "Milo Darcy, how long have you worn that?"

"You know how long—starting my third term. More than eight years serving the voters."

More like serving yourself, I thought. "Then you know that when Denise left Axle, she lost her standing. That's a three-dollar word that means—"

"I know what it means—she lost any legal objection to the place."

"Including us walking into the house."

"But she only left for a job in Billings."

I laid my hand on Milo's shoulder. "As an experienced sheriff going on his third term, you picked right up on her lie about taking a new job. Figured she left Axle for another man. No." I waved my hand around the yard. "Ol' Denise is probably in some other feller's lucky arms, just like you figured. You coming?"

Without waiting for an answer, I turned and walked across the yard. When I stepped onto the porch, I grabbed my pocket knife, expecting to jimmy the door. But like most ranch houses in Wyoming, the front door was unlocked. No reason to have it any other way out here.

Milo was close on my heels as I stepped inside. All the

curtains were drawn, and I pulled those covering the long windows aside to let some light in. We stepped into the sitting room where I'd always paid Axle for my booze when I came here. Milo started past me, but I held him back. "Don't be in such a rush."

"But Axle's getting bigger by the hour."

"He's not going to pop in the little time we'll be in here. Just stop and look for a moment."

Sunlight through the window cast a perfect angle across the room. Dust motes we'd kicked up shone like faint snow and deposited on the furniture and floor and the fixings. But not heavy enough to suggest the room hadn't been cleaned in a month. Whenever I would come here to buy hooch, I noticed that Denise kept a neat and tidy house, if not spotless. Like most ranch women did. With Denise gone, I couldn't imagine Axle donning an apron and grabbing a feather duster.

I squatted and looked across the floor, while Milo looked at me like I was crazy. The only footprints on the hardwood floors were ours walking in just now.

I stood and put my hands on my hips like Dad used to do sometimes at calving time when he was trying to figure out when a cow was going to calf. He was usually right. Just like I was certain I was right now. "No one robbed Axle before or after the murder."

"How you know that?"

"There's some valuable things the killers could have taken." I motioned to the wall where four scoped hunting rifles hung on an antler rack. "Those guns alone would fetch good money. Makes it real simple for you."

"Simple!" Milo said. "How can that make any of this simple?"

I smiled. "Because now you don't have to worry about solving multiple crimes. All you have to do is worry about who murdered Axle."

"Don't you beat all—"

"I do have my moments," I said. "But thank me later."

I walked around the room, trying to get a feel for what might have happened. Family photos hung on the wall, though I couldn't tell if they were from Axle's side of the family or Denise's. To be honest, they both looked a lot alike in the face and the body.

I walked into the large living room and stood in front of an upright piano next to an oak secretary, the drawers untouched, a picture of a wolfhound undisturbed. As I continued walking around the room, I could not spot anything that had been disturbed. Light passed over the fireplace mantel and—when the angle was just right—I saw where something had once rested there. All that was left was the outline of dust. I squinted and put on my reading glasses and judged that a picture frame had sat on the mantle. Recently.

"See something?" Milo asked, instantly beside me as if he wanted to learn how to investigate. Which he really didn't.

"No," I answered. "I'm just looking around. Guess all we know was that it was a plain murder, without theft involved."

"Suicide," Milo said as he followed me outside. "There was nothing in the house to suggest anyone robbed Axle, just like you said. And no reason to murder him. I'm sticking with suicide, just like I figured."

But something inside the house did jump out at me. The outline of dust on the mantle told me a picture had recently sat there. And the most prominent photo a family would proudly display for everyone to see was a wedding picture. If Denise ran off with another man, would she take her wedding photo with her? I doubted it. But I didn't doubt that she'd take the picture if she left with the intent of coming back. Had she left in a hurry?

Chapter 7

I helped Milo unload Axle at the Forever Rest Funeral Home in Thermopolis. The owner of the Forever Rest, Aaron Allright, whistled "Life Is Just a Bowl of Cherries," though I suspected Axle would disagree if he had any say. Aaron took Axle's head while I grabbed his legs. "Upsie daisy," Aaron said as we unceremoniously hauled the corpse onto a steel table in the cold room in back of the funeral home.

When we finished, Aaron wiped sweat from his face and from the wattle that served as his neck. "Whew," he looked around. "What happened to the High Sheriff?"

"He's in your waiting room," I answered. "He got a little green around the gills when the smell hit him." And me, too, though I wouldn't admit it to Milo that—between the odor of dead bodies and the acidic smell of formaldehyde—I'd gotten a little queasy, too. If the room didn't smell like putrefying bodies and old corpses, I'd have loved to spend time in here out of the intense heat. "He decided to take a breather."

Aaron smiled. "Perhaps this experience has the sheriff considering his own services," he held up his hand. "When the time comes, of course." He nodded to the bloated body under the pile of blankets on the table. "But something like this does make one ponder his own mortality." He stepped closer and looked up at me. "Have *you* thought of what . . . type of service you would wish when your time comes? I offer a ten percent discount on pre-pays."

Milo clued me in on the ride back to town. Folks hereabouts referred to the Forever Rest as the Forever Broke Funeral Home for the steep fees Aaron charges. Aaron's goal was to clinch a sale for funeral expenses while the family was still grieving, before he left the house with the loved one. I doubted if I could ever afford Aaron's prices. "I have plans to build my own coffin," I said, pleased when the smile faded from his face. "And I have a little spot of ground in back of my barn where I'm going to be planted. Where the horses can fertilize all the flowers mourners bring by."

Aaron backed away, wringing his hands. "It is, after all, a personal decision. But if you decide on something a little more . . . elaborate—"

"You'll be the first I get hold of to stick the forever juice in me, Aaron."

The smile returned, and I could imagine him already kicking figures around in his head. The only thing lacking was him measuring me for a coffin with a yardstick. "You do autopsies on homicide victims, being the county coroner and all?"

Aaron looked at the body encased in blankets that had threatened to burst on the drive over here. Every time Milo hit a bump, gas escaped, and the sheriff groaned, expecting Axle to explode. "In this heat, it is doubtful if we could learn anything—"

"But you *do* perform them?"

"I'm no medical examiner, but I do what I can. *If* Sheriff Darcy requests it."

Milo had argued with me the entire trip here that Axle's death was a suicide. Milo would jump at any chance to prove me wrong, so he could rule the death as self-inflicted. Nice and neat. "He'll request it," I said. "If you go to your waiting room and ask him."

"What are you looking for exactly, Marshal?"

I bent to the corpse and carefully peeled the blanket off Axle. If I didn't know it was him, I wouldn't recognize him. I pointed to the dark discoloration across his neck while I explained that I thought Axle had been strangled from behind. "I want you to see if his hyoid bone is broken or not. If it's fractured, that'll strengthen my case that Axle was murdered."

I followed Aaron to his waiting room. When we walked through the door, Milo jumped. Aaron asked if he'd order an autopsy, and Milo nodded to me. "Just to get Marshal Lane off my back, I want it."

Aaron looked to the door leading to his cold room. "If you're sure—"

"I am."

When Aaron left the room, I grabbed a cup hanging on a peg over a coffeepot and poured myself some. It tasted suspiciously like what I figured the forever juice would taste like. "Aaron gives a discount for pre-paid funeral services if you're interested."

"I have enough money," Milo said, "but I wouldn't give it to that vulture, the high prices he charges." He wiped sweat from the inside of his hat. "I still don't know what he can find out, not being medically trained."

"He's all you got," I answered. "All he requires is that you're present when he cuts Axle open."

The color drained from Milo's already pale face. "I have to go watch?"

"Relax." I nudged him with my elbow, and I thought he'd fall over. "You don't have to be there."

The air seemed to go out of him, and he slumped into a chair. "Thanks." He fished into his pocket and handed me a slip of paper. "Forgot to tell you, your girlfriend stopped by and handed me this."

"Girlfriend?"

"Some hottie." He frowned. "But she looked Indian."

I unfolded the note from Maris. She said she would meet me for supper, but she didn't say where. "She mention where she wanted to eat at?"

"She was unfamiliar with the town and wanted a recommendation. I told her Delmonico's was always busy."

"Because the food's good?"

"And the service is excellent," Milo grinned. "So, I sent her to Mom's. I know just how you enjoyed her fine . . . rustic cuisine."

I drove through the town, and it took me only minutes to turn onto Broadway. Even though handling a bloated, heavy corpse and a beside-himself county sheriff had given me an appetite, the thought of another of Lucille's meals tamped it down considerably.

Parking spaces in front of Delmonico's spilled past Mom's Diner, making it appear as if Lucille had customers. Which I knew she did not. I parked down the street across from Maris's Chevy coupe—given to her by her Uncle Byron when she left Oklahoma. She had parked it between a DeSoto sedan and a Ford Phaeton with a bale of hay in the back seat and two sacks of chicken feed strapped on top. I had hoped I could have made it before Maris did to warn her about Mom's.

When I walked into the diner, I saw I wasn't the only customer: Maris was seated at a booth across from Lucille. As Lucille talked, the cigarillo in her hand waved the air. When she spotted me, she rose and sat next to Maris. Maris looked like a younger Lucille, with her rouge cheeks and ruby lips. Her hair was pulled back in a tight bun, and her too-tight shirt barely contained the star pinned to her chest. Maris was trolling.

"Looks like you've been chowing down already," I said as I grabbed a napkin and wiped brown gravy that had dripped down her cheek. "What you think?"

Maris took a swallow of coffee to wash her food down. "This is my second helping," she said. "Lucille's almost as good a cook as Uncle Byron." She sopped the rest of the gravy up from her plate with a buttermilk biscuit. "Me and Lucille have been swapping stories. Seems like we got a lot in common—men."

I wisely let that pass and motioned to her empty plate. "What'd you have?"

"Pot roast," Maris answered as she pushed her empty plate aside. She shook out an Old Gold and used Lucille's cigarillo to light it. "With mashed potatoes and the sweetest corn—"

"I'll take that."

"Can't," Lucille said. Her ash dropped on the table, and she brushed it onto the floor. "Maris took the last of today's special."

"All right, then. What do you have?"

"Pork chops. I got the impression you liked it before."

Lucille's impressions weren't worth squat, and I ordered the chicken noodle soup.

"She's an amazing lady," Maris said as Lucille disappeared through the kitchen door. "Knows everyone and everything hereabouts."

"I wish she was an amazing cook right about now." Lucille hadn't brought my coffee yet, and I took a sip of Maris's. It wasn't as bitter as Lucille's last pot. Which wasn't saying much. "How'd the foreclosure go?"

Maris took a long drag of her cigarette and leaned across the table. "Don't send me up there to serve those hillbillies around Cody ever again."

"You're from Oklahoma, and you call us Wyomingites hillbillies? Must have made an impression on you."

Maris snubbed her butt out in what was left of the gravy on her plate. "The rancher was plumb friendly. Almost hospitable. Until I slapped papers on him. Before I knowed it, he whistled, and a dozen boys—big bastards—came out of the woodwork all carrying rifles. Except one kid about nine—he was toting a ten-gauge shotgun. They surrounded me, and the rancher said if I ever came on his property again, I might not get off in one piece, lady or not. What the hell kind of job did you favor me with?"

I finished Maris's coffee and sat back. "Who owned the paper on the ranch?"

"Stockman's Bank out of Miles City."

"I go there every year for their annual horse sale," I said. "I'll get hold of Stockman's and see if there's anything the rancher can do to work it out." Through the last few years, I'd talked with many a banker who held paper on ranches going under. They didn't want to take the property back—bankers didn't want to mess with ranches. Might get their hands dirty. Most would go out of their way to work out a deal rather than take back property they didn't want. "If the bank can't work something out, I'll go up to Cody myself and kick them off the place. Can't have them threatening one of my deputies."

"Well, you better take an army with you, 'cause those boys looked as mean as their pappy."

I shrugged. "I can be quite persuasive when I have to be."

"I can testify to that." Maris laughed. "So, tell me what's so urgent about a runaway girl that I had to beat feet back here?"

I filled her in about Will Lone Tree reporting his daughter missing after she hadn't come back home for four days. I explained that her supplier of booze—Axle Denny—had gotten himself murdered at his mountain home. "When we got to Axle's, we found him swinging. Ruined a good rope, too."

"I heard the mean bastard hung himself." Lucille came out of the kitchen balancing a bowl and plates and a coffee pot. She set a steaming bowl of chicken noodle soup in front of me along with a plate of biscuits. "But I doubt it."

"How'd you hear about it? We just carted Axle's body in an hour ago."

"An hour's a lifetime when you got friends with loose mouths." Lucille sat next to Maris and grabbed one of my biscuits. She looked at it for a moment before dunking it in my soup. "Can't keep a secret in this little town." She snubbed her cigarillo out on the heel of her shoe and stuck the snipe behind her ear before she started gumming my biscuit.

"You said you doubted Axle hung himself," I said to Lucille. "You know something?"

She motioned with the biscuit, and a crumb fell into my coffee cup. "For starters, he was too damned selfish to commit suicide."

"You knew him, then?"

"Axle never came in here," Lucille said as she refilled her coffee cup. Then, as an afterthought, refilled mine. "But Denise would, pop in whenever she came to town. Lord, the tales she told . . ."

I sipped the soup. It was runnier even than Yancy's concoction had been, but somewhere in the bowl there was bound to be chicken. If I could find it. "Tales?"

"Tales. She couldn't take it anymore," Lucille said just as she snatched my last biscuit.

I nodded to the empty platter. "You got more in the back room?"

"Cost you extra," Lucille said and disappeared into the kitchen.

Maris looked after her. "I like her. She's like Uncle Byron. Only crustier."

"She a *lot* crustier than Byron. Hell of a way she's running her business. Almost like she doesn't want any customers. How she stays afloat is beyond me."

Maris lit another cigarette and leaned back. Her shirt snagged on a piece of wood sticking out of the rough booth back, and she picked at the splinter. "She's probably got nothing else to do with herself, like a lot of folks nowadays. If she's like Uncle Byron, running a café keeps her mind off bad times."

Lucille returned with more biscuits and sat beside Maris again.

"You were telling us you doubted Axle did himself," I said. "Milo figures he might have been depressed 'cause he knew Denise ran off with another man."

"I can relate to that," Maris added. "Went to greener pastures myself a time or two."

"A time or two for you is every week, but don't bring that up around Yancy," I told her. "You broke his heart bad enough as it is." Yancy and Maris had hit it off the couple weeks she and her Uncle Byron came up from El Reno for a visit. After I'd hired her, I thought there was a budding romance developing. Yancy thought so, too, until Maris went running through those greener pastures she referred to. I thought she'd beat her addiction—men. Apparently I was wrong.

I turned to Lucille. "So, you don't think Milo's theory that Denise ran off with some other guy holds water?"

"About as much water as my bladder," she laughed. "Which isn't long before I have to run to the water closet." She snatched a biscuit just as I reached for it. "You see photos of Denise?"

"I have," I said, though I didn't mention I'd actually met the woman more than once.

"Then you know she and Axle could almost be twins. Except Axle's boobs are—were—bigger."

"If she didn't run off with some guy," Maris said, "maybe she did move to Billings to work in a cannery."

"I'll call bullshit on that, too," Lucille said.

I moved my spoon around in my soup and finally landed a tiny piece of chicken. As in Yancy's antelope stew, the meat had eluded me until now. "You seem to know a lot about Denise's situation."

"I know a lot about most people's situation around here." Lucille took a sip of her coffee and scrunched up her nose. Even she didn't like her own coffee.

"You made it," I said.

Lucille ignored me and set her cup down. "Denise came into the diner whenever she was in town."

"More for the conversation than the food, I'd bet."

Lucille shrugged. "Probably. But the last time she came in was a couple weeks ago. She said she was scared. Bad. Axle's moonshining operation was sliding, as if money wasn't tight enough in the hunting off-season."

"That sure sounds like she went someplace for a job—like that cannery."

Lucille grabbed the half-smoked snipe from behind her ear and lit it. Sparks fell onto her lap, and she batted at them with my napkin. "As much as she might have needed a job," Lucille said as she handed my napkin back, "she needed to get out of there worse. She said Axle's competition paid him a visit the morning she was in here."

"What competition?"

"Some geek in a new suit. Dressed like he was fixing to enter some dance competition or something. Came to the house and threatened Axle. Said he was going to be sole distributor hereabouts of liquor, Denise said. The guy informed him of that right before Axle put a boot in the guy's rectum and put the run on him."

"Sounds like Axle had a handle on it." I squinted in my bowl and spotted one more piece of chicken. That made three so far. But who was counting. "And I'll wager again that you can tell us just who Axle's competition was."

"Sure," Lucille said. "Same as Denise figured. Nest of Italians—that Napoli bunch. Got a fancy place they bought for county taxes on Kirby Creek a few miles north of town."

"Did Sheriff Darcy mention them?" Maris asked me.

"He did not. Maybe he's not aware of them."

Lucille shook her head. "That pompous ass is aware of the Napoli bunch, all right. The high sheriff's just so worried about his own cushy job that he keeps his nose buried in their asses. Rumor has it that old man Napoli contributed a sizeable amount to Darcy's reelection this time around."

"I'll ask the sheriff about the Napolis tomorrow." I left the rest of my soup on the table and forced down the coffee as I digested what Lucille said. If someone had visited Axle and threatened to shut his business down, I'm surprised they made it away from his place alive.

I paid Lucille and asked for a receipt. At least the government was paying for this feast.

I left her a tip, and she pocketed the quarter. As Maris and I were leaving, Lucille called after me, "You're the second person who came in here asking about Axle lately."

I turned back to her. "The second? Who was the other one?"

"Some great big Indian." She turned to Maris. "No offense. From the Wind River Reservation. Only seen him in town a time or two. Will something-or-other. Said he was going to speak personally with Axle. I figured he was just another one of Axle's moonshine customers as he sure didn't seem the type to afford a hunting trip with Axle."

"Anything else?"

Lucille flipped her butt into a spittoon, but it bounced off the rim and landed on the floor. "That's about it, except that—as mean as Axle was supposed to be—he'd have little defense against that big Indian."

"Why didn't you tell me about this before?"

Lucille started picking up dirty plates. "I guess that massive tip you left jarred my memory."

Maris walked with me to where I'd parked the panel down the block. "What the hell did you get yourself into? We're supposed to be paper-servers. Evict delinquent ranchers because the banks tell us to. Investigating murders is not *our* job."

"And how is that job going for you?" I asked. "Pretty exciting, isn't it?"

Maris sighed. "About as exciting as trimming my toenails."

I watched a buggy pulled by a mule trotting by and wished I was on mine on my way up to that trout stream. "Right about now, we're it. The government doesn't send any of those citified Department of Investigation hot shots to the middle of nowhere. Hell, the last one they sent out this spring got lost in the Tetons, and it took me a week to find the fool. He was lucky some grizzly didn't eat him."

"I see your point." Maris leaned against the panel truck and patted her pocket. "You got a smoke? I'm out."

I shook out a Chesterfield for her and lit one for myself. "Someone's got to take the initiative, or else that blowhard Sheriff Darcy will be more than happy to rule it a suicide. Lazy bastard. And Darla Lone Tree's disappearance is probably connected."

"That's a stretch . . ."

"Is it?" I said. "Just too coincidental. Her coming up missing about the time Axle was murdered. That's why I need you to go to Wind River and get with Yancy—"

"In what way do you mean 'get with Yancy'?"

"Not in the way you're thinking. If Lucille is right—and the unofficial town crier probably is—Will paid Axle a visit recently."

"So now you think Will killed Axle?"

I dropped the butt on the ground and stepped on it. "He's sure capable. I know just how his temper can get away from him. I can see him talking to Axle in the hardest way and going too far."

"And you don't think one of the Napoli bunch killed Axle after he kicked the dog shit out of whoever the Italians sent to shut him down? They could have returned with reinforcements."

"Occam's Razor."

"What the hell's that?"

"One of those normally useless things I learned hitting the books in the hospital when I was mending up after the war. Some fourteenth-century Franciscan friar came up with the theory to explain scientific assumptions, but I've found it pertains to our work as well. Means that when two theories come to the same conclusion, the simpler of the two is probably right. My guess is that Will beating Darla's whereabouts out of Axle and going too far is the simpler."

"I'd look closer at the Italians—"

"If car loads of men roared up to Axle's, he'd see them half a mile off, and they wouldn't get far. I'd have found their bodies, and their car, within rifle range of Axle's house." I climbed behind the wheel and started the Ford. "But take Yancy with you when you talk with Will."

"What will you be doing?"

"First, I'm going to soak in the mineral springs. Then I'm going to find a motel that accepts government payment."

Maris grinned. "Wanna' share the room?"

Chapter 8

When I entered the courthouse, a kindly, white-haired lady walked down the hallway towards the clerk's office. I stopped her and asked where Milo's office was. She directed me to the office at the end of the hallway. Her nose turned up, and she sniffed in my direction. "Mineral springs?"

"You got a good smeller."

She smiled, and twin gold teeth smiled back at me. "If you'd lived here as long as I have, you'd smell the sulfur, too. Feel good?"

"Felt great," I answered and had started walking to the sheriff's office, when I stopped and followed her back into her office. "You're the clerk of county courts."

"They do hire smart marshals nowadays," she said as she opened her office door. "Whatcha need?"

"Axle Denny—"

"Heard he was found hanging yesterday."

"They do hire smart clerks nowadays," I said.

She grinned and tipped an imaginary hat. "So?"

"Could you find property statements Axle had filed? I heard he bought some land to set aside for hunting a few years ago," I told her, though I knew he'd talked about the land sale during one of my booze trips some years before. "I'd like to see what he used as a reason for the application."

"Folks don't need much of a reason if they got money to pay the taxes—"

"Humor me," I said.

"Guess marshals have more spare time for foolishness than clerks do," she said and disappeared into a huge walk-in safe containing county records. She returned with a brown folder with Axle's name scrawled across the top. "Take your time," she said. "I know you have it."

I took out the many papers Axle had filed with the clerk's office through the years, until I reached the one where he had bought the section of land from a rancher next to him who went belly up. In the application for transfer, Axle explained the location and terms of the sale. I cared nothing about those particulars. What I *did* care about was that the application was in Axle's own handwriting—neat. Legible. With excellent sentence structure as though he were an educated man. Nothing at all like the suicide note we found in his horse barn. I closed the folder and walked down the end of the hallway to the sheriff's office.

I expected a receptionist to greet me, but none sat at the chair on the other side of the counter, so I walked into Milo's office unannounced. He sat behind an enormous mahogany desk holding a receiver to his ear. He held up his hand for me to wait a moment and soon slid the receiver onto the horseshoe, ending his call. "Just what the hell do people expect me to do?"

"Problems?"

"I've had cattle thefts in the county since last summer that I haven't solved. One of the sisters'—Mary Ann Mobley's—Model A roadster was taken in front of the post office while she was inside mailing a package, and it was found out of gas north of town. Jody Well's Indian Chief was stolen off the street in broad daylight last month and reported wrecked in the park. Now this." He tossed his pencil on his desk and pointed to the phone as if it were the cause of his woes.

I waited for him to continue his rampage. "A . . . taxpayer

reported someone shot his pet squirrel."

"You mean some squirrel living in his house like a dog?"

Milo shook his head and dug his pack of Mail Pouch out of his pocket. "No. He claims it's a squirrel that lives in his tree. Comes up and eats out of old man Napoli's hand every morning. Somebody had the stones to shoot the critter right out of the tree in front of his house."

"That Italian who lives off Kirby Creek?"

Milo stuffed tobacco into his cheek and squinted at me. "You know Gustavo Napoli?"

"No." I took off my hat and sat in an overstuffed chair that smelled of fresh-tanned leather. I thought about telling Milo I'd heard the Napolis had contributed to his reelection but figured I'd hold that close to my vest. For now. "But I learned he is—was—one of Axle's competitors."

"I heard that the last year or so as well, but—like we both agreed before—moonshining is none of my business, if they don't do anything else wrong in my county." Milo stood and walked to the window. He opened the blinds and said over his shoulder, "If I confirmed the Napolis were bootlegging, I'd have to do something. Maybe even call in the US marshal," He faced me and grinned. "And we wouldn't want that, would we?"

"I find it interesting that you brought up that it's none of your business if they did nothing else illegal besides moonshining," I said, running my hand over the smooth leather of the chair. "I don't begrudge a man taking a nip now and again. For medicinal purposes, you understand. Or the men peddling their bathtub gin. But if they get into some war with another bootlegger that results in his murder—"

"You're not on that murder kick again." Milo dropped down in his chair. "Axle committed suicide."

I told Milo about the suicide note, and how different it was from the land application on file with the clerk of courts. "I looked at both writing—someone else scribbled that suicide note."

"Or how about this," Milo argued. "I'm thinking Denise wrote that application with the county. She was the brains of that team. No doubt she filled out the application for him."

"And notarized his signature that was night-and-day different than that on the note?"

A faint rap preceded a woman in her twenties as she sauntered in. She wore a skirt that ended right above her shapely knees, and a long-sleeve blouse that fit tighter and lower than it ought to have. She didn't even look at me as she carried a tray of eggs and toast and pork chops—that looked a lot more appealing than Lucille's pork chops—and set it in front of Milo. She unfolded a checkered napkin and draped it over Milo's lap. Her eyes met his and lingered a little too long for my thinking, and she sashayed out of the room.

"Damn good secretary," he said as he tucked the napkin under his chin. "Brings me breakfast from Delmonico's every morning." He looked at the door. "Should have married her."

"Then you wouldn't have some of the goodies you have now." I patted the leather chair that cost more than I made in a month. "You might even have to drive a truck like me."

"I got my own money," he snapped. "I don't need Roberta's."

"But hers helps." I smiled.

"Did you come in here to tell me what a grifter I am because my wife's family has money?"

I leaned forward, and Milo drew back. He knew I wasn't there to share his breakfast. "Why didn't you tell me Axle had competition from the Napolis? Were you *ever* going to mention it?"

Milo shrugged. "I didn't think it was important. Old man Napoli keeps to himself. I doubt he'd risk committing murder just to trim the competition. He and his boys stick to themselves. Come into town to do some shopping couple times a week. Polite, all of them. Since they've moved here, it's like Thermopolis has had a mini-injection into the economy."

Milo used his *fork* to slice the pork chop. *Tender.* "Like I said, I've heard he was dealing illegal liquor, just like I heard Axle was. And the word is the Italian's product is far superior to Axle's tarantula juice."

I picked up an empty glass sitting on the edge of the desk and sniffed it. It brought back bad memories, and Milo grabbed it from me and put it in his desk drawer. "*That's* the reason Axle lost business. People will buy the finest booze they can afford. Besides, since the Napolis bought that place out of town, I've had no complaints. Until today."

"Today?"

Milo nodded to the phone. "That was old man Napoli reporting someone shot his squirrel. First time I've had to go there in a long time."

"Either way, I need to speak with him."

"Why? Axle's death—murder or not—is county jurisdiction. There's no need to speak to Gus." He smiled. "Unless you have papers to serve him."

"I'm dealing with a very upset father looking for his runaway daughter. It just so happens, she was buying booze from Axle—"

"That's got nothing to do with the Italians."

"It is if Axle wasn't there when she stopped by—like if he was swinging in his barn by then—and she went to the other place she knew sold hooch—the Napolis. Besides"—I reached over and grabbed a slice of Milo's buttered toast, but he said nothing—"Denise Denny said some fancy dancer paid Axle a visit a few weeks before we found him dead. One of the Napoli bunch more'n likely."

Milo grabbed a pencil and pushed his breakfast aside.

"Where'd you find Denise? I need to interview her, just to rule out murder."

"She told a friend in town—"

"What friend? I'll talk with her, too."

I thought it better to keep Lucille's name close to my vest as well. As Lucille herself said, you can't keep a secret in this small town. "Just someone I bumped into on the street. Point is, I need to find someone who has seen Darla Lone Tree, even if it was briefly while she stopped at Axle's. Or if she went to buy hooch from the Italians. You're welcome to come along."

Milo finished the last of his pork and eggs and dabbed his mouth with a napkin. "Can't. I got real police work to do."

"Like looking for a squirrel killer?"

"Good day, Nelson."

I stood and smoothed my denims. "Can you at least give me directions to the Napoli place."

Milo nodded to the outer office while he grabbed the phone receiver. "Ask my secretary. All Emily's got to do all day is sit around and make men drool. Answer the phone now and again." He laughed. "She'll give you directions."

I stepped into the outer office and walked to the counter. Emily sat at a pine desk ringed with cigarette burns where people had set smoldering butts at the edges. Probably not Emily. She gave the appearance of someone who kept herself—and her work area—spotless. Even as she read a *Colliers* propped open by a paperweight as she layered color on her long nails. Long because, I suspected, she rarely typed. As most secretaries did. But then I figured Milo kept her around for her other attributes.

"Sheriff Darcy said you could give me directions to the Napoli ranch."

She ignored me until she'd finished her nail and capped the bottle. She waved her hand in the air to dry the polish as she motioned for me to follow her to a wall map. "Go north like you're heading to Worland until you hit Lucerne." She traced the hard-packed road with her finger and leaned closer to see. I knew where Lucerne was. I just enjoyed standing close enough to smell Emily's Chanel #5, though I wondered how she earned enough being a county secretary to afford the racy cologne. "Turn east to this dirt road that parallels Kirby Creek, and drive four miles. Turn at the mailbox, and go the winding road. Can't miss it: big house that sits in a valley north of the creek."

"So, you've been there a time or two?"

"What's that supposed to mean?" she blurted out. And backed away from such a simple question.

"Just figure you've been there, by the way you describe the place."

"I drove past there once."

Emily obviously didn't want to talk about the Napolis. But I did. "What's old man Napoli like?"

"How should I know?" She stepped around me and retreated back behind the counter.

"I was trying to get a feel for what he's like before I talk with him about my runaway girl. And, as it sounds like you've been there—"

"All I can tell you," she said as she hid behind her open *Colliers,* "is that I wouldn't call him old man Napoli. He's a little sensitive about his age."

CHAPTER 9

I drove the seven miles north of Thermopolis to the little hamlet of Lucerne and turned east like Emily said. As a young man, I'd passed lush alfalfa fields on both sides of Lucerne on my way to Lander or Riverton or the Ft. Washakie rodeos. Now, dusty dry fields struggled in this drought, and farmers tried to keep their crops alive. But why? With farm prices remaining at a fraction of what they were before the Crash of '29, farming seemed almost a waste of time. Like the farmers were marking time, doing what they could, until the drought ended, and they could once more feed their families. Hell, most folks around here didn't even realize the market crashed three years ago. They just did what they could to survive.

The road paralleled Kirby Creek, meandering between low hills of scrub brush and cactus and trees stunted by the drought. Off to the south a few head of steers grazed on whatever they could paw out of the dry ground. Interspersed among the cows were a few head of sheep, their wool hanging in loose and scraggly patches on their backs as they cropped what the cows missed.

Emily had pointed out that the Napoli ranch—what they called their land, consisting of two sections (small by Wyoming standards)—lay across a wooden bridge. As I drove the creaking bridge over the creek bed that had dried up years ago, my thoughts turned back to Emily. Not because she was stunning, even if she hadn't drowned her face in makeup, but because she had some unique relationship with Milo. I'd learned early on not to trust information between lovers, if they were indeed that. Perhaps things hadn't gotten any further than a fantasy between them. Either way, it was something I'd file in the back of my mind for later.

I turned at the mailbox—painted red and green and faded by the sun, the colors of Italy—with the name *NAPOLI* stenciled on the side in bright white letters.

The grade gradually rose as I drove north toward a high spot in the road. When I reached the top of the hill, I could look down upon a sprawling ranch house seemingly as big as the courthouse in Thermopolis. Thirty yards away sat several outbuildings, a blacksmith shop by the looks of one stack, a smokehouse the other. Ringing the north side was a shelter belt of struggling trees. A two-story barn wore fresh paint to match the mailbox: blood red with bright white trim. Most farmers and ranchers hereabouts forgot the last time they could afford fresh paint, and their buildings looked weathered and cracked, unlike Napoli's. Nowadays, all the country folks could hope for was that the grasshoppers wouldn't eat what little paint remained on their own buildings.

A lean-to was attached to the barn, and a small open-ended equipment shed sat beside that. A bright orange Allis-Chalmers tractor—replete with rubber tires, which no farmer or rancher here could afford—had been backed into the shed. Hay forks were mounted on the front, but I doubted if anyone down in the valley had ever harvested even a shock of hay with it.

The ranch house was no more than a quarter mile away as the buzzard flies, but the drive winding down to it took a half mile of dusty road. When I neared bottom I saw better what I'd spotted from on top. The log ranch house drew my attention the most, and I stopped the truck for a moment. From this angle, I could see it was a single-story ranch affair, twice as long as it was wide. Rocking chairs and round tables sat under a covered porch that ran the entire length of the front of the house.

Parked neatly in front of the porch were two Cadillacs and a Packard with a hood as long as my panel truck. The sun shone off their newly washed bodies, unlike a Pontiac pickup, dented and dirty, with barrels of something lashed to the bed, parked away from the fancy cars so as not to contaminate them.

As I descended into the ranch yard, I caught movement in my periphery: sun glinting off something in the trees to the east. I'd been around enough bunters, many with scoped rifles, to know I was being watched and tracked. How many armed guards did Gustavo Napoli have around his house? Were they to protect his bootleg business? If so, his operation must be bigger than Milo let on. Or was the old man just paranoid? Like me.

As I drove into the yard, two young women perhaps Emily's age crossed the yard. They stopped and stared, and one said something to the other before they scurried to the barn and disappeared inside.

By the time I'd stopped beside the Packard, two men had emerged from the house. Both in their twenties; both shorter than me by several inches; both muscular. Blue eyed, and paler than Lucille—who looked like she was a step away from the Forever Rest—they displayed no weapons, though I sensed they were armed. One casually picked his fingernails with a long, thin-bladed knife, while the other looked up the hill as if he were studying something. But it was me they were studying.

An almost imperceptible nod from the one picking his nails, and a man stepped from the house. His grey hair had whitened around the temples and stuck out of a broad-brimmed Panama straw hat as if he were headed to some beach near Hollywood. He wore the collar of his silk shirt turned down, and a silk handkerchief jutted out of his shirt pocket. He owned those high cheekbones of someone perpetually smiling, and his twinkling eyes followed me as I shut the truck off.

He said something over his shoulder to a man in his twenties, perhaps thirties—it was hard to tell when a person is dressed like he's going to a dance, with his tight leather pants and silk shirt open to the waist to show off his thick gold chain. My first impression was one of a weasel as he rolled a toothpick around in his teeth. He came to the old man's shoulders, and his eyes darted around, never focusing on one spot. He played with his pencil-thin mustache as he watched me climb out of the truck. When he turned his head, I saw one eye sported a nasty, dark bruise, and he whispered to the old man through lips that were swollen and split.

"Howdy, friend," the old man said, trying his best to sound like those Texan cowboys who came up north on the rodeo circuit every summer. But his thick Italian accent betrayed him. "You lost?"

The two husky men parted and took up positions to either side of the old man. They wore denims and pressed flannel shirts left untucked, bulges betraying their weapons. And the shine of their cowboy boots told me it was unlikely they ever saw a cow. The one pocketed his knife, while the other one hitched up his Levis over the belt holster hidden under his shirt. "I'm looking for Gustavo Napoli."

The old man twirled his white handlebar mustache, and a smile spread across his face. "You have come to the right place, young man. I am Gustavo Napoli. But my friends call me Gus. You a friend?"

But as charming as he appeared at first, I'd call him Gustavo. Just in case our friendship wound up in the outhouse. "I'm certainly no enemy at this point."

His eyebrows arched upwards, and the twinkle returned to his dark eyes. "At this point? But come. Sit." He motioned to wicker chairs clustered around a large glass-topped table on the porch. He said something to a woman standing just inside the screen door right before he slapped the weasel on the back of the head. "Where are your manners? Introduce yourself."

The younger man's gaze darted past me, until it finally settled on my chest. "Marco Napoli," he said. "My father's son."

"And thank the good Lord I have but the one," Gustavo crossed himself. "Sit."

"Then these are not your sons?" I nodded to Gus's muscle men, though I doubted they were related to Gustavo, with his dark complexion, his prominent bone structure. Those two appeared almost refined, in a way that rattlers are refined from garter snakes.

Gustavo laughed. "Heavens, no. But I would be proud if they were. They are the Twins."

Even though they held similarities, I failed to see any resemblance, and Gustavo caught my look. "Yosef and Rafael Rosenbaum. They are not really twins. They are cousins I adopted when their parents were killed in an automobile accident back east. But enough of me and my Jewish . . . stepsons." He nodded to my badge as he sat in one of the chairs. "Tell me who graces my house, and why are you here?"

"Nelson Lane," I got out just as the woman walked from the house carrying a tray with glasses and a sweating pitcher of iced tea. I drew in a sharp breath as I watched her walk—no, glide—across the porch to the table. She was much younger than Gustavo, about my age, and her rayon dress clung to her curves. Which were impressive. She wore little makeup—I concluded she needed none—and the odor of her cologne as she walked past me reminded me of Emily at the sheriff's office. Her bobbed blond hair was made up in perfect finger waves, and the diamond studs in her ears matched a ring of them adorning her feathered cloche hat. She looked at me, and I thought I detected a slight wink.

"This is Rosie Manning," Gus said as he wrapped his arm around her legs and drew her close. "Love of my life, and heir to all this." He waved his arm around the ranch yard. "If my lazy son does not get to work soon."

Marco glared at his father and walked down the porch steps toward the barn. "Damned kids," Gustavo said, drawing Rosie nearer him. He kissed her lightly on the forehead before he swatted her behind. "We do man talk."

"Of course," she said right before she poured tea and disappeared back into the house.

He pointed to the barn and spoke to the Twins. "It is all right. Go see if Marco needs help."

Gustavo opened a humidor sitting on the table and took out a cigar. He snipped the end with a pearl-handled cutter and slid the box toward me. "Never got the urge. But I'll have a cigarette if you don't mind."

Gustavo lit his Cuban and leaned over and lit my Chesterfield. "Now what brings you out here from Thermopolis? Here to find the rascal who shot my squirrel, I hope." He pointed to a dead squirrel lying at the base of a cottonwood tree twenty yards from the house. "Whoever shot her cut the tail off and was gone before we could catch him." He leaned closer. "But I didn't realize US marshals normally investigated trespassers."

"We don't." I dropped two sugar cubes in the glass of tea and stirred. "I'm looking for a young girl—"

"Whoa!" Gustavo said. "I don't know what you've heard, Marshal—"

"I haven't heard anything." I explained that I was looking into a runaway—Darla Lone Tree—from the Wind River Reservation.

"And someone told you this Indian girl is here?"

"No." I snubbed my butt out in an ashtray made out of a hollowed-out elephant foot. "Her father believes that Darla went to Axle Denny's, looking to buy moonshine."

"I still do not follow you, Marshal."

"One of your . . . employees paid Axle a visit a few days before he was murdered."

"Murdered!" Gustavo stood and began pacing the porch. "I never knew he was murdered."

"Then you knew Axle?"

"I knew he was—"

"A competitor?" I finished. "Someone who took business away from you."

"Now see here, Marshal—if you're here to make an arrest—"

I held up my hand to stop him. "It's not my job to enforce liquor laws," I assured him. "Unless I absolutely have to. I am looking for this runaway, and she might have been at Axle Denny's ranch a time or two while one of your people were there. I need to know if any of your people saw her there."

"Rosie," Gustavo called, and she appeared in the doorway. "Go to the barn and bring back Marco. And the Twins, too."

Rosie bounded down the stairs toward the barn, and I found it hard to avert my eyes from that bounce.

"Striking, isn't she?" Gustavo said as he caught me looking after her.

I nodded.

"She, too, is Jewish. I met her in Chicago after my first wife died."

After Rosie led Marco and the Twins to the house, she brushed past me and went inside. Gustavo pointed a finger at all three when they'd stepped onto the porch. "The marshal needs it straight—did any of you visit Axle Denny lately? He is looking for a young Indian girl who ran away from . . . her tribe? Is that the term?"

"Close enough." I fished Darla's photo out of my vest pocket and handed it to the Twins. They shook their heads, and one of them—Yosef, I think—said to Gustavo, "You know we just returned from a visit back home this week."

"And you?" I handed the picture to Marco. "Been at Axle Denny's lately, maybe when this girl was there buying liquor?"

Marco's hand crept to his eye that showed little sign of the swelling going down. The dandy Axle had beaten and run off his property would have serious injuries, and I was surprised Axle let Marco off so easy. But he shook his head, even if he didn't look at the picture.

"There you have it." Gustavo threw up his hands and turned once again to Marco and the Twins. "Go. Leave me and the marshal to visit."

I watched them walk to the barn and asked Gus, "What kind of work do those fellers do, anyhow?"

Gustavo waved his hand around. "Ranch work, of course. I bought this property to develop it into a working ranch."

"No offense," I said, "but that boy of yours has hands soft enough to be in a Palmolive commercial. And the Twins are wearing jeans so tight a fart couldn't get through the denim, let alone allow them to swing a leg over a saddle."

Gustavo shrugged. "So, they are young. They are learning."

"And are they learning the moonshining business as well?"

Gustavo poured himself another glass of iced tea but didn't top mine off. Guess that was my cue that I wouldn't be staying for lunch. "I thought it was not your job to enforce liquor laws."

"It is not. I'm just trying to get a grasp on what's going on hereabouts." I motioned to the barn. "That barn, for instance, wouldn't contain a still or two by any chance?"

"It does not."

"Then you wouldn't mind me taking a peek inside?"

"I would," Gustavo said. He turned his chair so it faced me and knocked the ash of his cigar into the elephant foot. "Your runaway Indian girl is not there. But if I allowed you to go inside and you found operating stills, well, of course you would have to take enforcement. No?"

"I might. Or I might not."

"That is something I cannot chance." He tossed the last of his tea out and set his glass on the table. "But I will pass the word that you are looking for this runaway. Rosie," he called, and she came onto the porch. She gathered up the tray and glasses and headed for the house. For the second time as she passed me, she winked so faintly I almost didn't catch it.

"Feel free to come back any time for a visit, Marshal." He smiled wide, and the sun glinted off two gold teeth on one side of his mouth. "I enjoyed our conversation."

I hated to admit it, but I enjoyed talking with Gustavo, too. Compared to the thugs he employed, he came across as educated, with a certain amount of panache. I had to keep reminding myself he was some kind of gangster. What kind, I didn't know. But I would find out.

When I opened the door of my truck, I looked back at Gustavo, who had been joined now by Rosie. He stood on the porch with his arm around her thin waist. I motioned overhead. "I see you have phone lines running to your house." *Something that ninety percent of ranch folks couldn't afford.*

Gus looked at the taut lines that must have been installed when he bought the spread. "Is it not great to be truly modern?"

"It is," I answered. "But how did you know I drove in from Thermopolis."

"What's that?"

"Thermopolis," I repeated. "You asked me earlier what brought me out here from Thermop. I didn't mention where I started from."

I left that hanging, thinking back to Lucille and how a person couldn't keep a secret in a small town. Especially if someone had access to a telephone.

CHAPTER 10

I double-clutched the truck to coax it out of the basin above the Napoli Ranch, all the while feeling as if I were being watched. When I was with the 3rd Battalion of the Fifth Marines at Belleau Wood, I would often shudder when I knew I was being watched. Across the open wheat field, a German sniper lay in wait, picking off whatever hapless American showed himself. But I'd been wounded by fire during a frontal assault, not random sniper fire. Even though I felt the same now, it might be nothing more than the aftermath of meeting Gustavo Napoli. But I doubted it.

When I topped the hill going out of Gustavo's valley, the feeling subsided, and I stopped on the road. Needing to rid myself of tea, I climbed out and conducted dust control as I thought about Gustavo. Ol' Gus. Just one of the boys. Friendly—even charming, I hated to admit. Just wanting to be left alone and mind his own business as he supplied liquor to people wanting it. As in every other part of the country.

But an idyllic ranch operation like Gustavo's suggested it was not the same. His son would be more in place pimping girls on the streets of Chicago, and the Twins could find jobs as circus wrestlers by the looks of them. I laughed as I pictured any of those three throwing a leg over some gnarly mustang who didn't want to be ridden that morning.

Then there was the constant feeling of being watched as I approached, and when I drove away. I'd remember that if I ever came back to talk with Gustavo again.

I buttoned up, so wrapped up in my thoughts that I nearly didn't see a rider approach from my blind side. The side I lost during the Great War. A skinny kid rode a long-haired pinto not twelve hands high on the road approaching where I was stopped. His unruly red hair whipped across his face when the wind gusted, and he brushed his bangs out of his eyes while he kept an eye on me. He wiped sweat with his shirtsleeve and put his floppy hat back on. He carried a rifle across the saddle, and I wondered if he had any more guns hidden inside his tattered and badly patched bib overalls. He reined his horse a few feet in front of my truck. "Howdy," he said, but there was little friendliness in his raspy voice.

I nodded to the rifle. "Nice day for hunting, but I don't recall anything in season right now." I rubbed the back of my head. "Step down from there. I'm getting a stiff neck."

He got down from an ancient McClellan cavalry saddle. Except for a chunk missing from the pommel, and barbed-wire gouges in the high cantle, the boy kept his saddle well oiled and properly adjusted for the pony.

"You're new hereabouts?" the boy said. As I rubbed my hand over his pony's lathered withers, I thought he was awfully forward with his questions. I liked than in a kid. I pulled my vest back, to reveal my badge.

"You a truant officer?" he said, his hand clutching the rifle stock. " 'Cause I meant to go to school that last month—"

"US marshals don't enforce truancy laws."

His shoulders slumped, relieved. "Then why are you here?"

"I'd ask you the same thing. Come around that horse for a moment and hang that rifle from that piece of rope on your saddle."

"It's only a .22."

"Humor me," I said. "I've had a case of the jitters once today already."

He looped a rope around the stock of the rifle and let it dangle from the horn as he walked around his mustang. He stood nearly as tall as me. But bean pole described the kid perfectly. I guessed him to be early teens, and he had a lot of filling out to do. "You live hereabouts?"

"Me and Dad's got forty acres over that hill. We run a few cows and a hog now and again. But I done my chores today," he blurted out as if I were going to haul him before his tribunal of a father.

"I believe you did." I offered my hand. "Nelson. But you can call me Nels."

"Can I call you Marshal?"

"If you like."

The kid broke into a broad smile and took my hand. "Never met a real live US marshal. James Kincaid." His grip was firm, the calluses deep.

"Well, Jimmy—"

"James." The smile faded for a moment. "I go by James."

"James it is, then." I leaned back against the Ford and shook out a cigarette. James eyed the pack, and I suspected he lit up at times when folks weren't around. "Now what's that you're hunting this summer?"

He turned to a gunny sack tied to his saddle and opened it. He reached in and took out two jawbones from coyotes. "County pays a fifty-cent bounty. I'm making some go-to-town money." He nodded to the road leading to the Napoli Ranch. "You come from there?"

"I did. Had a talk with Gustavo Napoli at his house."

"You meet the Twins?"

I lit the Chesterfield and ground the match out with my boot. "Wasn't much of a meeting, but, yes, I saw them. Why?"

"They're mean bastards—"

"That any way to talk?"

James smiled. "I talk . . . a whole sight harsher about them when I'm not around strangers." He stepped closer and looked up at me. "You go down thataway again, Marshal, you watch your backside."

"Thanks for the advice." I snubbed the cigarette butt out in the dirt. "But I need to get into Thermop." I had opened the door to my truck when I noticed a small flour sack looped over the pommel. "You got some other hunting . . . proceeds in there?"

James nodded and grabbed the sack. When he opened it, I saw a dozen squirrel tails bouncing around the bottom, and he closed the sack again. "Feed store gives a dime a tail," he said as he hung the sack from his saddle again.

"You weren't by any chance hunting squirrels on the Napoli Ranch this morning?"

"Early, like maybe six o'clock or so? When everyone would be asleep?" He grinned. "Of course not. The Twins would string me up if they caught me."

Chapter 11

Yancy sounded out of breath when he picked up the phone at the tribal office. "You sound like you just ran in from the outhouse."

"I wish it were that simple," Yancy said. "Nels, you gotta' do something about Maris."

"Whoa. Just what's going on with her?"

"Maris is . . . trying to find Darla in the oddest places."

"That's what I wanted her to do," I said.

"You don't understand." Yancy seemed to be pleading. "She's asking every single guy she comes across if they've seen Darla. Asking in her own way. You know what way I'm talking about."

I did know, and I rubbed my temples to stem a rising headache. I'd hoped that when Maris moved here to Wyoming she would get that itch out of her system. Apparently, she had not. I felt ashamed of myself for thinking it, but if she got results and found Will's daughter by bedding half the male population of Wind River, it just might be worth it. At the least, I assured myself, her addiction was only her form of entertainment.

"Relax," I told Yancy, though I knew it pained him to see her with other men. After all the ladies he had been with, Maris was the only one who had stolen his heart. And kept it. "As I recall, you've had a couple ladies on the hook since you and Maris broke up."

"Drunks drown their sorrows in booze," Yancy said. "I drown mine in women."

"It'll work out," I told him, though that sounded a little lame, and I quickly changed the subject. "Now what did you want to tell me besides Maris is bedding every guy she comes across?"

"One of my sources here on the rez saw something." Yancy sipped something, and it sounded like gurgling on the other end of the phone. Probably his nasty coffee. "This witness said he went to Axle's one day last week to buy a jar of shine. When no one answered the door—guess he was swinging from the rafters by then—he drove to Napoli's place. He heard they sold booze and figured the Italians would be more than happy to sell him a bottle."

Yancy just about choked on whatever he was drinking, and I waited until he'd recovered from his coughing fit. "So, my source said that when he went to Napoli's to buy some hooch, those Twins put the run on him. Roughed him up some just for fun before they kicked him off the ranch."

"All that proves is that the Twins are mean bastards, in the words of James."

"Who?"

"Just someone I met on the road today."

"Listen," Yancy insisted, "don't you think if illegal liquor is their business, they'd want to sell as much as they could?"

"A lot of these guys—especially those who come from the big cities like Gustavo did—don't trust anyone. They live and die by being cautious," I said as I thought back to the lookouts secreted in the trees around Gustavo's place. "Maybe they thought this source of yours worked for revenuers." I processed the scene in my mind: a potential customer comes to Gustavo's to buy moonshine. They don't know him, don't trust him, so they put the run on him.

"There's more," Yancy said. "This feller says he was picking himself up off the ground after his beating and was staggering to his truck just as a car pulled into the yard and three women piled out."

I didn't see a lot of earth-shattering information here. I appreciated Yancy beating the bushes to find someone who might know about Darla, but he had a habit of over-dramatizing things. "So, Gustavo's ranch hands got needs. They'd want women to come around—"

"But such young needs?"

"How young?"

"My source said all the girls that bailed out of the car looked his daughter's age."

"How old is this witness?"

"Your age."

I laughed. "At my age, every girl looks young." Especially Polly, who just turned fourteen last month. "And they probably did to this feller as well."

"Well, you better do something," Yancy said. "Between Maris bedding half the male population of Wind River, and Will Lone Tree kicking the shit out of the other half, it's driving me nuts. What if one of the girls the guy saw was Darla?"

"All right," I told Yancy. "I'll check with Sheriff Darcy. If he hasn't heard anything about her whereabouts, I'll take a drive back out to Gustavo's."

"Thanks." Yancy breathed a sigh over the phone. "But hurry. By the time you get back out there, Maris will probably have a couple more notches in her garter belt."

When I walked into Milo's office, Emily jumped down from the edge of his desk where she'd been sitting. She smoothed her grey, pleated dress and glared at me as she scurried out of the office. "Don't you ever knock?" Milo asked.

I smiled after Emily. "I didn't realize you were knee-deep in—what—dictating a letter to her?"

Milo held up a piece of legal paper. "As a matter of fact, I was just telling Emily to mail this off. It's a letter to the state investigators in Cheyenne."

"About what?"

"Axle Denny," Milo answered. "I'm closing out his case. Death by suicidal hanging."

I pulled up the same leather chair that cost as much as I made in a month and scooted close to his desk. "I disagree. I believe there's enough evidence to show he was murdered."

Milo opened a humidor and grabbed a fat black cigar that looked like something a dog left on the lawn. "What evidence? That Axle still had his sidearm strapped to his belt, and his horse and mule needed food and water—that evidence?" He snipped the end of the cigar and lit up. "I'll stay with the suicide note and his revulsion at selling booze to reservation kids."

"What did Aaron find when he cut Axle open?"

Milo shrugged. "Haven't talked with him. Don't matter no how. Aaron's not a doctor."

Milo was beginning to piss me off. He knew Axle's death was county jurisdiction, and I had no say in it. I changed the subject before I reached across his desk and throttled him. "I paid Gustavo Napoli a visit this morning. Nice feller."

"I told you he was a decent old man."

"But he's hiding something out there in his barn. He wouldn't let me look."

"Don't you think it just might be his cookers?" Milo dropped the cigar cutter in a little tray beside the humidor. "He wouldn't let me look, either."

"You asked to look before?" I asked him.

Milo's face drew a blank. Which was an improvement on his lame expression. "Well, no. I never had any good reason to look, 'cause I already know what's in there—his stills." He threw up his hands. "And Lord knows, I don't want to touch that here in

Hot Springs County. I'd be rode out on a rail if I busted the only source of booze hereabouts. But you're not here to tell me about your nice little visit with Gus."

"I'm checking if you've heard anything about Darla Lone Tree's whereabouts."

Milo lit up the smelly little cigar and blew smoke rings upward where a ceiling fan blew the stench around the office. "I've put out feelers to everyone I could think of. If I knew where she was, I'd tell you, believe me." He leaned back and relit the cigar that had died out. "No offense, but it would get you out of my county sooner. Folks hereabouts are getting nervous having a US marshal in town for the last few days."

"Have I arrested anyone yet?"

"No, but folks are wondering whose ranch you're going to serve papers on next."

"And I'll bet that you are doing your civic best to put them at ease?"

Milo smiled. "I do what I can."

I stood and started for the door. Milo was as useful as Ex-Lax in a diarrhea ward, and I was wasting my time.

"Headed out so soon?"

"I got to go back to the Napoli Ranch," I said as I put my hat on. "One of the tribal police got word that three young girls bailed out of a car and ran into Gustavo's barn a couple days ago. It's a long shot, but I'm going to ask him again if I can just look in his barn for Darla."

"I'll follow you out there," Milo said. "I need to serve a summons to a derelict that's been squatting on abandoned land for the last year. Then I'll take that damned squirrel report Gus has been bugging me about."

Milo picked up the receiver on his desk phone and tapped the switch hook. He paused when he saw I remained standing in front of him. "Mind, Nels? I got to make a call to the little missus and tell her I might not be home for supper tonight."

"Far be it for me to stand in the way of true love," I said and shut the door behind me.

Emily sat at her desk hiding behind an open *Good Housekeeping.* Somehow, the magazine didn't fit her, but it was large enough she could pretend as though she didn't see me leaning over the counter. "Emily, is it?"

She nodded but didn't look up from the magazine. Didn't make eye contact.

"How long have you worked for Sheriff Darcy?"

"Seven months," she said but didn't look at me. "Why?"

"I'm thinking you'll go far in life."

She glanced at me warily out of the corner of her eye as if I were leading her into a trap. Which I was, of course. "I'm thinking you're good at your job. Those directions you gave me to the Napoli Ranch were right on target. Simple, yet informative. I bet you give people who come in just as good information."

She sat straighter in her chair. "You think so?"

"Absolutely." I took out my pack of cigarettes. "Mind?"

A faint smile tugged at her mouth. "Not if I have one, too."

I shook out one for each of us and struck a match on the corner of the counter. Her hand circled mine as she brought her cigarette to the match, and she blew it out. "What else can a girl do in these parts? Jobs are hard to find. I was lucky to land this one."

"You have an education?"

She waved smoke from her face. "I was going to graduate from school two years ago, but I had to quit and help Momma work the ranch after Papa died."

"And I'd bet you were a hard worker."

Emily leaned on the counter. "I got fed up with ranch work. Dirty all the time. Hands cracked like I was some clodhopper. I told Momma she needed to sell out while she could and move to town. But you foreclosed on the ranch before she could, and she lost everything."

Emily told me her last name, and I recognized it as just one of the many ranches we foreclosed on outside Green River a couple of years ago. "What did you do before you came to work for Sheriff Darcy?"

Emily shrugged. "Little of everything. Little of nothing."

"Well, a smart young girl like you *ought* to be off the ranch," I said. "I'm figuring you for bigger and better things."

"You really think so?"

"Of course." The other thing I figured on was that no one ever complimented her on her intelligence. Men always focused on her beauty, be my guess.

We spoke some more, and Emily slowly let her guard down. Until I asked about Gustavo. "He's got a first-rate spread there. Ever been to the ranch?"

Emily backed away from the counter. "Been there in what way?"

I shrugged. "Just for a visit. It seems like there are a lot of good looking young fellers working for Gustavo."

Her gaze darted to Milo's office door for the briefest moment. "I have a boyfriend," she said just as the high sheriff walked out of his office.

"If anyone calls," he told Emily, "I'm out to the Napoli place taking a report about his pet squirrel. Then to Kincaid's rat trap of a ranch to serve him a court summons."

Chapter 12

Milo's Buick had thirty more horses under its hood than my Ford. But his car wasn't sprung to take back-country roads very fast, and he bottomed out in ruts in the road. I had to slow to allow him to catch up, and I wondered why a county sheriff didn't have something more suited for his job. Unless he rarely made it out into the county.

When I arrived at the bridge leading towards Gustavo's drive, I once again felt the urge to tamp the dust down. By the time I'd pulled alongside the road and climbed out, Milo had caught up. He got out to stretch and looked up the road to where I'd seed James disappear on his pony yesterday. "Soon's I talk with Gus about that stupid squirrel, I'm heeded to Kincaid's place. Or I should say the Myerson place that he's squatting on."

"This Myerson sign a complaint on something?"

Milo filled his cheek with Mail Pouch and slipped the tobacco back inside his vest. "Naw. Myerson abandoned his property when grain prices went to hell. No one knows where he lit out to."

"So, the summons is not for trespassing?"

"I'm working on that angle. But, for now, the summons is for neglecting his kid. Son-of-a-bitch Kincaid's been raising his son to be a damned outlaw."

"How so?" I asked, grateful that I hadn't told Milo about meeting James yesterday.

"Kid roams the county on that scraggly-ass pony of his. Getting into trouble. There's been a dozen calls where people reported seeing someone matching the kid's description sneaking into their brooder houses, stealing chickens. One rancher across the road from Lucerne thinks the kid stole one of his fat steers." Milo shook his finger at me like I was James's pappy. "And folks swear it was James that stole Jody Wells's Indian motorcycle and wrecked it. I just can't prove it. Yet. If I could find Myerson, I'd tell him how Kincaid's been squatting, and that he took over what few steers still roam the place. Get him to swear out a warrant for stealing his fat critters."

It had been so long since I'd actually seen a fat steer, it was hard to imagine. The more likely scenario was that Myerson found one of his scrawny steers torn up after coyotes got to it and just abandoned it when he abandoned his ranch sudden-like. "Ever caught this Kincaid kid stealing?"

Milo spat a string of tobacco juice that was less than impressive. The wind carried it back toward him, and it splattered on the toe of his shiny cowboy boot. "Never caught the kid outright." He wiped his mouth with his bandana. "But I caught him once riding that old swayback mustang of his. Kid had a running iron in a gunny sack tied to his saddle. But I couldn't prove he'd actually used it."

"If you haven't caught him, what's the summons for?" I asked as I zipped up and turned to Milo.

"Truancy," Milo answered proudly.

"I'd say that ranks right up there with investigating squirrel murders."

Milo hitched up his jeans. "It's the only charge I can prove. Once I serve old man Kincaid and get the kid shipped to the reformatory, I guarantee the crime rate in this county will drop dramatically."

I climbed behind the wheel and shut the door. "I hope you

serve them. I hate to see anyone getting away with those terrible deeds."

We started down the steep winding road leading to the Napoli ranch, and I got that overwhelming feeling of being watched once again. As we neared the yard, I finally spotted a piece of cloth fluttering in the wind on a hill overlooking the north side of the house. I stopped three hundred yards from the ranch house and chanced a look through my binoculars. A man sat on a tree stump on the other side of the house, watching in our direction, his rifle propped against the stump as he sipped from a silver flask. He sure wasn't standing lookout for the squirrel killer, and I stowed my binos. And filed the position of the spotter away in my memory. Just in case.

Milo finally caught up with me, and we drove the rest of the way into the yard. By the time we pulled up in front by the hitching rail, the Twins had already taken up positions on either side of the porch. They reminded me of flankers we'd send out to spot Germans at the Wood. Some words passed between the Twins, and they split up: Rafael, with his blond cowlick, moved to stand beside a long, sleek Lincoln with orange Colorado tags, Yosef by a Chrysler with Montana plates. They kept the cars between them and us, as if they expected trouble. I would expect nothing less from bodyguards, for they certainly served Gustavo in that function.

Two more ranch hands emerged from in back of the house, and the bald man I was acquainted with smiled as he sauntered up to my truck. "You looking for poachers, Lane? Or are you looking to evict someone from their property? 'Cause these folks"—he waved his hand at Marco and Gustavo walking out of the house—"might not be so easy to serve."

"Dan Dan," I said as I climbed out of the panel. "I hear a village somewhere is missing their idiot. You best run along and check in with them." I grinned back at him. "And leave us adults to visit like civilized folks."

"Who you calling an idiot?"

I exaggerated a sigh. "Anyone whose folks give him two first names has gotta' be an idiot."

Dan Dan's face turned crimson all the way down to his thick neck, and he stepped toward me, his fists clenching and unclenching. Dan Dan Uster fancied himself a hunting guide, but he was more like a poaching guide. I had arrested him and a client two years ago for poaching a bull elk out of season in the Big Horns and turned him over to the game warden. Dan Dan had competed with Axle for hunting territory around the state, and their bad blood was a thing told around fires at night. I'd never had much of an opinion about Axle as a human being, but at least he respected wild game and the statutes that protected them. Even if he respected no other laws.

"I heard you got out of the slammer," I told Dan Dan. "Too bad you're not still there, being someone's girlfriend every night."

"I ought to kick the shit out of you—"

"But, of course, you won't." Dan Dan would be a handful in a fight, with his barrel chest and thick shoulders honed from a lifetime of hard work and wilderness travel. But my hands were unusually large, and he knew I'd used them boxing in the service. "Now unless you have business with me, I'd suggest you move along before I find something else to arrest you for."

Milo looked on with some amusement before he climbed onto the porch and shook Gustavo's hand. "There, Milo." Gustavo pointed to the tree in front of his house. "Right there is where someone murdered Mabeline."

"Mabeline?" Milo asked.

"My squirrel. She came down and ate right out of my hand every morning. Whoever shot her came hunting early before any of us were even up. Walked right into the yard. Now you going to take a report and find out who did it?"

I wasn't so interested in someone shooting the squirrel. What interested me was that James had waltzed right into the yard before any of the guards were awake. Ballsy. If I were James, I'd remember that Gustavo posted no guards that time of day.

"Well, Milo?" Gustavo pressed. "You going to find the killer?"

Milo looked over his shoulder at me and rolled his eyes. "Of course, Gus. Let's go inside, and I'll get the particulars." He turned to me. "Excuse us while I take a report." He walked back to his car and grabbed a notebook from the front seat. He followed Gus into the house, leaving me with the ever-pleasant Marco.

"The old man says make nice to you," Marco said. "So, sit."

Dan Dan began to speak, but Marco cut him off. "Why don't you and Ernie go and see if Rosie needs any help."

Dan Dan glared at me a moment longer before he turned on his heels and led the younger man beside him to the barn.

"Looks like you and Dan Dan know each other."

"Intimately," I said. "I gave him that misshapen nose the last time I arrested him. He was foolish to take a swing and . . . well"—I smiled—"he fell down some stairs a few times before I finally got him inside the jail cell at Grey Bull."

Marco laughed as if he thoroughly enjoyed hearing about other people's pain, while the Twins stood impassive beside the cars looking on. "I can relate to that."

"But I didn't know Dan Dan was the working kind. What does he do for your father?"

"Is that an official inquiry?"

"Just curious," I answered. "Dan Dan's sole saving attribute is that he's one hell of a woodsman, even if he takes game out of season whenever he can."

Marco stuck on Old Gold between his teeth and lit a match. Stalling. He saw me eying the cigarette but didn't offer me one.

"If they're good enough for Babe Ruth, they ought to be good enough for some Italian kids from Cicero."

When I didn't validate his remark about the Great Bambino, he lit up and nodded to Dan Dan disappearing inside the barn fifty yards away. "To answer your question, Dan Dan comes in handy in other ways. He knows this country very well. He knows where we should put . . . men to watch the place."

"Do you need someone watching the ranch?"

Marco smiled and flicked his match away. Yosef walked to it and snubbed it out. I'd almost forgot about them, they were so quiet while we talked. Like good soldiers tasked with action only when needed. "Let's say we like to be protected."

"From squirrel killers?"

"From trespassers," Marco snapped. He stood and paced the porch in front of the wicker chairs. "And from people who aren't invited." He looked down at me, the veins throbbing in his forehead, his breathing barely controlled. "Just remember that if you ever feel the need to come snooping around making official trouble for us."

"I *will* remember that." I wanted to tell him that Dan Dan might have pointed out the best spots from which to watch anyone approaching. But the man up on the hill was about as sneaky as fireworks on the Fourth of July.

Gustavo came out of the house with Milo on his heels, puffing on a fat White Owl cigar. Guess Ol' Gus saved the good Cubans for himself. "Sheriff Darcy tells me you'd really like to get a peek inside our barn," Gustavo said. "Still worrying over that runaway girl?"

I stood abruptly. Marco jerked back, but the Twins instantly moved away from the cars and moved toward me. They stopped when Gustavo nodded to them. One more thing to remember about those two. They were pros. "I got it on good authority that three young girls were driven here a few days ago, and that they went into your barn. At least one looked like an Indian girl."

"Marshal," Gustavo said as he sat in a chair and looked out onto his ranch yard, "I have ten men working for me. Mostly *young* men." He slapped Marco on his chicken chest. "With more hormones than common sense. Like this one. And sometimes we bring their girlfriends out here to . . . take the edge off of them. That was all they were. I can assure you that your Indian girl was not among them."

"Then you wouldn't mind my looking? Just to verify she's not there."

Gustavo tilted his head back and laughed heartedly. "You are persistent, even if you learned nothing during our last visit. No"—he nodded to Milo—"neither of you can look. If—and I'm not admitting anything here—there's an operating still in my barn, you and the sheriff would be compelled to take action. Just like we discussed before."

"But we'll keep our eyes peeled." Marco grinned. "Just in case your runaway comes around."

"Then we're done here." Milo turned to Gustavo. "I will file this report immediately." He turned his head and winked at me on the sly. "And see if I can catch who killed Mary—"

"Mabeline," Gus corrected. "Her name was Mabeline."

"Of course." Milo grinned. He was walking to his car when Gus stopped him. "Can you give one of my ranch hands a ride into town?"

"Can't," Milo answered. He wiped tobacco juice off the door of his Buick before climbing in. "I got to go up the road to that coyote Kincaid's place and serve him a summons. Might take me a while to put the sneak on him. Wary son of a bitch." He fired the car up and made his getaway before Gustavo insisted.

"Then you, Marshal Lane—do you have room in that"—he looked over my panel truck—"thing of yours?"

I watched Milo's Buick struggle to get up the hill leaving the ranch. "Room for how many?"

"Just one," Gus answered. "One of my cars threw a water pump yesterday in town, and it's ready to be picked up from the mechanic."

"Sure," I said. "Why not."

Gustavo turned to Yosef. "Run down to the barn and get Charlie."

Gustavo's muscle ran the fifty yards about as fast as I could have driven and came back in moments leading a twenty-something—it was often hard for me to tell an Indian's age—man. If this was Gus's ranch hand, he damned sure wasn't a real cowboy. The man was dressed in leather pants, and his starched white shirt lay open mid-chest. His medicine bundle—shaped like a turtle and dyed red and green—hung by a gold-colored chain around his thin neck, and his pointy boots were shined so that he could see himself in them. "Marshal Lane will give you a ride into town to pick up the Caddy," Gus said.

Charlie slid into the passenger seat, and Gus walked around and shut the door. "And Charlie"—he waged a finger at him—"be *very* careful."

"I will, Mr. Napoli."

As I started out of the yard, I looked as casually as I could to the hill in back of the house. The man who'd watched Milo and me approach earlier was nowhere to be seen. He had moved, and the move had Dan Dan Uster written all over it. He would have told anyone watching the road to move his position now and again. Just like I'd advise the lookout, were I in charge. It just reinforced my opinion that Dan Dan was savvy enough to be a dangerous man.

As we drove past the barn, Dan Dan stuck his head out of the door, and I stopped. "Be a minute, Charlie."

I set the brake and climbed out. Dan Dan met me halfway

from the barn, his face flushed, his jaw muscles tightening, as if he wanted a rematch of our last encounter at the county jail two years ago. "You here to make trouble for me with Gus?"

"Not if you give me an honest answer."

"I'm always honest." He patted his sweaty, bald head with his bandana. "Whether or not I chose to answer is another matter. But ask away."

"You and Axle Denny had words more than a few times."

Dan Dan shrugged. "I've had cross words with a lot of folks." He paused. "That's right, Axle done hung himself. And good damn riddance, too. But what's that got to do with me?"

"Where were you this past week?"

"Here. Working. What are you getting at?"

"I think you know what I'm getting at. Axle didn't hang himself. Someone did the hanging for him. As in, someone murdered the man."

"And you think *I* did it?"

"You had a hell of a good motive—get Axle out of the way, and all the prime hunting spots are suddenly available."

"Why now after all these years?" Dan Dan asked. "If I wanted him gone, don't you think I would have done so before now? I'd have loved to string him up, as much business as I lost to him. But the fact is, I was up above Dayton scouting the high country, getting ready for fall hunts." He grinned. "I'm a legitimate hunting guide now. I follow all the rules. Besides, I have a steady job, here with Ol' Gus."

"Just what do you do for the Napolis?"

Dan Dan took a pouch of Pinch Hit from his back pocket and stuffed his cheek with tobacco, no doubt stalling, figuring what to answer. "You could say I'm Gus's go-to man. At least that's what Marco calls me."

"Go-to for what?"

Dan Dan smiled. "For whatever unpleasant thing he wants done."

"Like paying Axle Denny a visit last week?"

Dan Dan didn't answer as he turned and walked back to the barn. "I'd say have a good day, Marshal," he called over his shoulder. "But I don't really care if you *ever* have another good day."

Occam's Razor was being put to the test.

Chapter 13

The entire way into Thermopolis, Charlie said no more than a few words and a grunt, despite my trying to talk with him. I learned he'd been working for Gustavo for the last six months, but he said little besides that. When I pulled up to Willie D's Repair Shop, Willie was just closing his doors. "Good thing you weren't five minutes later," he told Charlie, "or it would have been tomorrow before you could pick up the car."

Charlie started to pay Willie for the repair, but Willie laid his hand on Charlie's arm. "Keep it," Willie said. "Mr. Napoli will pay the bill the next time he's in town."

Gustavo's warning for Charlie to be careful must have sunk in, because he cautiously stepped onto the running board without scuffing it and slid behind the wheel of the new coupe. When he started the car, sixteen cylinders of Cadillac power roared to life.

Willie stepped close to the car and took a neckerchief from around his neck. He bent and rubbed fingerprints away from two of the six shiny hood ports nearest him. "Damned if I couldn't work on that beauty all day," he said with a distinct Georgia accent. He had drifted up to Wyoming when just a youngster, escaping the memory of his folks working their fingers to the bone on a cotton plantation. The Civil War had freed them physically, but not mentally. Willie had never apprenticed with a mechanic, never had formal training. But he was one of those rare individuals who could pick up anything mechanical and figure it out in moments.

"I take it you work on all of Gustavo's cars," I said as I watched Charlie motor away from the repair shop.

Willie laughed and tied his bandana around his neck. "I'm the only repair shop for miles. I work on *everybody's* car."

"Don't know if I'd trust Charlie to drive something that nice."

Willie chuckled. "Charlie is Gustavo's gopher. I sees him driving those fancy cars everywhere. Don't let the kid's fancy clothes fool you—he just runs errands for Mr. Napoli." He wiped his hands with the bandana. "Board's set up," he said sporting a sly smile. I'd first met Will when my old Dodge broke down coming through Wind River Canyon. After fixing the Agony Wagon, Willie offered to tear up the bill if I beat him in a game of chess. Double or nothing. The accounting officer later questioned the inflated repair bill on the Dodge when I turned it in for reimbursement. Twice what it should have been. And I've been trying to beat Willie in a game ever since.

"I feel lucky today," I bragged, "and would beat you for sure." I checked my watch. "But I have just enough time to make it to the state bath house for a mineral soak before they close for the day."

I made a beeline through the state park and ran into the bath house. I quickly changed into some baggy shorts and a shirt the attendant handed me, and I plodded barefoot down the ramp to the pools. I passed an elderly couple just finishing their soak, the strong odor of sulfur coming off their dripping swimsuits. The old bowlegged cowboy nodded as he passed and disappeared into the changing room.

The water was customarily hot, and it took me a moment to settle down into the pool. But that was all right—I was alone and in no rush. Just like when I was a youngster. Whenever Dad and I drove to Riverton for the annual bull sale back in fat times, we'd stop at the bath house after a nice meal at the diner that had folded a couple years ago. And whenever I finished competing in the local rodeos, I'd take time to soak in the mineral springs, letting the incredibly hot water and minerals sponge the aches right out of me. The pools always seemed to make getting thrown and stomped a bit more palatable.

I settled down into the pool and sat on a ledge under the surface. I swished water over my chest and neck and thought back to my wasted day at the Napoli ranch. And finally realized it wasn't wasted after all; that I had learned some things that might prove useful. One, during my last two trips to see Gustavo, I concluded he was one paranoid SOB to have men on guard duty watching whoever drove in. Perhaps his moonshine business *was* a lot bigger than I'd figured. Especially now that his only competition had been conveniently found hanging from the rafters of his horse barn.

Secondly, that paranoia spilled over into the hiring of Dan Dan Uster. He was more than a go-to guy, as he'd brushed it off. But why him? Gus didn't need Dan Dan to lean on people when needed—he had the Twins for that. I could only conclude that Dan Dan had been hired because he was the best man to tell Gustavo's guards where to sit, where to watch, how to best defend the ranch should it be necessary. Besides the occasional visit by the sheriff whom you had in your pocket, and the US marshal looking for a runaway girl, Gustavo must have felt some compelling reason to post guards constantly. Some reason besides guarding a bootleg operation.

Thirdly, I'd spotted a way I could sneak into the barn for a look-see. Besides Darla Lone Tree, I'd developed a curiosity as to just how involved Gustavo's illegal liquor business was. It wasn't my job to enforce liquor laws. But Gustavo's attitude caused me to make it an exception. Even if it meant waiting a little longer to catch some pan-sized trout.

I closed my eyes and dozed, lulled to sleep by the pain leaving my muscles, the water seeming to pull the aches from me, when splashing woke me. Rosie Manning walked down the steps and into the pool. She wore her hair pulled back in a tight chignon and held by a bone clasp, but it was her tight bathing suit that drew my attention. I held my gaze a little too long, and I looked away, embarrassed. She laughed when she caught me staring. "You mind sharing your pool?"

"It's open to the public," I said, more a stammer than coherent speech.

"That's what I understand." She made her way to my end of the shallow water and sat with her back against the sides of the pool. "If Gustavo owned this, he'd be charging for it. And making a lot of money to boot."

"Then let's thank God he's not in charge." I moved away a few feet to give Rosie room. "The Indians meant it to always be open to anyone wishing to use it."

She opened her eyes. "You mean some of those . . . how you say it out here, redskins, owned this?"

I let it drop, figuring this was Rosie's first foray into the wild West. "Shoshone Chief Washakie and Arapahoe Chief Sharp Nose graciously agreed to deed this land to the government so it would always be free for people, back just before the turn of the century."

"So even Gustavo couldn't break that agreement?"

I nodded.

"Good," she said and closed her eyes again. "At least there'll be one venture he can't sink his mitts into."

"Like the moonshining business?"

"That. And other . . . businesses he's made money from."

"Like?"

She waved her hand around, and steam rising from the mineral pool drifted around her face. "Every time I come here, it seems it gets foggier."

"The Shoshones called the water *Bah-gue-wana.* Smoking waters. And you still haven't answered my question."

Rosie opened her eyes, and a wry smile crossed her lips. "Marshal Lane, do you really think I would say anything detrimental about my—"

"Benefactor?"

"I was thinking lover." She grinned and closed her eyes again. "At least this place has one thing going for it—these mineral pools," she said, avoiding the path our conversation was headed.

"Do I detect a hint of resentment about being here in Wyoming?"

She scooted closer before I could move away, and her arm brushed mine under the water. "This place is boring. There is nothing to do here."

"Then why are you here?"

"Why else?" She brushed wet bangs out of her eyes. "Because Gus wants to be here. And where Gus goes, I go."

"So, you're . . . expected to love wherever Gustavo takes you?"

"Love and enjoy," she said, looking me in the eye.

"And where was home before moving here with Gustavo?"

"Chicag—Marshal, I forgot for a moment you are a lawman. Used to eliciting information from people. Even when they don't want to tell you things."

"Just making conversation," I said and avoided looking into those inviting blue eyes.

"Okay, Marshal. Let's say you were just making conversation." She moved closer and turned in the water to face me. "I lived in Chicago with the family."

"So, your family is from Chicago?"

She frowned then, and even with her face scrunched up, she looked stunning. "My family immigrated here from France when I was a baby. They lived in New York just long enough to die in a railcar accident. I was farmed out to an orphanage and ran away on my fourteenth birthday. I fled to Chicago to seek my fame and fortune, so to speak. I found neither, but I did find my second family."

"I don't understand—"

"My new family," she said, and I heard some cynicism creep into her voice. "Gustavo and Marco and the Twins. They're my family now, and I go where they do. That is why I am here in the sticks." Her hand flicked a water bug off my shoulder. "And where is your family?"

I never talk about my family, except to Yancy now and again, but found myself telling Rosie everything she asked. "My wife, Helen, died from diphtheria eight years ago, leaving just me and my daughter. She's fourteen now."

"She takes care of herself when you're in the field?"

"Helen's sister and her husband take care of Polly. I see her when I can." I fought the urge to tell Rosie that—ever since Helen died—my sister-in-law didn't trust Polly to live with a one-time drunk. Someday perhaps. But, for now, our arrangement worked out the best for all.

Rosie moved closer in the water, and, for some reason, I could not bring myself to move away. Even while avoiding looking into those eyes. "You have your excitement, being a wild-west marshal. But for me"—her arms draped around my neck—"I have to make my own excitement. What would you suggest, Mister Lawman?"

I shrugged off her arms and moved away. "I'm no betting man, but if I were, I'd wager that if Gustavo saw you in the pool here with me real close-like, things would get a lot more exciting for you than you expected."

Rosie turned away and sat on the ledge beneath the water. "What Gus don't know won't hurt him. As far as he's concerned, I drove into town this morning to pick up some groceries and do a little shopping." She smiled at me. "My turn for a wager."

I nodded.

"That you have leads on that runaway Indian girl?"

"I have my suspicions about where she's at—"

"Which figures to be somewhere on Gus's ranch? That's my wager."

I paused long enough to mull over what she'd speculated about Darla Lone Tree. The long wager was that whatever I told her, it would go straight back to Gus. The short wager was that Rosie just needed a little excitement to spice up her life. And the intrigue of me pestering Gus to look at his barn was enough to whet her appetite. "Three girls were brought to Gustavo's ranch last week. One of them an Indian."

"Girlfriends of some of Gus's ranch hands," Rosie said. "Nothing more. I was there when those girls bailed out of the car, and when the boys piled out of the barn after them. Those fellas"—Rosie moved closer and leaned against my shoulder—"get all horned up and aren't worth sand until they get it out of their system. Don't you remember what it was like being young and . . . with needs?"

"That seems like a lifetime ago," I answered and moved away from her. "These ranch hands you mentioned: are there actually enough cows to keep them employed?"

"Gus runs some shorthorns in a pasture to the west—"

"How many?"

Rosie pulled a shoulder strap up that had fallen south. "Maybe thirty head."

"And how many hands does Gustavo employ?"

She shrugged. "Ten or twelve, not including the Twins and that nasty man Dan Dan Gus hired."

Rosie confirmed my suspicions, though she didn't realize she had. Twelve ranch hands to manage thirty head of cattle. One good cowboy could do that by his lonesome. Meaning the other eleven or so were doing something else for Gus. Like running moonshine and standing guard.

"But don't worry about those fellas," Rosie said, lowering her voice as if she were worried someone was close enough to hear her. "It's those Twins you need to be cautious around."

"You telling me I need to worry about one of your . . . family? And I thought you Jewish folks stuck together."

"It's been so long since I thought of myself as Jewish, I'd almost forgotten. But not the Twins. They were working for the Jewish mob in Cicero when Gus took them in."

"After their folks were killed in a car accident?"

Rosie looked sideways at me. "If that's what Gus told you."

I thought it best not to press the issue just now. Later, perhaps, I'd be able to draw more of the Napoli family history out of her. But for now, I was grateful for what she'd told me so far. "And little Marco? What's his story?"

She laughed nervously. "He's one crazy SOB. The kind who pulled wings off insects when he was young. He stays away from me, though. I threatened to tell his father he tried bedding me one night back in Chicago."

"Some son," I said. "Making time with his father's woman."

"Worse, he said he'd make sure Gus went for a one-way ride somewhere. Thought he'd impress me, but nothing about Marco has ever made an impression."

"Why don't you tell Gustavo about it?"

Rosie shook her head. "For one, he wouldn't believe me. For another, I am afraid that—for all his suave demeanor and boyish charm—Gust would as soon see *me* take that one-way ride as not."

"I'm locking up," the caretaker of the bath house yelled from the office.

"Closing time." Rosie moved a little closer. "But you

remember what I said about the Twins—you watch your butt." She pinched a cheek under the water. "Because it's such a nice butt."

Rosie mounted the steps, water dripping seductively off her sleek body. "If anyone asks," she said over her shoulder without looking back, "it took me longer to go shopping than I planned."

I waited until she had entered the women's changing room before I stepped from the water. I started toweling off even before I reached the top of the steps as I headed for the men's changing room. I wanted to be well away from Rosie by the time she came out of the bath house. If what she said were true, saintly Ol' Gus had any number of bad men he could have sent to follow Rosie when she went to town. And I didn't want anyone to think we purposely met in the pool.

CHAPTER 14

When I walked into Mom's Diner, Maris was just finishing her supper. She sat across the table from Lucille, and I slid in the booth beside Maris. "I suppose you'll want something to eat, too," Lucille said, a cigarillo dangling from her lips, which I'd grown to expect from the old woman.

"This *is* a diner. But depending on what your special is tonight will depend on if I eat."

"Fair enough."

"What's the special?"

"Steak and potatoes."

"That sounds good."

"No," Lucille said. "That sounds like I'm out of it."

I looked around at the empty diner. "You have a run on your special today?"

Lucille just shrugged.

"Well then, bring whatever you have made." I watched Lucille disappear into the kitchen carrying Maris's plate and wondered just how the hell Lucille could stay open.

"Be easy on her," Maris said, wiping a bit of gravy off her shirt front. She caught me looking and smiled. I quickly looked away.

"She seems a little perturbed tonight."

Maris jerked her thumb at the back door. "Lucille's chickens started fussing this afternoon—"

"What's she keep chickens for? Surely not for all the chicken she puts into her soup."

"For the eggs," Maris said. "Anyways, Lucille saw some peckerwood was running off with a hen tucked under each arm this morning."

"Wasn't hens. It was two pullets he stole," Lucille said, emerging from the kitchen with soup that looked suspiciously like the stew I'd had yesterday. Except more watered down. "I had a dozen pullets that just went through their first molt. Another month and they'd be able to lay eggs. And now they're gone into somebody's stew pot."

"At least *someone's* going to find meat in their chicken soup."

Lucille glared at me and set the bowl on the table.

"Did you see who stole your chickens? 'Cause if you did, it'd give Sheriff Darcy something to do beside investigating squirrel murders."

"I got a look at him all right. Was that Kincaid kid that lives up north."

I scooted from the booth, but Lucille stopped me. "You're not going to call Sheriff Darcy, are you?"

"I aim to."

"You keep that pompous bastard away from here," Lucille said. "He couldn't find his ass with both hands." Another ash fell from her cigarillo, and she brushed it off the seat. "I'll take care of that thieving little bugger myself."

I tucked the napkin under my chin and looked at the runny soup. "Don't look so glum," Lucille said as she headed for the kitchen. "That's just a warm up. The entrée is on the way."

"You'll love this meal," Maris said. "Lucille outdid herself with the liver and onions."

I cringed. "Liver and onions?"

"Deer liver, at that." Maris lit a cigarette and dropped her match in her empty coffee cup. "And the onions were exceptionally tart."

It had been thirty years since I'd eaten liver and onions. Whenever we butchered a steer to hand out for Christmas bonuses for the ranch hands, all Mother insisted on keeping for us was the liver. Dan and I both held our noses when Mother served up plates of it. One year I managed to sneak the entire pile of liver from the larder to make coyote bait. Dad never said how the liver had disappeared, and he never complained.

Lucille came from the kitchen, and I could smell the liver long before she got to the table. She set the plate of liver and onions and wilted peas in front of me and went back to the kitchen. "Holler if you want seconds," she said.

I picked at one edge of the liver, but the odor nearly made me retch, and I concentrated on the peas that hadn't rolled into the liver.

"You can work around corpses that have rotted in the sun for weeks, but you can't stomach liver?" Maris asked.

"My nose can take only so much," I said as I speared a pea and hoped conversation would take my mind off supper. "What did Will Lone Tree say when you talked with him?"

"We made small talk, as we Indians like to do—"

"Like you're doing now," I said. "Just give me the headline version."

Maris snubbed her butt out in her coffee cup. She could have gladly put her cigarette out on my plate. Be an excuse not to eat the liver. "Will is determined that Darla's not going to end up like her mother—dead drunk and froze to death in a snow bank. He'll do whatever it takes to make sure that don't happen."

"Including killing the man who supplied his daughter her booze?"

"I asked him that very question," Maris said and picked up a fork. "You going to eat that?"

I patted my stomach. "The peas filled me up. Help yourself. As soon as you tell me about your talk with Will."

Maris took out her pocket knife. She sawed off a strip of liver and sat back gnawing it. "He said that if he would have talked to Axle about selling Darla alcohol, he might have lost it. Will was so mad, he could see himself killing Axle. But he made a concerted effort to stay away from Axle just for that reason. Will said Darla didn't need to go through life without a mother and with her father sitting in prison. That's why he finally called Yancy."

"So, you came up with nothing?"

Maris chewed, and chewed, and chewed the tough meat before swallowing. She reached over and took a swig of my cold coffee. "I didn't say we came up with nothing. Will said he talked with Darla's best friend, Wanda Bent, yesterday. She wouldn't say a thing to Will—he got the impression she was afraid of him."

"I can empathize with that."

"And he finally admitted that a woman might have more luck getting information out of Wanda. Yancy's going to hunt her up tomorrow for me. And he's going to find Darla's boyfriend and interview him."

"Some kid on the rez?"

Maris sawed off another piece of meat and moved my cup closer. "Will wasn't sure just where he is, but Yancy got wind the boyfriend's working for those Italian guys you talked with."

I took out a piece of scrap paper and the pencil stub I kept in my vest pocket. "What's the boyfriend's name?"

"Charlie Grass."

"Charlie? Did Will give you a description?"

Maris laughed. "Did he ever. He can't stand the kid. Will said before Charlie went to work for that Napoli bunch, he dressed like any other ranch hand on the rez. Will said the last time he picked up Darla for a date, he was dressed like some pimp out of Billings."

"This Charlie," I asked, "is he about five foot seven or eight? Thin?"

"You a mind reader?"

"Not quite. But that sounds like Napoli's hand I gave a ride into Thermop to pick up a car."

"You better find him and talk to him before Will finds him. Charlie might be sipping his supper through a straw while his jaw mends up. Or worse."

Chapter 15

As I left the hotel the next morning, the desk clerk stopped me and handed me a note. "If you need privacy, use the phone in the lobby."

I walked through the lobby lined with murals painted decades ago by some unknown artist depicting battles between the Shoshone and Arapaho, between the cavalry and Sharp Nose's braves. The lobby phone was located in a booth too small for me to fit into, and I dragged the phone and cord out and set it alongside a wilted flower on an end table. Yancy sounded as if he'd just woken up at tribal headquarters. My guess was that he started staying there when he got fed up sleeping in his tipi. "I found Wanda Bent," he said. "She was staying at her aunt's place in Ethete."

"Give me directions, and I'll head over there."

"No good," Yancy said. "Wanda's scared to death of being seen with an Indian policeman, let alone a federal marshal."

"Then how the hell am I going to talk with her?"

"Is Maris still in Thermopolis?"

"She's got a room at the motel," I said and quickly added, "but not in adjacent rooms from me, if that's what you're wondering next. Why?"

"I think I could talk Wanda into riding with me into Thermop," Yancy answered, "if you and Maris can meet her someplace there's not too many people."

"Bring her to Mom's Diner," I said without hesitation, knowing it was a sure bet there wouldn't be anyone there to see Wanda. "I'll buy her breakfast."

"Not if you want her to cooperate with you," Yancy laughed. "I've ate at Mom's before."

I rousted Maris from her room, and she answered the door in a long, flannel shirt. I didn't even want to know if she had anything underneath it. "Yancy's bringing Wanda Bent in to Mom's. She might just talk with you."

"Maybe she's got more liver." Maris rubbed her eyes.

"Yeah." I cringed. "Maybe liver and flapjacks."

By the time Maris walked into Mom's, Lucille had just placed a plate of flapjacks—without liver, thank goodness—in the middle of the table. "Bon appetite," Lucille said as she poured coffee, weak and tepid.

"You got any tea bags?" I asked.

"Thought you wanted coffee."

"I do. But in lieu of that, bring some tea bags to give this"—I held my cup to the light—"to give this some color."

Lucille stood with the coffee pot in one hand, her other hand on her hip, giving me what-for. "You insinuating that my coffee is weak?"

"I'm not insinuating anything," I answered. "I'm flat out saying it: Lucille, you gotta' put more grounds in that pot of yours."

"You want good coffee," she snapped, "go next door to Delmonico's. You want conversation, stay here and drink what I bring. Now eat your flapjacks."

She stormed into the kitchen, and I smeared butter on my flapjacks—or at least some butter-lard combination that ran off the stack like a dirty, warming snow bank.

"Thought you said Yancy was going to be here," Maris said.

"You miss him?"

She guffawed. "Of course not. Just professional curiosity is all."

I pointed with my fork, "So that's why you wore denims a size too tight."

"I did not—"

"And button that top button before he gets some notion."

Yancy entered the diner and held the door for a girl half again as wide as he, but not nearly as tall. She kept her eyes to the floor as Yancy led her to the booth. He motioned for the girl to slide over and took a seat beside her in the booth. He smiled across the table at Maris while he adjusted his new silk neckerchief. She smiled back until she caught my wink and looked away.

"I didn't know you were coming," Maris lied.

"Well, I knew you'd be here," Yancy blurted out, and I had to step between them, so to speak, and referee.

"This young lady must be Wanda," I said.

"It is," Yancy said about at the same time he spied the coffee pot sitting on the hot plate on the counter. He stood and brought a cup for him and set another one in front of Wanda, but she just stared at the tabletop. Yancy topped our cups off before returning the pot to the counter. "Tell the marshal and Deputy Red Hat what you told me at your aunt's house."

Wanda remained silent and would not look at me, but that was not uncommon. Traditionally raised Indians were often taught not to meet a white man's gaze. "Please," I said. "We need to know what you know so we can find your friend."

"I went to the Napoli Ranch with Darla a few times," Wanda said, almost a whisper.

I waited for more, but she continued staring at her coffee cup.

Maris laid her hand on Wanda's arm. "What happened when you went there?"

"Please tell them," Yancy said.

When Wanda said nothing, Yancy told us that Wanda and Darla regularly went to Napoli's for a couple of days at a time. "When Darla didn't come back this time, Wanda thought Darla was out with her boyfriend someplace."

Wand raised her head, but she did not look at me. "We got a job a few days a week cleaning for the Napolis."

"The house?"

"The barn," Wanda answered.

"I'd have thought Gus had enough ranch hands to clean manure that he wouldn't have to hire young ladies—"

"It was not manure we cleaned up." Wanda focused on Maris. "It was rooms in the barn we cleaned."

"Rooms?" I asked. "The stalls?"

Wanda remained quiet.

"Tell us, little sister," Maris said. "We need help finding Darla."

Wanda nodded and spoke to Maris. "There are eight rooms in the barn. Fancy rooms. Big beds with nice floors." A smile crossed her face for a brief second. "Lots of beautiful lights."

"Is that where you and Darla stayed when you were cleaning?"

Wanda shook her head and paused when Lucille came out of the kitchen. She set a glass of buttermilk in front of Wanda, who grinned. "How did you know—"

Lucille tapped the side of her head. "I know a lot of things, sweetheart. Enjoy." And she returned to the kitchen. I wondered just how the hell *did* Lucille know Wanda liked buttermilk.

Wanda took a long sip, and Maris leaned over and wiped the white mustache from the girl's upper lip. "Darla and me slept in a room in the upper loft. But it wasn't nice like those down below. We slept on army cots. Used a chamber pot. Sometimes we didn't even have a blanket."

"Then who were the rooms below for?" I asked.

Wanda met my gaze then, and for once she was defiant when she spoke. "Girls. Girls come and go to the ranch. Many girls. And some men."

"Did you know any of the girls?" Maris asked.

"I've seen one or two around the reservation, but they were older than me and Darla, so I didn't know them very good. And I didn't know the white girls at all." Tears started then, and Maris dabbed Wanda's cheek with the napkin and handed it to her. "We heard . . . things downstairs at night. Partying. But when we woke in the mornings, the rooms were empty. And Mr. Napoli paid us to clean them. Change bedding, and straighten up."

"What kind of partying was going on down there?"

Wanda shook her head. "I do not know. But Darla sneaked down the ladder one night and listened at the doors. When she came back up to the loft, she was smiling. All she could say was, 'We are going to be rich.' "

"What did she mean by that?" Yancy asked.

Wanda kept quiet.

"Tell us," Maris said. "Please."

"I cannot," she answered. She shook slightly, and I knew Wanda could tell us if she chose. She was just too frightened.

"We can protect you—"

"Ask Charlie," Wanda said. "He knows."

Neither Yancy nor Maris could elicit any more information out of Wanda, and Yancy said it was time to run her back to the reservation. As he led her to the door, I called after her, "I'm just glad you're out of there."

She stopped abruptly. She half-turned toward me, and I saw the tears had returned. "I am going back there, Marshal."

"For heaven's sake, what for?"

"Money." Wanda wiped her eyes with the sleeve of her shirt.

"It is the only job hereabouts. And my aunt cannot work anymore."

Maris tried talking her out of going back, but she ignored her and left the diner ahead of Yancy.

After they left, Maris and I kicked around what Wanda meant. "I'm thinking those girls in that barn were brought in for partying," Maris said. "Paid a few bucks and sent on their way." She pointed to my flapjacks. "You aren't hungry."

I slid the plate across the table. "They're cold, but help yourself."

Maris grabbed a fork and started grazing. "We had some girls lured to Ft. Reno last year," she said, referring to the army remount station in her old Oklahoma jurisdiction of El Reno. "Soldiers offered some lucky bucks for girls to snuggle up, and in return they'd make enough to get out of town. At least for a while."

"Like they ran away?"

"Some," Maris answered between mouthfuls. "Most were old enough to be on their own. The runaways got arrested, usually in Oklahoma City, where they went for the fast life. Some never returned, and we figured they'd hopped a freight train and were living the low life somewhere in California."

Lucille came back into the dining area, a damp, dirty towel slung over her shoulder and the stub of a cigarillo smoldering from behind her ear. "I think your hair's about to catch fire," I mentioned in passing.

Lucille knocked the cigarillo to the floor. She dipped her hand in my coffee and slapped her smoldering hair with the liquid before snubbing the butt out with her shoe. "I overheard your conversation," she said when she'd regained her composure. "A couple girls from Lander came in last month. Dressed like they were fixing to go out and cut a rug—all dolled up." She laughed. "They must not have been any smarter than you were, to come in here for a meal."

"Tell me about them," I said as I sipped a glass of water. At least Lucille couldn't mess up water.

"They talked real loud so even I could hear them."

"Like just now when you had your ear to the door listening to Wanda?"

"You want to know about them or not?"

"At least *I* do." Maris smoothed things over.

"All right, then. They were real giddy, like they was already tanked up. But they weren't. Didn't even complain about the food. And when I asked them what they were so happy about, they said that after tonight they'd have enough money to go to Hollywood and try out for the movies."

"What's that got to do with Gustavo?" I asked her.

"Maybe not him. I don't know. But when I asked where they intended getting the money, they said one word: Marco. And that nasty little SOB at the Napoli Ranch is the only Marco I know."

"Getting rich is how Darla put it to Wanda that night when she come back from downstairs," Maris said. "Maybe Darla is there after all." Maris slid out of the booth. "Guess we better pay the Italians a visit."

"I'm thinking that would not be a good idea," I said. "About one more trip out there, and his thugs are going to make their play for me."

"I never knowed Nelson Lane to shirk a fight."

"I'm not," I said and followed Maris out of the booth. "But Sheriff Darcy has some rapport with Gus. If anyone can talk the old man into letting him look in the barn, it'd be Milo." I wanted to tell Maris that I felt as if someone were following me, and right now I didn't want anyone to think I was zeroing in on Gustavo and his crew. I had spotted the same old Chevy four times in two days, hanging back just enough that I couldn't see the driver or get a good look at the car. The one time I made a bootleg turn and went after it, the car had more *oomph* than it looked and easily outran my truck. What perplexed me was the car: it should have been new. Shiny. Like all of Gustavo's vehicles. But it wasn't.

"Good luck getting Sheriff Darcy off his ass," Lucille said. "He might get a callus or something doing real police work."

"What about me?" Maris asked. "What you want me to do?"

"Something even more boring than serving eviction notices."

"You want me to do surveillance work?"

I dabbed a smear of runny syrup from Maris's cheek. "Get Yancy to spot you when he can. But we either have to cross off Will Lone Tree as Axle's murderer, or elevate him on the shit list."

"I thought we were trying to find Darla?"

"We are."

"Then why are you sticking your nose into Axle's death when Sheriff Darcy's already ruled it a suicide?"

I wanted to tell Maris that—in some convoluted way—I owed Axle something for selling me liquor all those years, even if it destroyed my relationship with my daughter and brought an early death to my wife. "I'm convinced Darla's disappearance and Axle's murder are connected."

"That's a stretch," Maris said. She took out her pocket knife and began whittling an Ohio Blue Tip into a toothpick. "Darla came up missing *about* the time Axle was . . . murdered, is all."

"Just the same, sit on Will's place. Follow him when he leaves. And when Yancy can spot you, find Denise Denny's sister. She lives a few miles from the reservation somewhere outside Lander."

Maris threw up her hands. "Is that all you want me to do, boss? And just when am I going to get any sleep?"

"You know those young bucks you've been keeping company with lately?"

"What about them?"

I winked at her. "It's not like they let you get any sleep anyways."

I was walking across the street when I became aware that another person was walking just behind me, and I turned sharply. Rosie Manning seemed to be running to catch up with me. "Those long legs make it hard for a girl to catch you."

I stopped and waited for her. She looked around and threaded an arm in mine. "You look like a man on a mission."

"Aren't you worried you'll be seen?"

"Marco is busy, and if the Twins see me, they could care less. All they care about is . . . protecting their money tit. Let's walk to that little park about a block north of here."

The sun had not cooked the walkway yet, and a cool morning breeze wafted over Rosie, carrying with it just the right amount of cologne to entice a man. But not quite enough to entice me to take another man's woman away. Especially someone with the resources Gustavo Napoli had. Still, Rosie knew things that might help me find Darla.

We sat at a bench in the small park at the center of town. Ducklings dipped their heads into a tiny pond and came up shaking water off while their mother looked on. Protecting. Just like I should be doing. If Gustavo or his boys saw Rosie and me sitting together, it would be bad news for her. Unless they already knew about it.

"Is there a reason you're risking being seen with the enemy?"

Rosie laughed. "You don't look like an enemy to me."

"And kindly old Gustavo Napoli doesn't look like someone who's knee-deep in illegal liquor."

"That's why I came to talk with you." She sounded confident, sure of herself, but she kept looking around as she spoke. “Marco is trying to convince his father that you are a danger to his business.”

“And Marco believes I’ll move to shut the operation down?”

She nodded.

“But he’s not worried about the other lawmen around, like Sheriff Darcy.”

“Milo is a frequent visitor to the ranch. He and Gustavo get along well—”

“Because Milo is in his pocket?”

Rosie looked away. “I’d rather not say any more about that.” She turned in the bench to face me. “I’d rather talk about you—”

“Because Gustavo asked you to?”

“Is it that obvious?”

I waved my hand around the park. “Here in the open, sitting arm in arm with me? Don’t you think that screams ‘getting close to the enemy’ ”?

Rosie moved away slightly and reclaimed her arm. “So, I can go back to Gustavo and tell him you saw through his ruse and wouldn’t say shit?”

“That’s about the sum of it,” I answered.

“Good.” She smiled. “I didn’t feel right about it anyway.” She took a silver cigarette case out of her purse and flipped it open. “Smoke?”

“French?”

“Lebanese tobacco.”

“I’ll stick with good old Chesterfields.”

I lit both our cigarettes and settled back on the bench. She watched the ducklings, enthralled, like she’d never taken the time to watch such wonders before. “You really are new to this?” I waved my hand around the park.

“What’s it like, out there?” She pointed north to where the

Big Horns lay. "The wilderness?"

"Never been there?"

"I'd be so useless, I'd get lost."

I laughed. "About as lost as I'd get back in Chicago."

"But back in Chicago there is no . . . beauty. No freedom like there is out here. Only bad things where I come from."

I'd rarely thought much about what Rosie called the wilderness. It just was the mountains. It is where I grew up. It is where I hunted, and where I took friends to experience the beauty of the land. "It is where that trout stream lies lonely, waiting for me to drop a fly on the surface," I told her. "This place is unlike any other left in this country."

"Take me there," Rosie said. She smiled wide, and a twinkle erupted in her eyes. "Take me to that mountain stream. Could I roll up my dress and take off my shoes and wade across it?"

"You could."

"And feel the cool water rush over my bare legs?"

Rosie had transformed herself from a woman of the world into a little girl desirous to experience a beauty she'd only heard about. "Take me, Nelson."

I thought about that, and how easy it would be to saddle a pony for Rosie. We could ride above the tree line, to where the cruelty of this world could never find us. To that cool trout stream that I knew. "I would love nothing else," I said. "Perhaps after I find Darla Lone Tree, and when you break with your . . . lover."

Her smile faded then, and she stood. "Sure," she said. Gone was the little girl. Back was the gangster's woman doing what she could to protect what was her man's. "Just as soon as Gustavo allows it."

As she walked away I stopped her, and she waited until I caught up with her. "A moment ago, you would have given the world to be free of Gustavo and all he represents. You *can* be free. If you choose."

"Do any of us really have a choice in this life?"

"I believe we do," I answered, thinking back to my choice to drink my wife to death. And my choice to get clean. "It can be hard, but I will do whatever it takes to help you. If that's your choice."

She stood looking up at me, and for a moment her expression softened. The little girl was back. If only briefly. "I believe you would. You are a good man, Nelson. The world needs more good men." This time she looked around nervously, as if people were within earshot. "I will give you one tiny scrap of information: Erik Esterling quit the sheriff's race to go truck driving."

"I heard," I said. "At a lot more money than he'd make as sheriff."

She laughed nervously, her head on a swivel, but no one was near to hear her. "Gus pays most of his salary. He arranged for Esterling to land the driving job."

"So Milo could remain in office?"

"Yes," she said. "So that buffoon could remain just where he is."

"Does Milo know Gustavo paid his opponent to drop out?"

"I doubt it," Rosie answered. "But it shows just how serious Gustavo is about keeping what is his. Now all he's got to do is continue giving the High Sheriff the runaround whenever he comes snooping." She backed away and looked over her shoulder. "And Gustavo will go to *any* means to protect what's his. Remember that, Nelson Lane, when you feel Gustavo is just like your old grandpa."

CHAPTER 16

Emily sat behind her desk looking at ads in the same *Colliers* as she was that first day I saw her. "Sheriff Darcy is on a business call," she said as she turned a page. "I'll let you know when he's available."

"That's all right," I said. "I'd rather visit with you anyways."

She warily brought the magazine down and looked over it. "Visit about what?"

"You." I shook out a cigarette and leaned over the counter with the pack. She eyed me suspiciously before pulling one out. "You gave me good directions to the Napoli Ranch—"

"So you mentioned yesterday."

After I lit our cigarettes I dropped the match into the spittoon in front of the counter. "I got to admit that even with your excellent directions, the place was a little difficult to find. When I asked you before if you've ever been there, you said you drove past there once. For someone who's only been by there that one time, you sure rattled off directions like you knew the place."

"Nonsense. Like I said before, I'm from Green River. How would I know my way around the country here?"

"I'm thinking you know your way around *quite* well, Emily."

She had half turned in her chair as if she intended leaving when I pressed my point. "What brought you here in the first place?"

"Is there a reason for your interest in me? I'm just a secretary."

"I think you're more than just a secretary." I looked at Milo's closed office door. "Let's cut to the chase. When I asked if you'd ever been to the Napoli ranch, the first thing you did was bull-up on me. You took offense when there was no reason to."

"All right!" Emily snubbed her butt out in an ashtray the shape of a rooster sitting on the edge of her desk. "I worked there once."

"Cleaning rooms?"

Her eyes widened. "Who told you that?"

I smiled. "I have sources. What I'm getting at is that, at some point, you had the courage to fight your way out of there."

"Don't give me too much credit," she said as she looked down at the floor. "I didn't have courage. I got lucky when Sheriff Darcy stopped to take a rustling report last year. And he offered me the job as secretary."

"Answering phones?"

She nodded.

"Typing reports?"

"Of course."

Typing reports, indeed, I thought as I looked at her fingernails, which were too long to be much good banging away on a typewriter. I suspected Milo had hired her for her other obvious attributes. "Tell me what it was like working for old Gustavo."

A little light on the side of her desk lit up, rescuing Emily, and she nodded to it. "Sheriff Darcy is free now if you want to see him."

I thanked her, but not before I told her we needed to have another nice visit soon. I wanted to know just how it was working for the Italians. And just what was going on in that barn of theirs.

"This better be quick," Milo said when I entered his office. He put his hat on and grabbed a pen and notebook. "I got another rustling report to take."

"At Napoli's?"

Milo used his bandana to polish silver *conchos* on his gun belt before he strapped it on. "No, a spread on the other side of Highway 20, across from Lucerne." He looked around a final time before heading out. "Just what do you need before I leave?"

I explained that I had a witness from the reservation who had worked at Napoli's ranch along with Darla Lone Tree.

"What witness?"

"Just a friend of Darla's who came into town to talk with me. They went to work at Gustavo's a couple weeks ago cleaning rooms a couple days a week."

"What rooms?"

"Apparently, the Napolis have converted the barn into some sort of hotel."

"Rooms like Emily once cleaned," Milo said. "This witness of yours thinks Darla is still there?"

"She couldn't say. They left together a few days after working there and returned to the rez. That was the last time she saw Darla. But she talked about going back to Gustavo's."

"You think your runaway might be there?" Milo repeated.

"Might be."

"And you want me to go back out to the Napoli ranch?"

"You'd get more help from them than I would. Gustavo already thinks I want to shut his moonshining operation down."

"I got no time—"

"Send your deputy."

Milo stopped and hung his head. "I hired no deputy to replace Esterling when he quit. It's just me." He faced me. "But we can change that. Raise your right hand."

"What?"

"Your hand. Raise it."

I did.

"By the power invested in me, I deputize you for the county

of Hot Springs." Milo smiled. "Now go forth and question Gus to your heart's content. 'Cause I got cattle thieves to catch."

Chapter 17

I turned off Highway 20 and slowed. This would be the third time I'd been to Gustavo's in as many days, and I was in no hurry to get there. When I left Milo's office, I waited a moment and looked around the neighborhood but failed to spot the car that had tailed me before. I was getting paranoid, I told myself, and found myself stopping at a pay phone down the street. When Polly answered the phone at her aunt and uncle's house, she was ecstatic to hear my voice. "When you coming home, Papa?"

"Soon," I answered her. "Just make sure you do what Sissy and Homer say."

I hung up, so grateful that Sissy and Homer had been there for Polly. They had welcomed her into their home in my dark days of the bottle, giving her stability I could not, showing her the decent side of life that her alcoholic father had failed to. And since recovering from the booze, I felt it prudent to let Polly continue living with them. At least until the time I was certain I wouldn't fall off the wagon. And for some reason, I had felt the urge to hear her voice.

I kept looking over my shoulder as I drove the winding road among sage brush and stilted junipers, driving past land that amazed me could still support ranchers like Kincaid, and my thoughts turned to James. He apparently was an enterprising young feller. From making pocket money killing other people's squirrels, to stealing chickens from Lucille, he had managed to eke out a living as best as a fourteen-year-old could do in these hard times. I thought if I could get him back in school, there'd be no limit for someone like him. If I could do that, I'd be satisfied that something positive had come out of this mess I was involved in.

When I passed the rickety Kirby Creek Bridge and turned north, I stopped long enough to watch my back trail. Someone might hang back far enough that I wouldn't be able to see them. But they wouldn't be able to control the dust their car kicked up on this road, and I saw none. Satisfied I wasn't followed, I continued.

When I reached a hilltop and started down the other side, a Model T sat catawampus on the road. Steam rose from the radiator, and a young feller in patched overalls sat on the running board with his chin on his hands. I pulled up short just behind him and climbed out. I reached for the water bladder I always carried as the man walked toward me. "I just don't know what's wrong with this old flivver," he moaned. "This is the second water pump that went out this month."

"Open the hood," I said and uncorked the water bladder. I handed it to him, and he laid his hand on the radiator cap before jerking it back.

"Best to wait a while," I said.

"Good thing you came along," he said. "I hate walking in this heat."

"Live hereabouts?"

He chin-pointed toward the south. "Me and the missus got us a little place over that hill a few miles," he said. The cap cooled off enough for him to remove it. "But I work in the oil patch over at Hamilton Dome."

"That's a far ways to drive every day."

He agreed, rapping his knuckles against the hood. "But I'm lucky to have anything to get me there, let alone this old T."

The man trickled water into the radiator, and I noted that he didn't hardly look big enough to work the rigs. I had known oil men and others when I went to El Reno on that fugitive warrant this spring, and all of them were hard men. Dirty men. The stink of their work—the oil men claimed—never left a man. The stench of crude stayed with you week in and week out, and one never shook the smell of oil, they swore.

The rig worker kept me in his periphery as he finished pouring water down the radiator. He spoke to me as he did so, but I wasn't listening. I was observing: the polished boots that didn't match the patched bib overalls; the perfectly manicured fingernails; the lack of that stench oil men perpetually reeked of.

He dribbled the last of the water into the radiator and set the bladder on his running board. "Thanks," he said over his shoulder as he reached through the door.

I caught the blur of something familiar in his hand as he jerked free of his car door. He pivoted towards me as he swung a short-barreled shotgun my direction.

But I had already unsnapped my holster, and I drew my gun.

By the time his muzzle came to bear on me, I had fired twice. Both .45 slugs caught him mid-chest, and he dropped the shotgun, staggering back, a look of painful surprise crossing his face. He hit the side of his car and slumped onto the running board for a brief moment before rolling onto the dirt.

I kicked the shotgun aside and holstered my automatic while I bent to him. I held his dying head as if I could take back the moment. "Who the hell are you?" I'd killed my share of men in my life and figured every damned one of them deserved it. But that didn't make it any easier killing some mother's son, and it sure didn't make it any easier to live with myself the next morning. "Why the hell did you try to shoot me?"

Dust blew around the young man and clouded his vision as

he tried to focus on me. "You're the federal marshal," he said as if that were all the explanation necessary. He spat frothy blood, and a smattering pasted itself across my vest front. I wanted to shake him, tell him how utterly foolish he'd been. But I knew he had mere moments before he was gone. "I don't know you."

"But you know my boss." He coughed and violently shuddered in my grasp.

"Who—"

"Kiss my ass, hayseed." He forced a smile a heartbeat before his eyes glazed over, and he went limp in my arms. I eased his head onto the road and shut his eyelids.

I stood on shaky legs and grabbed the water bladder. I took off my Stetson and poured water over my head before taking a drink. There was just enough to wash the man's blood from my hands, and I scrubbed off what I could before drying my hands on my trousers.

When I was finished, I bent to him once again and butterflied his pockets. Inside one of his overall pockets, I found a thick envelope. I studied the lettering with a name scribbled on the front but could not make it out, it was so sloppily written. The envelope contained money. I laid it out on the hood of my truck and counted it: five hundred dollars. Even a driller didn't make that in a year.

I stood and looked around, the feeling coming on once again that I was being watched, causing the hairs to stand up on the back of my neck. I popped the magazine from my automatic and inserted a fresh one as I continued looking around.

But I never spotted him until he moved.

James Kincaid rode his pony slowly towards me from the safety of a stand of cottonwood thirty yards off the road. He reined his horse in front of the dead man's Model T and hung his .22 rifle from the pommel by a rope. "Didn't know if you were gonna' need help with this feller or not. Apparently not," he said.

Any other time, I would have figured a .22 was useless. But I'd seen how many squirrels James had killed in one morning. "Were you sitting there all this time?"

James took a plug of tobacco from his back pocket and bit off a chaw. I felt obligated to berate him for using tobacco but thought it not quite right to do so with a dead man lying at my feet. "I seen him pull his jalopy to the side of the road. I figured he was after me and thought he'd seen me," James said, "and was waiting to put the grab on me when he got out and uncapped his radiator to make it overheat." James spat a string of juice that barely missed the man. "Wondered what he was doing till I seen you drive up the road."

"Know him?" I asked.

"Frankie Love. Works for old man Napoli." James chuckled. "Or I should say, he used to work for him."

"Doing what?"

James shrugged. "Odds and ends for Mr. Napoli. For one, he's been trying to put the grab on me. I think Mr. Napoli figures I stole one of his cows last year." He wiped his mouth with the back of his hand. "Frankie Lovelino—he always went by Love—was one of those dandies Mr. Napoli brought with him from Chicago."

I walked around to the rear of my panel and opened the back. For once I was grateful that McColley Funeral Home once owned the truck. Made it so much more appropriate to haul this dead feller in. "I'd better get Frankie to the sheriff's office."

James's eyed widened. "You ain't gonna' drive me to town to be a witness, are you?"

"That bother you?"

James pointed north where—over several deep valleys and as

many tall hills—lay the Napoli ranch. "They've been trying to get their mitts on me for a long time. I'd hate for them to succeed."

I walked closer to him. "Straight now—you steal Napoli's cows?"

"I might have found one wandering on the road, but it wasn't worth much." James scooped the tobacco out of his cheek and let it fall to the ground. "The cows they have wouldn't be worth the trouble to steal, all scrawny like they ain't been fed. Don't know why Mr. Napoli even keeps them around."

"Now chickens are another thing?" I said.

James looked away. "Dad and I do like our chickens."

I bent to Frankie, wrapped my arms under his armpits, and lifted him. "Run along," I told James as I dragged Frankie to the back of the panel. "I reckon I don't need your say-so to back me up about what happened."

James turned his horse towards the Kincaid ranch. "Thanks, Marshal."

"And get back to school when it starts up again," I yelled at him as he rode away.

Chapter 18

I sat in the front office of the Forever Rest Funeral Home beside Milo, who shook his finger at Aaron Allright. "You don't have to be so damned happy."

Aaron picked his coffee cup up from where it sat on the display casket in the showroom. He frowned and used his shirtsleeve to rub the coffee ring away before setting the cup back down. "It is not that I am happy for the deceased." On cue, he wrung his hands, and his mouth turned down. But only for a second before the smile returned. "It's just that Mr. Napoli pays. I have so many non-paying customers nowadays, it's refreshing to have a customer who pays up front."

"Your customer is dead."

"It was a slip of the tongue," Aaron said. "I meant Mr. Napoli pays on *behalf* of the customer."

An hour earlier when I pulled in to the sally port of the Forever Rest with Frankie Love laid out in back of the panel, Aaron looked over the dirty bib overalls Frankie wore today. He scowled at the tattered hat, and he groaned. "Not another hobo. Why couldn't you kill him in Washakie County? They got more money for indigents."

"Frankie here worked for Gustavo Napoli."

Aaron's demeanor changed instantly. "Well, then," he told me, "this man deserves the best service." He tapped a nice mahogany casket sitting in the sally port. "And Mr. Napoli always tips generously."

"And you'll talk Gus into the most expensive casket." Milo sat beside me. He'd been testy ever since I called him to the funeral home about another death. "Vulture," he said under his breath.

Aaron wrung his hands again. "I charge what the market will bear. Besides, this man deserves a . . . nice send-off." He nodded in my direction and tipped his porkpie hat. "And since Marshal Lane came into town, my business has picked up."

"Don't plan on it continuing," I said.

The Cadillac Charlie Grass picked up yesterday from Willie D's shop pulled up to the large plate-glass window. Aaron stood abruptly and reached under the counter beside his desk. He came away with a plate of oatmeal cookies and set them on the display casket before folding his hands and standing solemnly by the door waiting for Gustavo and his entourage.

The Twins climbed out of the car first and glanced around the funeral home before entering. A moment later, Marco scooted from behind the wheel and held the door for Gustavo.

He stood looking around Aaron's waiting room dressed like he was already at Frankie's funeral. His dark sharkskin suit was set off by a boutonniere stuck in his lapel, the bright red flower matching the red silk handkerchief jutting out of the sleeve of his suit. He took off his homburg and smoothed his hair before he handed it to Marco. "I understand I need to identify one of my employees."

"Just a formality," Milo said. "This way."

I waited until Gustavo and the Twins followed before falling in behind. On the way to Aaron's cold room, Milo explained that Frankie had set an ambush for me, but he had failed fatally.

We got to the cold room, and I thought it wasn't quite cold enough, to judge by the odor. Frankie Love lay naked on a polished hardwood table. His eyelids had fallen open, and he seemed to look accusingly at me. "He one of yours?" Milo asked, already knowing Frankie was one of Gustavo's ranch hands.

The old man's legs buckled, and Marco wrapped an arm around Gustavo's waist. Marco led him to a chair and helped him sit. "Frankie Lovelino," Gustavo said and slapped the table hard enough that one of Frankie's eyes seemed to wink. "He stormed out of the house this morning after we had an argument."

"About what?" Milo asked.

Aaron stood silently to one side, and I could almost see him counting up funeral expenses already.

"Him," Gustavo looked up at me. "Frankie was concerned the marshal would make trouble for me. Even when I assured him that Marshal Lane wasn't concerned with moonshiners, he still wanted to do him harm." He stood on wobbly legs and brushed Marco's hand off his arm. "But Frankie always had a temper, ever since I took him in."

"Maybe Frankie's concern was justified," Marco said, and he stepped closer to me. "Frankie knew the marshal has been snooping around the ranch." He craned his pencil neck up to look me in the eye. "Maybe you *are* planning to make trouble for us." Marco took a step back, and his fists clenched. I braced myself for Marco's punch, which would have been only slightly more damaging than Frankie's when he was alive.

"That is enough!" Gustavo said and stepped between us. "What Frankie did, he did on his own. His death was not the marshal's fault. For God's sake." He crossed himself. "The marshal had to defend himself."

He spun Marco around by the arm and shoved him toward the door. "Go outside." He looked at the Twins. "You two go with him. Make sure he does not do anything rash. The last thing we need right now is trouble here in a funeral home."

Gustavo shook his head as he looked at Marco storming out

the door. "Youngsters nowadays—they know nothing," Gustavo said and faced me. "I am sorry, Marshal. My son has a temper not unlike Frankie's. They grew up in the same neighborhood. Played the same children's games. Kissed the same girls. Marco should have been upset—not at you, but at Frankie for doing such a foolish thing as trying to kill you."

He sat back down and took out a pack of Old Golds. He offered us each a cigarette, but we declined. Except Aaron. He took one. Then—as if preparing for later—he took two more and stuck them behind his ears. "Frankie's father was one of my drivers in my freighting company in Chicago before I sold out and moved here." He laughed, but there was no joy in it, and his mouth turned down once again

Aaron lit Gustavo's cigarette and stood beside the body. "Frankie was always so sickly. When his folks died, I *had* to take him in, he was so puny. Other boys called him a runt. But he was just small for his age."

"I need to ask you," I said, "how much you paid Frankie."

Gustavo's eyes narrowed, and he snubbed his cigarette butt out on the side of the table. "I paid him fifty dollars a month." He waved the air to clear the smoke from his face. Or to stall while he thought of an answer. "Which is pretty generous in these times. But he knew he could have had more if he needed some. Why?"

I took the envelope of money from my vest pocket and pulled the greenbacks out. "There's five hundred dollars in there."

"What?" Gustavo asked. "Where the hell did he get that much money? Can I see the envelope?"

I handed Gus the envelope filled with money, and he turned it over while he traced the illegible writing with his finger. "He stole it from me. Damn him." He kicked the table leg. "Frankie stole it from me."

"Do you usually leave that much money lying around where

anyone can make off with it?"

"I have a safe," Gustavo said. "The money was in there. But only I know the combination."

"And Marco knows it, too?"

His face paled, and he closed his eyes. "Marco knows it, too."

I took the money back, and Gustavo tried to snatch it from me. "This is evidence," I said.

"Evidence of what? Frankie is dead."

"If I find out that your son paid Frankie to set me up and kill me, I *will* make trouble for you. And this will help make the case."

"Are you threatening my family?" Gustavo asked. "If you are, never come to my house again. You are not welcome."

I wanted to shout at him that my threats were real, and that I would soon come to his house. And that I would find a way to get a look into his barn. But what I really wanted to do was go outside and choke the life out of Marco for causing me to kill his friend.

Lucille's special was vegetable soup. Being a carnivore, I craved meat. But after a day of dealing with Gustavo's thug, I was hungry for anything. Even if it was soup with all the taste and texture of mop water. "Call Yancy," Lucille said and handed me a note. "Needs to talk to you right away."

While I stuck a nickel in the pay phone, I actually saw Lucille add extra grounds to her coffee. I recognized the number as the Wind River tribal police office and asked the operator to stay on the line until someone picked up. When Yancy did, I waited until I heard the operator disconnect. "What's the emergency?"

"No emergency," Yancy answered. "Just a problem. We lost Will Lone Tree."

"What do you mean, you lost him?"

"Maris found Denise's sister living in Lander and interviewed her. Denise is hiding in a boarding house in Grey Bull."

"Still doesn't explain how you lost Will. I thought you were teaming with Maris to dog him?"

"I'm getting to that. With Maris gone, that left just me to watch Will's place. I drove back into Ft. Washakie to grab a quick bite and visit the outhouse. By the time I got back, Will was gone."

"How are you sure he left his ranch?"

"Truck's gone."

"Maybe Lucille took it to town or something."

Yancy laughed. "As tiny as she is, she couldn't reach the pedals."

"You might be right," I said. "At least put the word out. We need to find Will."

"Already have," Yancy said.

"And just what did Denise's sister tell Maris?"

"Not much more than I already told you. Her sister said Denise was scared to death when she moved out."

"Of Axle?" He hadn't seemed the type to rough up his woman, but I'd learned in this job never to assume anything.

"The sister didn't know—Denise just went up to Grey Bull to hole up. Only one Denise told she was leaving was her sister. But Maris convinced the sister she needed to talk to Denise."

"Keep me posted if you find Will."

"I'll do that," Yancy said. "Fixin' to beat the bushes now and look for him. What's up on your end?"

I explained the circumstances leading up to the gunfight with Frankie Love, and how Gustavo and Marco were upset for different reasons. "I'd wager Marco paid Frankie to kill me. I can't prove it yet, but I'm working on it."

A tinkling over the door announced another customer. I looked just in time to see a couple poke their heads in long enough to retreat back outside. Probably to Delmonico's.

"What's the plan now?" Yancy asked.

"The plan is, you find Will and hope Maris locates Denise. I'll find her and send her up to Grey Bull." I explained that Gustavo said Frankie had a younger sister back in Chicago—Gustavo said he would have someone locate the sister and tell her Frankie was dead. "As for me, my next move it to call a deputy US marshal working out of Chicago. If anyone knows Frankie, he would. I'll ask him to make notification to Frankie's sister, because I suspect Gustavo won't actually do that."

"One thing you've always hated was to kill a man and not have his next of kin notified. I like that in a man."

"Thanks for the compliment. I think."

CHAPTER 19

I returned to my table, and to the special of vegetable soup, thinking about Will Lone Tree. I still wasn't convinced he had killed Axle Denny, though I knew Will's temper could override his common sense, especially where his daughter was concerned. Will was little different from me—if I learned some moonshiner was pushing booze on my daughter, I might be tempted to find some abandoned water well and drop the bootlegger headfirst into it.

But where did Will go? He might have found out where Denise Denny went and drove to Grey Bull to learn what he could about Darla. But the more logical scenario was that Will assumed the Napolis knew more than they did, being competitors with Axle when he was alive. Would Darla have gone to the Napolis for her booze if Axle was . . . unavailable last week? Recalling my drinking days, I would have travelled to the gates of hell itself if that's where my next bottle was waiting for me.

Lucille poured me a cup, and I braced myself for it. But it was strong, with no bitter taste that I'd come to associate with her coffee. Perhaps she wanted to draw customers after all. Except for her food.

I sliced open one of her biscuits sitting on the plate beside my bowl. Steam rose out, and the inviting odor of a fresh buttermilk biscuit overcame my trepidation, so I broke off a corner. A sweet taste surprised me, but not as much as the soup. Thick with fresh vegetables and chunks of chicken, it tasted superb.

Lucille came from the kitchen, dressed more like she was going on a date than cooking. Her cotton dress was pressed neatly and stopped just above her ankles. The feathers sticking out of her hat bobbed as she walked, and her shoes had been shined. I told her how I appreciated that she'd finally gotten the food right.

"Don't thank me," she said, taking off her hat. "Thank Delmonico's. I've been gone all day, trying to find out about that thief-of-a-kid Kincaid. Had to buy some soup and biscuits from next door to get me by until I got a chance to cook."

I wanted to tell her she ought to feel free to look for James anytime, if it meant eating this well. She busied herself cleaning glasses and cups on the counter—she really only needed a couple of each, no more customers than she ever got—while I finished my meal. I checked my watch.

"Would you mind stepping into the kitchen for a couple minutes? I need to make an official call."

"Now you're telling me what to do in my own place? Go to the sheriff's office and make your call."

"I don't want Milo to hear what I'm talking about."

She grinned wide then and tossed her apron aside. "You don't trust Sheriff Darcy then?"

I shook my finger. "Don't start rumors." It was the first thing that popped into my head. It wasn't so much that I didn't trust Milo as that I didn't want Emily overhearing what I had to say. She had lived at the Napoli ranch once before Milo lured her away. Someone had tipped Gustavo's bunch that I was headed there that first day. And probably yesterday, when I had my run-in with Frankie Love. "I just need to make this call alone."

"In that case . . ." Lucille headed for the kitchen. "Take your time."

I walked to the phone on the wall and dug a fistful of dimes and nickels out of my pocket. When I tapped the switchhook, the operator told me to feed the phone fifty-five cents, and she put me through to a Chicago operator. When Ed Crane came on the line, his gravelly voice sounded as if he were sick. But then, he always sounded like he was under the weather. "US Marshal's Office."

"How's my favorite deputy marshal?" I asked.

"Who the hell's this?"

"Nelson Lane."

Ed groaned. "What the hell you need, 'cause that's the only time you ever call is when you want something."

"At fifty-five cents," I told him, "I can't afford to just call and chat."

"Understood. What 'chu need?"

"I need you to look up a next of kin for me."

Silence on the other end of the line that I calculated cost me a hefty dime. "You think I got nothing better to do than piddly shit like that? I got a stack of foreclosures I haven't even had time to look at yet. And as many subpoenas for federal court. In case you haven't heard, the Volstead Act has us kind of jumping, holding court for bootleggers. Maybe you got time for the little stuff out west, but here in Chicago, we're damned swamped."

"Remember that nice fall bear I . . . you got three years ago? And that five-by-six bull elk the following winter?"

"That's blackmail."

I smiled. Ed had wanted to bag a black bear, and I'd baited some up above Sheridan for a month before he came out to hunt. And the following year, he wanted a trophy elk, and he had that rack hanging on the wall of his office, too. If anyone ever found out that Ed missed all his shots at both animals—and I had to kill them for him—his reputation as a mighty hunter would evaporate within the Chicago office. "Of course it's blackmail. But official blackmail."

"All right." He sighed. "Who do you want me to find?"

I told him I had killed Frankie Lovelino, and I wanted his sister notified. "Gustavo said she was living somewhere on Chicago's south side with a one-legged pimp. If you can find her and give her the bad news—"

"Nope."

"What's that?"

"I said no," Ed answered. "Because Frankie Love's got no sister."

"How do you know that? Did you get invited over to Frankie's house for Thanksgiving dinner or something?"

There was rustling on the other end of the line, and I knew Ed was fishing his pipe and tobacco pouch out of his vest pocket. He drew out his explanations over a pipe full of Prince Albert. At fifty-five cents for three minutes, I hoped the tobacco burned quick. "I only know this because that little bastard Frankie Love was in trouble from the day he was old enough to pick pockets and steal apples. And break into businesses. And jack cars. And if the witness to his last crime—a bank heist where a guard was murdered—hadn't come up dead, Frankie would have been somebody's girlfriend in Joliet."

"Maybe I got it wrong. Maybe Frankie's folks live there. The dad was one of Gustavo Napoli's drivers—"

"Old man Lovelino's truck was firebombed as it crossed the Wisconsin line with a load of moonshine. Rumor was that Capone personally ordered the old man killed." More pausing, and I imagined the fire went out of Ed's pipe. "How do you know about Gustavo Napoli?"

I told him that Gustavo and his boys had bought a small ranch on the outskirts of Thermopolis, but they kept to themselves. Except for running booze, is all.

Ed laughed over the phone just before the operator came on and told me to stick in another fifty-five cents. Ed's information was getting expensive. "Old Gustavo thought he was a player here, too. Rolled with the big boys, he did. But when it looked like Capone or Bugs Moran would put Gustavo out of business permanently, he pulled up stakes. I always wondered where the old rascal ended up. But you watch your butt, Nels."

"I heard that warning before. From somebody a lot prettier than you."

"No, I mean it. Gustavo might seem like a distinguished old gentleman, but he's more like a nasty old fox. You follow the presidential election, Nels?"

"Of course," I answered. "Here in the Wild West, we can even vote when we want to."

"Smart a—"

"Ed, this is costing me."

"All right. But I mention it because at the Democratic convention here this last summer, Franklin Roosevelt didn't have enough delegates to beat Al Smith. Somehow or other—money changing hands, no doubt—Gustavo got involved. And on the fourth vote, or was it the fifth, some state's delegates changed their vote to support FDR, and he got the nomination."

"Gustavo was responsible for that?"

"He was."

"If he had that much influence, why not stick around Chicago? If he was a player, he'd be in fat city there."

"Ask him if he ever met Roosevelt," Lucille yelled form the kitchen.

"Who's that?"

"A nosy little old woman who runs a diner here's got ears as sharp as a dog."

"I heard that," Lucille said.

"To answer your question," Ed continued, "remember that Capone threat I mentioned? Scarface might have been serving time in Atlanta for income tax evasion, but good ol' Alfonse still had people on the outside who'd put the muscle on whoever he gave the nod to. Including a relatively small-time operator in the moonshining business named Napoli."

I started to hang up before it cost me another half a buck when I asked, "you ever run into a woman named Rosemary Manning in your travels back there?"

"Foxy lady? Looks like she could be a professional girl?"

"That's her."

"Because she *was* a professional girl. High end. Had a nice, tidy black book on a few attorneys. Couple politicians. A judge in the circuit court. I met her once. Nice lady, though. Gustavo used to sneak into her apartment on the north side and visit her. That's before Gustavo's wife unexpectedly died of a café cardiac while they were dining at home. Alone. At least that was Gustavo's version. Always wondered what happened to Rosie, too."

I thanked him and had started to disconnect when Ed told me to hold on. "Had to dump my ashes. But I wanted to tell you that if Rosie Manning and Frankie are out your way, Marco and the Twins must be there as well."

"You must be one of those carnival fortune tellers," I told him. "Marco and the Twins live at Gustavo's . . . ranch. They're one big, dysfunctional family."

"Then you had a chance to size Marco up?"

"Little man complex," I said. "Likes to push his weight around. Which isn't much."

"Don't let his size fool you," Ed says. "He is pure nutso. A sociopath is how the prosecutor referred to him on the last murder charge that got dropped. Now the Twins—they're cunning."

"They are Gustavo's protection, by the looks of them."

"And good protection they are, too," Ed said. "Contract killers before Gustavo took them on. They were deep in with the Jewish mob, until they got too hot even for them. Remember those wolves we saw chasing after that big old buffalo a couple winters ago?"

"The ones you wanted to shoot, but I knew you were too crappy a shot to hit them?"

"Funny man. Point is, those wolves just loped along behind that old bull. Biding their time. Until they saw their opportunity and *wham*! They went in for the kill. The Twins are like that, too. Bide their time. Wait for the right moment. Then they make their move. You got wolves in Bison?"

"Just the two-legged kind," I answered, then on a hunch: "You have any unsolved murders there last week?"

Ed laughed. "Nelson, we got more unsolved murders than Carter's got little liver pills. Why?"

I told him one of the Twins mentioned they had returned to Chicago last week to see family. "If they still freelance, perhaps they're connected to a body or two your way."

"I've got a meeting with some of the CPD detectives this afternoon, and I'll run it by them. But I can tell you the Twins are like Frankie."

"In what way?"

"They got no family. Here or anywhere."

CHAPTER 20

It wasn't a chore to find James Kincaid—I just drove past the Kirby Bridge, pulled to the side of the road, and waited. The sun was setting, and the temperature was finally dropping enough that I didn't have to constantly wipe my face with my shirtsleeve. Long about the third cigarette, I caught movement out of my periphery. James emerged from a deep draw walking his horse.

"Did they believe you about the shooting?" James tied his pony to my bumper and sat on the running board. "You got the makin's?"

"You're too young to smoke."

"That's what Dad's always telling me." He grinned. "But what do grown folks know?"

"We know enough to use all our resources," I answered. "We know enough to take a while to plan things out before we do something dumb."

"You fixin' to do something dumb, Marshal?"

"All depends if you're going to help me or not."

"I help better with a smoke in my hand."

"Did I adopt you or something?" I tossed James my pack of Chesterfields. He lit up and exhaled smoke through his nose like he'd done it all his young life. He looked like a real pro. Until he started a coughing fit that would put a tuberculosis victim to shame.

I reached inside my truck and handed him my water bladder.

He took a long pull of water, his color gradually returned, and he handed me the pack of cigarettes back. "Now what do you need help with?" he said when he could breathe again.

"I need to get into Napoli's barn for a look-see."

James took another drink. "You're a lawman. Just drive down there and walk inside."

"Couple things wrong with that. For one, I have no search warrant—"

"That thing Sheriff Darcy served to Dad couple days ago?"

"No, that was a summons for you both to appear in court. I need a search warrant to barge into another man's property without his consent. And for that I'd have to go through Sheriff Darcy—"

"Who is on Mr. Napoli's payroll."

"I'm not ready to accuse him of that. Point is, no judge will issue a warrant without Milo's say say-so."

"What's the other reason you don't want to bust in there?"

"I'd just as soon not get my behind shot off. If you haven't noticed, ol' Gustavo's got about a dozen gunnies masquerading as ranch hands. Not to mention the Twins."

James eyed me warily. "What's this got to do with me?"

I sat on the running board beside him and tugged a boot off. A cocklebur—what the Indians sold to tourists as porcupine eggs—had gotten down inside, and it was driving me crazy. "Remember that squirrel of Gustavo's you killed—"

"I never admitted killing it—"

"You killed that critter"—I ignored his denial—"in the early morning. With no one the wiser. That tells me you know how to get down there without being spotted. I'd bet you could show me just how."

"Gambling's illegal."

"So is whatever the Napolis are doing down there." I pulled my boot back on.

"You're asking me to help the law?" he said. "That's contrary to my well-being."

"Is looking over your shoulder every minute you're out here, worrying if one of Gus's men will catch you, contrary to your well-being as well? You were ready to help me yesterday."

James stood and walked to his pony. He lovingly stroked the gelding's muzzle as he talked. "The only reason I was willing then was that Frankie Love's been after me."

"And you really think with him dead, the Napolis are gonna' give up on you?"

He kicked a dirt clod with his boot and thought about that. "I see your point."

He looked around and walked to a sage brush. He snapped off a branch and bent to the dirt. He began drawing the layout of the Napoli ranch—intricate. Detailed, with a good eye for composition. I wondered what he could do with a canvas and the right paint and a little guidance. "What do you expect to find in their barn?" he asked as he drew a trail that ran north of the ranch house.

"Besides liquor stills, I'm looking for Darla Lone Tree. She and Wanda Bent have been there numerous times. Darla might or might not still be there, but I hope to find some girl who might know where she is."

"They get a lot of girls in and out of there." James looked up at me. "And lots of fancy cars from out of state, too. Don't mean that runaway of yours is there. But if you really feel a need to put the sneak on the barn . . ."

He motioned to me, and I squatted beside his dirt drawing. "Only way to get in and out without being spotted is this here trail to the north. That mean-looking bastard working the ranch—that Dan Dan—usually posts a man here." He pointed to a stand of trees just above the house in the same spot where I'd seen the sentry the other day. "But if you stay to this trail down in this draw, they'll never see or hear you."

"That looks like a ways from the house."

"It is," James said. "But once you dismount—"

"Dismount from what? My mule's in my barn at home. And I don't want to chance asking Sheriff Darcy for a loaner. I got to go in on foot."

James exaggerated a look up and down my frame. "No offense, Marshal, but you're a little . . . old to be hoofing it that far. You'll need to go in on horseback." He stood and nodded to his pony. "Ride Precious. He knows the way. Lord knows, he's been there enough times."

I looked at the swayback mustang that had seen its best days about the time Herbert Hoover was inducted into Harding's administration a decade ago. The pony's hooves were overlong, the tail ratty and full of weeds and cockleburs, and one ear lay flopping against the side of its head where barbed wire had torn it some time ago. Besides, my feet would come close to dragging on the ground.

"Don't let his looks fool you," James said. "He's as sure footed as any critter on these plains."

When I walked to Precious, his head jerked back, and the whites of his eyes showed suspicion. As suspicious as I was as I eyed the ancient McClellan saddle with little or no padding. But James was right—I had to ride in, and right now Precious was it. "I might be a while getting in there and back out again. Where can I get your pony back to you when I come out of Gustavo's?"

"*If* you come out," James taunted. "The old man had a passel of goons watching the place. But if you insist on doing this, just ride Precious back here to your truck and turn him loose. He'll find his way home."

"Where will you be?"

James smiled. "I can find my way home as good as Precious can."

"Thanks," I said.

"One other thing, Marshal," James said. "Just in case you get caught—you might want to give me the rest of that pack of smokes."

James's lack of confidence in my abilities to put the sneak on Gustavo's barn was slightly less concerting than his desire to smoke the rest of my cigarettes. I stuck two cigarettes in my vest pocket before handing him the rest of my Chesterfields. He lit one and sat back on my running board. "Mind if I watch?"

That should have been my first clue that things would not go as smoothly as I'd hoped.

I grabbed my Springfield rifle and bent to Precious, quiet and unperturbed while he eyed me, the whites of his eyes like any other bronc I'd ridden. Which should have been my second warning. As I swung into the rickety McClellan, the mustang remained still

For all of three seconds before he hunched and, when he didn't throw me off, Precious sunfished as hard as most saddle broncs I'd competed on. My rifle fell from my hand, and my Stetson hit the pony's head before rolling in the dirt.

I looped the reins around my hand and tightened up on the bit, but Precious only leaped higher into the air. When we came back down, he stretched his neck around and tried biting my hand. All the while, the smiling James Kincaid smoked one of my cigarettes from the safety of the truck.

After what seemed like ten minutes—but was probably no more than half a minute—Precious stopped as abruptly as he'd started and ambled off the road. He bent his head to a clump of gramma grass and started grazing. "I should have warned you," James said, "that Precious is a one-man critter." James stood from the running board. "But I figured you were horseman enough that you'd let Precious know he's supposed to take you someplace."

"He always that friendly?" I panted as much as the pony. I took my rifle from James and blew dust off the action.

"Just toward folks he likes," James said and started across the prairie. I watched him disappear in the growing darkness and eased Precious towards the trail James had drawn for me.

The trail was all but invisible in the darkness, but I finally found it. Even though I could see nothing, Precious walked the uneven ground, stepping across deadfalls, around fallen rocks like he'd done so many times in the past with James on his back.

When I arrived at the top of a hill overlooking the ranch, James said I would be able to see the sentry stationed to watch the barn below. I looked out of the corner of my good eye, knowing a man saw more plainly at night using his side vision.

Nothing. No sentry.

Then music filtered through the trees. Music playing from a Victrola inside the barn, too far away to make out the song. But that was the least of my worries as I strained to spot the guard James said was always stationed there. But not tonight, and I could only surmise Gustavo was confident enough no one could approach on such a dark night that he'd pulled the guard. If only Dan Dan knew that, there'd be hell to pay, I was certain.

I climbed off Precious and tied him to a tree. I chambered a round and slipped the safety on before slinging the rifle and picked my way along the path James had described.

As I neared the barn I heard music—rising and falling with the whim of the wind—coming from inside. Along with laughter. I resisted the urge to sneak down right then and see what their little party was all about. But I knew whoever was inside would be dulled after a couple hours of drinking under their belts. Just enough they might not see or hear me enter.

So I sat with my back against a tree and my rifle resting across my knees while I took out a smoke. I cupped my hand over the match when I lit it and settled back. After I finished the smoke, I'd take a short nap. And when I awoke, I'd slip down to that barn and see what all the fun was about.

Chapter 21

Cries awoke me. Nasty cries. Frightened, desperate cries that pierced the night air and carried to where I sat upright.

I stood beside the tree and watched the barn door burst open. A man dragged a screaming woman outside while three other men stood beside a car watching. In the darkness and fifty yards distant, I could tell nothing about her. Except she was on the verge of hysteria. And her life was on the verge as well, I was certain.

The man dragged her to the open car door—a long sedan, possibly a limo—and tossed her inside a moment before the three men climbed in after her. I ran as best as I could to where I'd tied Precious. But before I could swing into the saddle, the car started up and sped up the hill, leaving the ranch. I knew I had no chance of catching the car, but I had to try.

I dug my heels into Precious's flanks and raced along the trail as much as a swayback mustang could race. I failed to see a deadfall that Precious skidded over. A large branch ripped into my ankle, and I held my feet high and out of the way of other trees that might have fallen across the road. As dark as it was, I could not see along the trail. And I thanked Precious for being a mustang familiar with this part of the ranch.

And right before I lost sight of the Napoli compound below, I saw the house was as dark as it was before this commotion, with no one rushing out to investigate. Like Gustavo and his boys were used to it.

By the time I reached my truck, Precious was lathered, breathing hard, and hadn't even had time to think about bucking me off. I climbed off and tied the reins loosely to the saddle horn before I slapped him on the rump. He trotted off across the prairie, and I jumped into my panel. There was only one way out of the Napoli ranch by car—by the gravel road—and I laid on the foot feed. By now the limo had me by twenty minutes, but I had to try to find it. For the girl's sake. I prayed she wasn't Darla Lone Tree, though injury to any girl would have been a tragedy.

When I arrived at the road leading out of Gustavo's, I stopped long enough to climb out and study the tire tracks. The car had skidded sideways speeding out of the ranch, and I had a direction: west toward the Worland Highway.

By the time I hit the highway, the sun had just begun to peek above the horizon. I stopped and grabbed my binoculars, stepping onto the running board while I glassed the area.

Nothing.

Except movement in the field towards Thermopolis. A farmer tilled his meager crops, the dust swirling around his tractor making him all but invisible.

I drove the panel truck off the road and across his field, bouncing atop the clumps of dirt that had baked as hard as bricks. The farmer saw me barreling toward him. He stopped his tractor and turned so the wind drove the dust onto his back. He dropped the bandana from around his nose and mouth and had rolled a smoke by the time I got to him. He patted his pocket for a match as I climbed out of the truck. "Howdy."

I handed him a kitchen match, and he eyed me nervously as he lit his cigarette. "You're that federal marshal." He nodded to my panel. "Don't get many crazy fools tearing up their trucks going across tilled fields. Must be important. You're not here to serve me, are you, 'cause I tried to make that last payment but—"

"I'm not here for you," I said. "I'm looking for a car."

"One of those big, fancy limousines, I'd bet."

"How'd you guess?"

He motioned to the road going east past his field. " 'Cause one drove by here a bit ago tearing up the road. In a big hurry, like someone was chasing them. Probably on their way to Wild Horse Butte."

"Where's Wild Horse Butte?"

The farmer nodded. "East a few miles."

"Show me."

He bent to the dirt and grabbed a twig.

"No, hop in my truck and show me where this place is."

"And leave my field? I have beans to—"

"That wasn't a request," I told him, snubbing my own cigarette out with the toe of my boot. "Unless you want me to check in on that payment you're in arrears—"

"I got no time for foolishness." He took off his hat and stepped closer. A big man as tall as me, but not as heavy in the arms and shoulders, with his jaw muscles working overtime.

"If you are going to jump me, do it now, as *I* have no time for foolishness. I can stuff you in the car bleeding just as well as not." I punctuated my threat by stepping within striking distance.

But he must have figured a few moments away from his field was worth more than a broken jaw, and he stomped to my truck. "I'll go."

He pointed me along a dirt road that seemed to drone on for miles, with no ranch houses to be seen, no standing cattle waiting a meal of hay or cake, nothing to indicate this was cattle country.

Then we arrived at a switchback.

Ahead off to one side of the road—perhaps a hundred yards—lay a lifeless form. I stood on the brake and skidded to a stop yards from the body. I was out of the truck before it settled back and ran to the body. I bent to her and gently rolled her over. But it mattered not if I was gentle or not: Wanda Bent's eyes had already begun to glaze over, and her skin had that pallid hue of one recently dead.

"Lord Jesus," the farmer said. He'd walked up behind me and stood looking over my shoulder at her. "I ain't never seen a dead woman before. Dead hogs and cows and—"

"Hey!" I yelled at him, and the farmer blinked repeatedly. "In the back of my panel is a blanket. Get it," I said as I eased Wanda's head onto the road.

He staggered off to the truck, and I figured giving him something to do would take his mind off Wanda while I looked her over.

Her lips were swollen and split where someone had hit her repeatedly. Her left temple showed where her skull had collapsed, and I studied the outline of the weapon—round, like a stick. Perhaps a broomstick or a pitchfork handle. Or gun barrel. Her dress lay torn nearly off her, and her underwear was ripped in half so the animal or animals could get to her easier. A ligature mark around her throat told me they had used something wide, a belt perhaps, to strangle Wanda.

"Here's your blanket, Marshal." The farmer dropped the blanket at my feet and quickly backed away.

I moved Wanda's body off to one side of the road and covered her with the horse blanket. "You said the limo was probably headed to Wild Horse Butte. Where's that?"

"Through that saddle." The farmer took his eyes off the

covered body long enough to point to two protruding buttes a couple miles east. "And off to the south a bit."

"What makes you so sure the car went there?"

The farmer pointed to the road. " 'Cause I been seeing cars come and go along that road for better than a year. Fancy cars. Like the one I seen this morning."

"What's at Wild Horse Butte?"

"A cabin," the farmer said. He tried rolling a smoke, but his hands shook, and tobacco spilled into the wind. I shook out one of mine and lit it for him. He brought it to his lips, his hands still shaking. "Hunting lodge. Or it's supposed to be. It's a party lodge, if one believes the rumors." He held up his hands. "But that's all I know. I mind my own business."

"Understood," I said and stood, my knees popping. "Now when you see Sheriff Darcy, tell him what we saw, and tell him this is his crime scene."

"The sheriff?" the farmer asked, looking around as if he expected Milo to come driving up. "When's he getting here?"

"As soon as you fetch him and bring him back."

"Me? I got a field to attend to."

Right about then, what little patience I had with this limp dick had run out. I grabbed him by the front of his bibs, and one of the straps broke as I bent him over backwards on my hood. "I don't give a rodent's behind about your field right now. You get your butt into town and fetch the sheriff. I don't care if you have to drive your tractor into Thermopolis. Just get to town and bring him back here."

"Okay. Okay, Marshal," he said as I let him up. "But where do I tell the sheriff you'll be?"

"Wild Horse Butte."

I pushed my panel truck as fast as it would go on the dirt road. It fishtailed on a curve, and the back end started coming around on me before I grabbed the mixer stick and shoved it into a lower gear. The truck straightened out, and, when I'd gone another mile, the road split off to the south, just like the farmer described.

Over a hill and just past some stilted ash trees, I saw the corner of a cabin seventy-five yards or so away. I inched the truck forward until I could see the front of the cabin. A long, low Chrysler limousine—dust caked on its once-shiny beige paint—was parked in front. Two men sat under a covered porch tipping Mason jars, and their heads turned my direction as I stamped on the brakes. I skidded to a stop right before a third man ran from the house, tossing long guns to the other two men.

I grabbed my rifle and bailed out of the panel towards a stand of cottonwood trees. I dove behind the largest one as automatic fire cut bark and branches off the trees around me. Pieces of wood rained down on me, and I scooted as low as I could get, pulling my hat over my eyes. More firing, bullets pinging off my truck, and I recognized that sound: Tommy guns. Thompson sub-machine guns. Six hundred rounds a minute would soon be coming my way from three Thompsons as soon as they gathered their wits and formed a plan of attack. My shit was weak if I stayed where I was. I could not compete with their firepower.

In back of the trees ran a shallow draw where rains had washed away soil to form a trench back when this country actually received rain. The gully was deep enough to hide me, and I created some distance between me and the shooters as I ran bent over.

I chanced a look over the rim. One man walked toward the tree I'd lain behind, while the other two shooters began to flank the tree where they thought I still was.

I dropped into the draw and ran hunkered over along it. By

the time the first man reached the tree, expecting to find me there, I'd retreated to where the trench petered out.

I was out in the open.

But I had distance. I was now more than a hundred yards from the nearest man.

Just as they spotted me I wrapped the sling around my arm. I dropped into a kneeling position, just like I'd done a hundred times in the Great War fighting the Huns, and many times since. I had carried this same rifle since joining the Marines in France. And although it didn't have modern telescopic sights like many hunting guns did nowadays, I knew just where it shot. I'd need to know. The closest man fired wildly, reloaded his Tommy gun, and continued. But his shots fell short of the tree. He hadn't spotted me yet.

But he would.

I let out my breath and tickled the trigger.

The big Springfield kicked hard and reassuringly against my shoulder. The man dropped, clutching his chest, as the man flanking the tree stopped and stared wild-eyed at his friend. He turned toward me and ripped off a string of bullets when my heavy .30 caliber slug tore off his lower jaw, and he was dead before his Tommy gun hit the ground.

The last man screamed and fired wildly as he advanced on me, his bullets kicking up dirt thirty feet in front of me. His Thompson ran dry, and he tossed it aside, drawing a large revolver as he continued firing as he walked, still screaming. I lined my sights up on his chest, then dropped my point of aim to his pelvis and fired. He fell to the ground, writhing in pain, firing into the air until his revolver, too, ran dry.

I loaded more rounds into my rifle with a stripper clip and pocketed it as I walked toward the last man. By the time I'd reached him, he had opened the cylinder of his gun and fumbled fresh rounds into the cylinder. But he shook so badly, the shell casings fell into the dirt, and I kicked the .38 away. He forced a look upward, blood oozing from his mouth, and I knew I'd hit a little higher than I'd wanted. If I ever hoped to get any information from him, it had better be quick.

I set my rifle aside and knelt beside him, easing his head onto the ground. "Which one of you killed the Indian girl?"

"We all did." He coughed. "We didn't mean to . . ." Frothy blood ran down his chin and the front of his suit.

I shook out a cigarette and lit it for him. He closed his eyes and took a deep draw while I asked him about Wanda. "I saw someone force her into the car at the barn. Why did you kill her?"

"We didn't mean to. Harry got a little too . . . carried away. She just died. We wasn't even finished with her."

"What do you mean finished?"

"It's been a while since you was with a woman." He coughed violently, and I lifted his head off the ground and turned it so blood didn't run down his throat. "They gave her to us—"

"Who *gave* you the girl? What the hell do you mean?"

His eyes closed, and I slapped him on the cheek to bring him around. "Just some kid we met in the barn," he said, and he dropped lifeless onto the ground. I closed his eyes and stood on shaky legs while I lit a cigarette for myself. Slowly my hand was losing the jitters as the adrenaline left me.

I looked around at the three men I'd just killed and felt not a whisper of remorse. They'd tried killing me, and they damn sure murdered Wanda, even if I believed this man who'd said they'd merely gone too far. As I often did when I survived something that should have taken my life, I felt so old and so worn out, I just wanted to hang up my badge and find that trout stream.

I used my other hand to bring the Chesterfield to my lips as I thought about what the thug said. In my years as a lawman, I'd come to know when to believe a man and when he was lying. But the one sure-fire time a man didn't lie is when he was knocking at death's door and he knew it. Like this man just now. He hadn't implicated Gustavo or his men, though he did say some kid in Napoli's barn gave them Wanda. In looking over her torn body as it lay dumped on the road, they must have raped her repeatedly, and she'd probably died during one of the attacks. Either way, I knew I didn't have enough to directly accuse Gustavo. But I had enough to pay the old man a visit once I brought Milo into this scene to process.

CHAPTER 22

Aaron Allright was in a foul mood as he bitched about Wanda Bent lying on the table in his cold room. "Just how am I going to get paid for her? Her aunt's indigent, and she had no other relatives. And don't expect the tribe to pay squat."

"Where would the tribe get the money?" Milo asked. "If she died on the rez they'd just take her out in the country someplace and put her up on poles until she rotted away."

I could not believe someone as ignorant as Milo Darcy kept getting elected. "They don't do that anymore."

"Well," Aaron said, "those Indians can barely feed themselves—"

"Drop it!" I said. "If the tribe comes up short, I'll kick in." After all, I wanted to say, I was partly responsible for Wanda's death. If I could have found Darla, perhaps Wanda wouldn't have felt compelled to go back to the Napolis, job or no job.

The smile returned to Aaron's face at the mention of a paying customer. "That's awfully generous of you, Marshal."

"Just don't pad your bill like you do with Gustavo Napoli."

"I resent that."

"Piss on your resentment." I took a step closer to Aaron. "Just tell me what you found."

Aaron stepped out of range, and Milo flipped his notebook to the autopsy page. "Wanda was strangled. And that is all we know."

I stepped to the side of the table. "You don't mind if I look for myself?"

"Suit yourself," Milo said. "But just remember, this is my case."

I pulled the sheet off Wanda and looked at her nakedness. Here in the funeral home, cleaned of all dirt and blood, her injuries were even more pronounced. Her bruises showed where they had begun discoloration before death, and her lip appeared more puffed and split than when I looked at her on the road. Where before I thought some object like a belt had been used to strangle her, the outline of finger marks encircling her neck stood in sharp contrast to the rest of her. But what did that shooter say before he died? *They each killed her.* I thought back to the dying man's words. "Did you check for rape?"

"Marshal," Aaron said. "She's not exactly a looker. I doubt if any man would want to have relations with her."

"Check her privates," I ordered, and Milo groaned.

"I'd better wait in the lobby."

Milo left, and I faced Aaron. He leaned against a wall smoking a cigarette from a silver holder. "You heard me, check her privates." I stepped closer, and Aaron looked around for an escape plan. But he was boxed in a corner. "Wanda Bent might not have been much to look at, but she was a decent human being. God help you if I hear another disrespectful remark about her."

"Okay, Marshal." He snubbed his cigarette out in an ashtray hanging on the wall. He smoothed his pleated, grey slacks. "You are right. It was unprofessional of me—"

"And dangerous, should I hear it again. Just check for rape. And let us know what you find."

I joined Milo in the front lobby. He sat in a chair, a little discolored around the cheeks himself. I leaned against a demo casket and lit a smoke. "Maybe you're in the wrong business."

Milo wiped his face with a monogrammed hankie and stuffed

it into the pocket of his starched, white shirt. "I grew up on a ranch. We calved, and we had livestock die in horrible ways—especially with the bears and the wolves. But this"—he pointed to the door leading to Aaron's cold room—"is something I didn't run for. This is the first bunch of homicides I've had since I was elected. And they began when *you* started nosing around. Besides Axle and Frankie Love and now Wanda Bent, there's those three out-of-staters you killed this morning."

"Excuse the hell out of me for defending myself," I shot back. "And just what did you find out about those three?"

"They're my case, too."

"I wouldn't want it any other way. I just want to know something about the men who tried killing me."

Milo pulled a piece of paper from his shirt pocket and unfolded it. "Two of them were from Detroit. One—the last man you shot—lived in Chicago. They're all connected men. But none have been arrested. Not a record in the bunch."

"Then what do you mean, 'connected'?"

"They liked the notoriety of being seen with gangsters," Milo said. "Makes them big shots. At least that's what the investigators said that I spoke with on the phone."

"You know the only gangster in these parts is Gustavo Napoli."

Milo stuffed his notes back in his pocket. "I wouldn't call Gus a gangster. He don't bother anyone. Keeps to himself. You said so yourself."

"Well, I know what I saw. Someone—working for him, no doubt—dragged Wanda Bent from good old harmless Gus's barn. Gus would damn sure know which one of his men it was."

"I'll pay Gus a friendly visit."

"*I'll* pay him a visit. And it might not be so friendly."

"I told you this is my case. You heard him the last time when he ordered you to stay off his property."

"I could care less. I want to know why those men were at his ranch, and how the hell Wanda Bent got mixed up in some shit that she had to be killed for. And you don't exactly have a sterling record when it comes to talking with Gus."

Milo stood abruptly, and his chair fell against the wall. He stepped closer, and the veins throbbed on his forehead as he met my stare. He had finally grown some *cojones.* "Stay the hell out of my county—"

"You kicking a federal marshal out? If you are, we might as well step outside and settle this now."

Milo paused, and I could almost hear the internal arguments going on inside his head before his shoulders slumped. He righted the chair and sat back down. "We'll both go out to talk with Gus."

Aaron walked through the door peeling off examination gloves. "I hate to say it, but you're right, Marshal. Wanda Bent *was* raped. Repeatedly. She has massive vaginal tears, and I got some semen samples." He turned to Milo. "If the sheriff's office will pay to determine the blood type of those involved—"

"No sense wasting taxpayers' money," Milo said. "We know the men who killed her are dead. That makes this a closed case." He held up his hand. "But we'll go talk with Gus tomorrow if you still wish—"

"I do."

"Will you be delivering the death notice?" Aaron asked me.

"Yancy Stands Close will tell Wanda's aunt." I motioned to a paper sack in his hand. "Are those the things she had with her?"

Aaron handed me the sack. "Rags is all that's left. Have the family bring a clean set of clothes for the girl."

I opened the sack, and the acidic odor of semen rushed out. Wanda's torn and bloody dress was wadded up on top of what was left of her underwear. Color caught my eye at the bottom, and I tipped the sack up. Clothes spilled on Aaron's clean desk top, and he scowled. But I didn't care; I wanted to see what was in the bottom of the sack. I picked it up—a small leather turtle, faded red and green paint on the back.

I turned it over in my hand. The last time I saw it, this was hanging by a gold chain around Charlie Grass's neck the day I gave him a lift into Willie D's. "Where'd you get this?"

Aaron nodded to his closed morgue door. "It was clenched in the victim's hands so tight, I had to break her fingers to get it free. Does it mean anything?"

"It might mean everything," I said and headed for my truck.

Chapter 23

As I walked to my panel with the sack of Wanda's clothes tucked under my arm, I ran my fingers over Charlie's medicine bundle in my hand. The three men I killed had waited outside the barn until Charlie Grass—I was now certain—dragged Wanda outside and shoved her in the car. The three out-of-staters being at Gus's was mystery enough. But was Charlie working on Gustavo's orders to get rid of Wanda, or on orders from one of his thugs? I was sure the old man wasn't pure as the driven snow. But then, after these many years as a lawman, I'd come to assume nothing.

I walked to my truck, the feeling returning that someone was watching me. I looked around outside the funeral home and shrugged off the feeling. Until I saw someone had flattened both front tires, and the feeling became stronger.

I unsnapped the strap of my holster and kept my hand close to my .45 while I scanned the area. I heard a car start up before I spotted it a half block down—a Chevy coupe, one door caved in, and missing the hood. I pulled my hat down over my eyes to shield them for the bright sun and finally recognized Charlie Grass behind the wheel. I was walking toward him when he put the car in gear and sped away. And right before he turned the corner, he looked my way.

And his expression of terror was unmistakable.

The Esso station towed my truck to Willie D's, and he agreed to patch my tires. I asked him to check the others as well, in case I had picked up things driving across the farmer's field that would puncture them. I just wanted to make sure I wasn't overreacting. But I also knew the answer even before Willie examined them.

I walked to Mom's Diner and phoned the hotel. Maris was waiting for my call, and she met me at the café.

Lucille came out of the kitchen when Maris entered. "Special of the day is grilled cheese sandwich," she said as she adjusted her bra under a flapper dress a size too small. For a seventy-something-year-old woman, Lucille was looking pretty hot today.

Maris walked behind the counter. She grabbed the pot warming on the hot plate and poured what Lucille affectionately called coffee. She brought the cups to the booth and sat across from me. "The town's all panicky about those men you killed."

"Panicky about what?"

"Folks know they used machine guns. They also know the law in these parts can't afford to buy Thompsons. They know those men were gangsters, and they are afraid more will come to avenge their friends' deaths. No one wants to get caught in a crossfire."

"That might be." I sipped the coffee and grabbed a glass of water to wash the bitter taste away. "But it'll be days before anyone arrives from Detroit or Chicago, if anyone comes at all. In the meantime, I plan to find out what the hell they were doing in Gustavo's barn. But you said you had some information?"

Lucille brought us both a grilled cheese sandwich. I eyed mine suspiciously and took a bite. "This has a different taste," I said. "Different, but good. Is it goat cheese?"

"Donkey," Lucille said, and I nearly spat the sandwich out.

"What are you doing milking a donkey?" Maris asked, but I noticed it bothered her none as she wolfed down the food.

"I traded rent on a building I have for the jenny. She foaled a couple months before I got her, and she just keeps giving milk. Pretty tasty, huh?"

I concluded I'd eaten worse and started on the rest of the sandwich.

"I'd take another if you got more cheese," Maris said.

"Soon's I take a break," Lucille said, and she sat in the booth next to Maris.

"Maris and I need to talk about some things," I told Lucille.

"Is it juicy?"

"It's private."

Lucille waved the air with her cigarillo. "Nonsense. Nothing's private in this town. Now, what you got?"

Maris shrugged. "Denise didn't run to Grey Bull like her sister said. She actually fled to Lander and is living under a different name—"

"Fled from Axle?" I said.

Maris shook her head. "Axle's the one that sent her away." She wiped melted donkey cheese from the corner of her mouth. "For her own safety."

"Something to do with that thug coming to their ranch and threatening Axle before he was murdered, I'd wager."

Maris finished her sandwich and shook out a Lucky Strike. "That thug was Marco Napoli, just like you figured. He paid Axle a visit a couple weeks before you found him hanging. Threatened to put a hurt on Axle if he didn't get out of the moonshine business. At least Denise said that's what they argued about, right before Axle lost his temper."

I thought back to Marco's beaten face where Axle did a soft-shoe on Marco's head. At least Axle got *some* satisfaction.

"Axle feared Marco would come back with help. Or ambush him on the road somewhere, and he didn't want Denise in the line of fire."

"Where's Darla fit in?" I asked. "Because it's too coincidental, her disappearing right when all this commotion went on at Axle's place."

"She *was* at Axle's when Marco threatened him." Lucille sat back, with a proud smile across her face. "You ain't the only ones who can detect."

Maris winked at Lucille. "She's right. Denise said Darla was at the house the day Marco showed up."

"Buying booze?"

"Denise wouldn't admit it. Still protecting her man, even though he's dead. But she said Darla was scared when Marco showed up, and she hid in the bedroom until he left."

"I wouldn't think that'd cause her to run away."

"Darla waited for an hour after Axle had beat Marco before she left. But she said before she drove off that she prayed Marco wasn't waiting and watching the ranch."

"Marco would know the girl," Lucille said. One of her false eyelashes had dislodged, and she pasted it back. "He was the one hired her and Wanda Bent to clean rooms, right?"

I eyed the coffee and opted for the water instead. I had endured enough punishment during the last few days. "Does Denise know where Darla is?"

"I asked Denise that," Maris said. "She has no idea, but she said she came to the ranch and talked with Axle every other week like clockwork."

"That would put her back at Axle's—"

"About the time he did the dangle of death," Maris said.

Willie D entered the diner. He walked to the table and tossed me the keys.

"Don't see you in here much," Lucille said.

Willie shook his head. "I'm too concerned with my health, Miss Lucille. No offense, but I go next door when I gots to eat out."

"No offense at all," Lucille said. "I encourage it."

"Both tires are fixed," Willie D said to me. "Someone sliced the sidewalls with something—knife be my guess. Maybe a screwdriver. And it's all gassed up like you wanted." He bent and whispered in my ear, "Your truck smells like dead people, Nels."

"A funeral home used to own it."

"I was thinking more like those men you shot up got a little rank."

"Thanks, Willie," I said. "I'll stick some flowers back there when I get a chance. Just so you don't have to smell it," I told Willie D before he left the diner. But I knew it would be a waste of time. Ever since McColley Funeral Home used the panel to haul dead bodies to be embalmed, and then to the gravesite, the truck had smelled like death. Another reason I got it for a song. But as much death as I'd smelled, it didn't bother me so much.

After Willie left, Lucille went into the kitchen to fix Maris another grilled donkey-cheese sandwich, and I took advantage of her absence to tell Maris about what I saw at Gustavo's barn the night Wanda was killed. "I'm sure it was Charlie who drug Wanda out. Just like I figured it was Charlie who sliced my tires—he was watching me when I came out of the Forever Rest."

"That's the other thing I was going to tell you—Yancy's got a line on Charlie."

"That's good—"

"Not really. Will Lone Tree found Charlie driving around St. Stephens. Smashed Charlie's car when he tried running him off the road. Luckily for Charlie, Will lost control and slid into a ditch. It took a team of drays from a rancher to pull that old International truck of Will's back on the road."

"Charlie got a shit-brown Chevy coupe with no hood and a

dented fender?"

"That's it," Maris answered. "The recent dent is compliments of Will this morning."

"What was Charlie doing on the reservation? Thought he was working for Gustavo."

"That's why Will was chasing him to begin with," Maris said, eyeing the fresh sandwich Lucille was bringing from the kitchen. "Darla was riding with Charlie."

"Refill?" Lucille asked.

"Oh, what the hell." I'd gotten shot at by three men with Tommy guns. I figured Lucille's coffee couldn't be any more lethal. I was wrong and grabbed for the water glass once again. "If Charlie was on the reservation, it's a safe bet that he was picking up Darla."

"Will said he limped his truck back home after he got out of the ditch and saw some of Darla's clothes missing," Maris said, taking a huge bite out of her sandwich.

"So, Charlie's been hiding Darla somewhere," Lucille said. "Why?"

"I thought you could detect?" I taunted her.

"Give me a break—I run the worst diner in town. I'm not a lawman. When it takes real detective work, I bow down to you professionals."

I zipped my mouth before I agreed with her. Even though her food wasn't fit for anyone, at least Lucille had a place where I could meet and discuss things without Milo or his secretary knowing. "Only thing I can speculate," I told her, "was that Darla was there when Marco and his crew returned and killed Axle."

"And that may be why Wanda Bent was killed," Maris said. "She knew where Darla was staying, and Charlie was afraid Marco would get out of her where Darla was."

"So, Charlie . . . gave Wanda to those men I killed." I was

supposing a lot of things. But what had me stumped was where Darla was this afternoon when I spotted Charlie watching me. I'd need a lot of help if I was to find out where Charlie was hiding her. Or I needed Charlie right in front of me within arm's reach so I could extract that information.

"Dessert?" Lucille asked. "Least I can do for listening to all this intrigue."

"I assume you put the word out to watch for that beater of Charlie's," I asked.

"And for Will's car," Maris said. "He told his sister he was fixing to fire up his Model A and hunt up that 'kidnapping son of a bitch,' is how he put it."

Lucille placed a plate in front of us, and a bowl of whipped cream in case we wanted topping for our spice cake. I took the first bite and thought I'd chip a tooth, so I slapped whipped cream on top to soak it a bit. "Tell me Will doesn't know where Charlie is staying."

"Wrong, boss," Maris said, chowing down on cake without a complaint. "He learned from some of the Ft. Washakie folks that Charlie is working for Gustavo and living out there. Probably in that party barn of his." She checked her pocket watch. "And he's probably headed to the Napoli ranch right now."

"Then that's where I better head, as soon as I grab Milo."

Maris hadstarted out of the booth when I stopped her. "I need you here I town."

"Bull shit. There's a chance to get some action—"

"I need you to call Yancy. Tell him to find Will and do whatever it takes so he doesn't bull his way into the Napoli compound."

"Isn't that what you're going to do?" Maris asked. "Bull your way onto the Napoli ranch?"

"I am," I answered. "But I'm going to do it with more panache than Will."

Maris followed me outside. She was walking me to my panel when I saw Gustavo's Cadillac pull up to the grocery store across the street from Delmonico's. Marco climbed out from behind the wheel, dressed like he was headed to a brothel rather than buying groceries. The explanation came a moment later when Rosie gingerly got out from the passenger's side. She had dark glasses on, but when she looked over at Marco ordering her inside, I saw the side of her face had swelled, and a dark bruise had formed on her cheek not under the glasses. They disappeared inside the store, and I led Maris to the corner of the diner. "Marco Napoli doesn't know you, does he?"

"Know me biblically or otherwise?"

"Any wise. Does he know you're a deputy marshal?"

Maris shrugged. "I never had reason to talk with him, so, no, he doesn't. Why?"

I nodded across the street. "He ushered Rosie Manning inside. She's been beaten. I need to find out what the hell happened—"

"You sweet on her, Nels?"

I might be, but I'd never admit it to Maris. "Just professional curiosity."

"I thought she looked like a professional girl," Maris said. "But what's that got to do with me?"

I waited until a ranch couple walked past us on their way to Delmonico's. "Unbutton those top two buttons of your shirt."

Maris smiled. "You old dog, you." She did as I asked. I reached over and spread her shirt open a little further before I unpinned her badge and pocketed it. "Now you're ready to distract Marco."

"And I thought you were finally noticing—"

"I noticed all along, but I'm just a little old to act on it." I led her by the arm to the corner of Delmonico's. "Give me five minutes to sneak into the back of the grocery, then lure our boy

Marco outside. I need ten good minutes to talk with Rosie."

I walked down the block and took a roundabout way into the alley. When I spotted Maris entering the grocery store, I waited another couple of minutes before stepping through the back door.

I walked the aisles and found Rosie with her back to me at the meat counter. Marco was visible through the plate-glass window out front putting his smooth moves on Maris, when I came up behind Rosie. "What happened to you?"

She jumped and began shaking as she looked around me for Marco. "You can't be seen talking to me—"

I reached down and took off her glasses. One of her eyes had nearly swelled shut, and a dark bruise covered a cheek. I gently ran my finger over her split upper lip. "Who did this to you?"

"You got to go—"

"Marco is being . . . entertained long enough for me to talk with you. Now who?"

She nodded to the front window. "Marco. Gus overlooked me talking with you at the bath house—he found out somehow. But he accepted my explanation that it was just coincidence we were there at the same time."

"It was."

Rosie smiled and winced in pain as her hand went to her lip. "You underestimate yourself, Nelson. Anyway, when I failed to elicit the information from you Gustavo wanted the other day in the park, he thought I was holding out on him. Remember you mentioned I was consorting with the enemy? That's almost the exact same term Gustavo used."

I kept an eye on the front of the store. "Let me take you to the sheriff's office and make a complaint—"

Rosie forced a laugh. "And trust that son-of-a-bitch Milo Darcy? I'd rather take my chances getting away from them on my own."

"I can take you away right now," I said. "I know people on the reservation who will hide you so deep, Gustavo or his psycho son will never find you."

She seemed to mull that over for a moment. But just for a moment. "I can't leave Gustavo. He would eventually find me, and things would be even worse for me. But Nelson"—she glanced at the front window again—"you watch your butt. Gustavo cares little about anyone but himself, and he can be ruthless."

"I can be a little ruthless myself," I said and saw that Maris was getting tired of talking with little Marco.

Rosie laid her hand on my arm. "I'll be all right." She looked around to make sure Marco was still outside. "But consider this—have you ever heard of a couple revenue agents who came up missing last year?"

"From the Casper office," I answered.

"Folks blamed Axle Denny for killing them. But it was the Twins who put the agents in the ground after they came snooping around Gus's ranch. They're buried out there somewhere."

"Where on the ranch?" I asked. I finally had something concrete to take to Milo, something serious enough that he couldn't back out of it. Even if he was in Gustavo's pocket.

Rosie shook her head and put her dark glasses on again. "I don't know. It's a big ranch. I just heard the Twins bragging about it. And bragging about a contract they fulfilled back in Chicago last week."

"What day did they come back?"

She calculated on her fingers and threw out a date a day before I figured Axle was murdered.

"When they claimed they went back for vacation, they were offing someone back there. I ran that possibility by a deputy marshal friend of mine in Chicago when I talked with him, but he hasn't gotten back to me yet."

Rosie nodded. "That just shows how dangerous they can be." She raised up onto her tiptoes and kissed my cheek. "You watch yourself, Nels. The world needs men like you."

"But I can protect you if you—"

Rosie smiled faintly. "Don't worry about me. I've been on my own since I was fourteen, living by my own wits. I'll think of something." She looked away. "And I'll come back here so we can go to that trout stream you talked about."

CHAPTER 24

I stopped at my hotel room long enough to pick up two more boxes of pistol ammunition and two more stripper clips of rifle ammo before I headed to the sheriff's office. When I walked into the room, Emily was just locking up to go to lunch. "Where's Sheriff Darcy?"

Emily jumped and began trembling but quickly regained her composure. "He had to go to the bank. The loan manager's daughter came up missing, and he's forming a search party."

"There's been a lot of girls coming up missing lately," I said, and I caught Emily looking away. "You know what happened yesterday with those men I killed—"

"How should I know?"

"You probably have few occasions to type reports for the sheriff, but I'm betting you typed his report about those three dead men."

Emily looked down at the floor.

"You know a young girl was dragged from Napoli's barn—"

"Just what do you want from me?"

"The truth. What's going on at that ranch?"

Emily pocketed the office key and had turned to leave, when I grabbed her arm. "Tell me what Gustavo's got going there."

"He makes illegal liquor—"

"Girls wouldn't come up missing because they saw his moonshine stills. Gustavo could care less about anyone seeing them." I tapped Milo's name on the glass office door. "Gustavo is protected."

Emily tried jerking her arm free, but I held it tight.

"What the hell's going on there?"

"All right," she said, and I let go of her arm. "Gustavo is running girls."

"Prostitutes?"

Tears began flowing down her cheeks. "More than that. He sells the girls, usually to contacts from back east."

She sat in one of the chairs along the hall wall and held her head in her hands. Her shoulders shook, and she cried. I gave her a few moments before I sat beside her. "Is that why you were at the ranch?"

She looked up at me through reddened eyes. Her mascara had run down her cheeks, and snot dripped from her nose. I handed her my bandana and waited until she blew her nose.

"When your office foreclosed on our ranch," she began, "I lit out. I had no place to go, only that I knew I wanted some excitement. So, when I heard that Mr. Napoli was hiring girls to clean his house, I asked for a job. Figured to save up some money and then light out for Denver or Billings. Some place with action. I didn't know at the time that he often took the girls who cleaned for him and sold them. If they were pretty enough to command a high enough price."

I took off my hat and ran my fingers through what was left of my hair. "So, the illegal stills are just a front—"

"—to draw attention away from his more lucrative business of trafficking girls."

"But how does that explain Wanda Bent? She wasn't exactly pretty."

Emily handed me the bandana back. "Some of the girls who aren't pretty enough to sell, Mr. Napoli's son pimps out to out-of-towners."

"Like those thugs I killed?"

Emily nodded.

"But you made it out of that snake pit."

A slight smile crossed her lips for the briefest time. "Sheriff Darcy took an . . . interest in me before I was sent back east. Offered me a job."

For whatever convoluted reason, Milo had spared Emily a life of being a kept woman for some gangster in the cities. I asked her to find Milo and have him meet me at the entrance to Gustavo's ranch road. "I'm going to have a look in that barn. Just as soon as I have a talk with the old man."

I took the long way around to get to the Napoli ranch, driving in from the east. I stopped in back of a stand of cottonwoods on the hill a quarter mile from the ranch. I uncapped my binoculars as I stepped from the truck. I steadied myself on the hood and glassed the house and barn. On the hill where I'd made the sentry the other day, two guards now sat with their backs against a tree. One cradled what looked like a shotgun, the other a lever action Winchester. Shotgun scratched his head and replaced his porkpie hat. He looked fashionable wearing his bow tie, while his partner wore a string tie to accent a bright white shirt that I could have seen at night. Both men screamed *big city*!

I swept the binos to the house and saw one of the Twins standing behind a corner of the house watching the barn and outbuildings. I knew the other Twin must be somewhere and finally spotted him lying prone under the tractor backed into the lean-to attached to the barn. A shotgun lay beside him as smoke from his cigar drifted upwards.

But no Dan Dan Uster.

The Twins *might* be able to hit with those shotguns, and those two goons on the hill *might* be able to hit with their long guns, but I knew for certain that Dan Dan *could* hit whatever he shot at. But no Dan Dan.

And that worried me.

Other movement caught my eye, and I shielded my hand from the bright afternoon sun. A paint mustang walked slowly across a field toward me, and I set my binoculars on the hood. James Kincaid rode toward me, rifle across his saddle, his floppy hat pulled low covering his carrot-top mop. When he got within talking distance, he didn't even greet me. "You got a smoke?"

"I thought we agreed you're too young to smoke. I bet your father told you the same thing."

"He also told me not to take game out of season, but I do now and again. But only when Pa and me gets a little gaunt in the belly. So, you have a pack?"

"What the hell," I said and tossed him my pack of Chesterfields. He stuck one behind each ear and stuck one between his lips before tossing the pack back.

"You goin' down there again?" he asked as he lit up. " 'Cause that would be pretty dumb."

"How so?"

"You were lucky the last time. They didn't figure you knew how to put the sneak on them."

"And why would this time be dumb?"

James inhaled a little too deeply and started coughing, while Precious looked over his shoulder at the boy becoming sick. James tossed the cigarette to the ground, and I stepped on it. "Those fools didn't expect anyone riding up their backside. They didn't even post guards last time. But now it's different."

"I saw they beefed up their watch."

James hopped down from his pony and tied off on my bumper while he walked around to my open window. He reached inside and grabbed my water bladder. "They're expecting you."

"It would appear so."

James poured water in his hat and held it for Precious. "I've never seen that many goons just sitting around. Watching. It's like someone tipped them off that you were coming."

"That's just what I was thinking." And I cursed to myself for being such a fool and telling Emily I was headed here.

"Why are you so bent on getting down to that ranch anyhow?"

I explained that Wanda had been forced into a car, and that she was later murdered by the three thugs I killed.

"I heard about that. Folks are saying it must have been a goodly piece of rifle shooting."

I just shrugged.

"You still figure to go down there with those men waiting for you?"

"Sheriff Darcy's secretary said Gustavo's been selling women. I'm thinking Darla Lone Tree might be held in that barn."

"They'll cut you down if you go there. Hand me your binoculars."

I handed him my binos, and he glassed the ranch. "I see the Twins and a couple others still in place. I don't see Marco or the old man, but that's not surprising. When you're the boss, you pay others to get their hands dirty." He handed me the binoculars back. "I suppose if we're going to sneak down there—"

"What do you mean 'we'? You can't come with me."

James started to argue, but just then a Model A Ford barreled down the ranch road from the west. I put the binos to my eyes and cursed my bad luck: Will Lone Tree struggled to keep his beater jalopy under control on the loose gravel road. It fishtailed as he lost control, driving into the ditch. He clipped a fence post before he managed to drive it back up onto the road. A moment later he disappeared down the hill that would take him into Gustavo's yard.

"Shit!" I tossed the binos into my truck. "James, you'll *have* to find the sheriff."

"And get me arrested for truancy?"

"James!" I grabbed him by the arms and shook him. "I need you to fetch Sheriff Darcy. Tell him that Will Lone Tree is hell-bent for the Napoli ranch, and it's not going to be pretty, however it turns out. I need you to tell him I'll need help."

"What about me? I can help."

I admired his courage, but he was a kid, after all. "I need the sheriff here. Tell him I went down to the ranch."

But you'll walk into an ambush—"

"I got no time to wait for help. If I do, Will's going to be cut to ribbons. He doesn't know what the hell he's getting into down there." I climbed into my truck. "Go find him. Now!"

I popped the clutch, and the truck lurched ahead. I fought the wheel while I fed a stripper clip into the top of my rifle. Before the day was up, I'd need every round I had.

Chapter 25

Right before I dropped over the hill that would lead me directly into Gustavo's ranch yard, shots echoed off the barn and the outbuildings. I slowed, taking just enough time to assess what was happening.

And it wasn't pretty. Just like I told James.

Will huddled, helpless, behind his car, all four wheels flattened by bullets, the windshield shattered. He had apparently not thought to bring a gun, relying—as he always did—on his size and strength to bull his way through situations. That wasn't going to happen this time. Incoming bullets pinged off his fenders, penetrating the door he lay behind. The Twins fired from the barn forty yards away, too far for their shotguns to be effective. Still, they winged rounds Will's way, the buckshot skidding off the metal of his trunk and doors.

But it was the two thugs up the hill who were causing Will the most grief. The goon with the rifle worked around to get a better angle on Will while his partner's submachine kicked up bullets faster than he could aim. Their attention was on the big man hunkered down behind his car, and they didn't see me on the road above.

I stopped the truck and grabbed my Springfield. I estimated the two shooters on the hill above the barn to be three hundred yards from me, and I rested my rifle on the hood while I adjusted the ladder sight. The Twins continued firing as quickly as they could reload their short-barreled shotguns—more an annoyance for Will at that range—while the two shooters up the hill walked their round in on Will.

I took up the first stage of the trigger and held my breath for a moment before letting it out. One thug stood and started walking down the hill toward Will. I lined my sights up on him and pressed the trigger. My bullet caught the man in his high chest, and he dropped right where he stood. His rifle skidded in the dirt. His partner jerked his head my way, and he stuck a fresh drum magazine into his Thompson. He began a steady firing in my direction, but his bullets fell far short of my truck.

He ran to the rifle lying beside the dead man and started shooting at me. I jacked a fresh round into my rifle and closed the bolt. The man's Homberg had fallen off his head, and his long, black hair fell down onto his forehead. He brushed his hair out of his eyes and shot. It fell twenty yards short of me.

Mine didn't. My bullet struck him just below the eye, knocking him backwards a few feet to fall against a tree.

The Twins stood and walked toward where Will tried making himself small. Which was impossible. He looked frantically around, but there was nowhere to go. Nowhere else to hide. He was trapped.

I jumped into my truck and sped down the hill towards Will's car. The Twins turned their shotguns on me, and I ducked under the steering wheel as their first volley shattered my windshield, showering me with shards of glass that cut my face and the back of my neck.

I sat up and drew my .45, leaning out the window and firing at them as I drove directly for them. They dove for cover in the lean-to as I narrowly missed them. I skidded to a stop beside Will. "Jump in the back—"

A shotgun blast tore into my passenger-side door. Pellets raked my shoulder and hit my rifle, taking a piece out of the stock. One of the Twins advanced on me, firing from the hip, while the other one worked his way around to flank me.

Shotgun blasts came quicker, hitting my panel with more regularity, and I dove out the door and scurried behind Will's car. Will followed suit, and buckshot pierced the side of the panel where he'd been a moment before. I dove to the ground, my shoulder bleeding, but the bone wasn't broken, and I scrambled to where Will squatted behind his Ford.

"That's just great," he said, peeking around the fender of his car. "Those two goons are coming for us, and all you got to go against those shotguns is that pistol of yours."

"You're the boob who got us into this mess," I said, pellets ricocheting off the car's fender and just missing my head. "Why the hell'd you come here anyways?"

"Charlie," Will shouted over the noise. "When I run into him by St. Stephens with Darla in the car, I figured he'd come here. After all, it's the only place he could hide her out."

"You damn fool, you should have called Sheriff Darcy or me."

"Since when did the law ever help us Indians?"

"Right now, this white lawman is the only thing saving your dumb ass."

"But for how long?"

"Until I run out of ammo," I said, leaning around the fender of the car and emptying the magazine at Yosef. I missed him, but my shots managed to force him to dive for cover, and we got a brief reprieve. For now.

"You got any ideas?" Will asked.

I quick-peeked around the car but couldn't see where Rafael was. "I got a plan," I said. "You run out there and draw their fire while I make my getaway."

He looked at me in disbelief. "You got no plan, do you?"

"As much of a plan as you had when you bulled your way down here." I popped the last magazine into my Colt and snapped the slide shut. I had seven rounds left. The two boxes I had grabbed from my hotel room sat on the floorboard of my truck where they'd fallen. The only thing I could hope for was that the Twins would get overconfident and expose themselves.

My hope lasted exactly a minute as they regrouped. They began working their way toward us, using the tractor for cover, flanking us to get a clear shot around Will's car. I snapped two quick shots and ducked behind the car again. "They're twenty yards from us," I told Will.

I fired two more shots in two different volleys at Rafael moving to one side of us before dropping back behind the car. I had one round left and debated on using it on Will. After all, if he hadn't come barreling his way into Gustavo's stronghold, we wouldn't be here facing the inevitable.

Yosef stood from behind the tractor, and I snapped a shot. It nicked him in the side of the neck, and he dropped back down. But my glee was short lived—the slide of my auto had locked back.

I was empty.

I sat with my back against the car beside Will. "Guess you gave it what you could," he said. "I only wish I could have gotten a look inside that barn to see if my little girl was there."

"Me, too," I said and looked around the fender. Yosef, bleeding from a superficial wound on his neck, trickled blood onto his white shirt as he walked slowly at us. He thumbed shells into his shotgun as he advanced.

I eased the slide of my Colt closed and handed it to Will. "Only chance we got—I'll stand up and Yosef will be concentrating on me. As mean as that bastard is, he'll want to drag out my misery as long as possible and won't shoot me right off. You get around to the far side of the car and point the thing at his head—"

"But it's empty," Will said.

"He don't know that. If he figures you got the drop on him, we might convince him he's about to be worm food."

"The only ones that'll be worm food is us. What about his partner?"

I shrugged. "Don't know where the hell Raphael is."

"This ain't gonna' work—"

"You got a better plan?"

"Not just now." He took my pistol and crawled around back of his car. When I figured he was in position, I stood with my hands high.

Yosef smiled and jacked a fresh round into the shotgun, the sound louder than I'd ever remembered it. "You're one pain in the ass," he said, wiping blood from his neck. "We got him," he called over his shoulder. Rafael stood from the far side of the lean-to and walked our way. "And a pain for Mr. Napoli."

"Where is that boss of yours?" I said, waiting for Will to make his move.

Yosef smiled. "Gone on vacation."

"Vacation from what, moonshining or selling women?"

"Guess that's no concern of yours anymore," Rafael said as he shouldered his shotgun.

"Drop it!" Will ordered. He stood apart from the car, my Colt in his shaking hand pointed at Raphael's head.

He glanced sideways at Will and laughed. "You even know how to use that thing, Indian? You forgot to take the safety off." His gun swung towards Will just as a shot rang out from somewhere up the hill that grazed Rafael's hand. Another shot clipped Yosef's thigh, and he ran for the safety of the tractor as two quick rounds kicked up dust behind him.

Another shot sent Rafael running for the barn, and I looked around for the shooter. Precious grazed in a flower bed running along the side of the ranch house as James pumped the slide of his .22 rifle, chambering another round. The distance from the house to the barn—forty yards—was a far piece for a .22. But not for James, who poached game at twice that distance, and he continued sending rounds down at the fleeing Twins.

They fired back at James from beside the tractor, but their buckshot fell far short, and James kept firing steadily. They looked a final time at me before they sprinted for a Cadillac parked by the lean-to. In a moment, they had motored up the hill and were gone from sight.

James took the loading tube out of his rifle and dropped fresh rounds in before stepping out from around the house. He grabbed his pony's reins and walked toward us.

Will and I stood, astonished, looking at James casually carrying his rifle in the crook of his arm, leading the swayback mustang toward the car. I took my Colt back from Will and reached into the floorboard of my truck for my box of ammunition. I began filling my magazines as James stopped beside Will's car. "No rush with that." He took the cigarette from behind his ear and struck a match on Will's fender. "Looks like they're plumb gone."

"I thought I told you not to come down here? Thought I told you to fetch Sheriff Darcy?"

"I don't fetch so good, Marshal," James said between coughs.

"You could have been shot by the Twins. Or by Gustavo and that psycho son of his, wherever the hell they are," I said. I looked around the yard, the barn, expecting Marco or Gustavo to start firing. Or worse, Dan Dan. But no one did, and I lit my own cigarette with shaking hands. *Damned adrenaline again.*

James shook his head. "I saw the old man and Marco light out of here long before the shooting started." He nodded toward the highway. "My guess is they're long down the road by now."

"I don't care a rodent's behind about Gustavo Napoli." Will started for the barn. "All I want to do is find Darla."

He headed for the barn with the same thought I had, and

James and I followed him. "Maybe you ought to stay out here until we see if it's safe," I said to James. "No telling what trouble's waiting for us in the barn."

"Couldn't be any worse than that little shooting gallery we just been to," James said and walked past me. But the barn door was locked, and I looked around for a bar or shovel to break the padlock when Will put his shoulder to the door. It burst inward and dangled by one hinge, as he kicked the door aside and made his way into the barn. I drew my pistol and followed him. I grabbed his arm to slow him down, but he jerked his arm away.

"At least let me check things out first," I whispered. "See if there's any more of Gustavo's thugs waiting for us."

"I don't have time—"

"Your bulling your way down here already damned near got us killed once today. A few more minutes won't hurt any."

"But if you find Darla—"

"Understood."

I button-hooked the door, leading with my gun, expecting to find horse stalls, cows awaiting milking, things a barn was built for. But the first odor that hit me wasn't the smell of horse shit or cow dung, but the odor of cooked mash. But not as strong as I expected for someone in the moonshine business.

Through the room with the one small liquor still I walked, expecting more of Gustavo's goons, but there were none. All there was were rooms converting the barn into a mini hotel. I holstered, and Will and James came up behind me.

"Some place." James whistled and stood looking around the barn in awe. A row of cribs—rooms just big enough for a girl and a client—lined one wall, while a wet bar took up space on the opposite wall.

"So, here's where that son of a bitch took my Darla."

"Might be," I answered. "We'll know as soon as I find the old man and have a talk with him."

"I'd do more than just talk," Will said.

"What I meant is that I'll talk with Gustavo by hand if necessary. But I have to find him first."

James walked into each room, looking at the cheap tapestries hanging on the walls of the cribs, the thick rugs on the floor to one side of the beds. A hat rack had been screwed to every wall, and a small table sat by each bed with a cheap table lamp. "M-m-marshal," James stammered and pointed to the last room.

I joined him outside the door, and he pointed. "Inside."

I looked through the door of the crib at two young girls, one some years older than the other. They sat on a bed, both chained to a ring in the floor. Will pushed me aside and stopped abruptly. Neither girl was Darla.

They began weeping and moved back as far as the chain would allow. I pulled my vest back to expose my badge and bent to them. I cradled their heads in my arms, and let them have their cry. "We thought you were those men coming back for us," one said between sobs. "Or we would have yelled."

I pulled away from them. "Who chained you up?"

The older girl looked at the younger. "Some man who works for Marco. He promised my sister and me here jobs cleaning rooms. Charlie Grass drove us here from Worland."

I bent to the shackles. "Where are Marco and his men now?"

"Charlie ran in here this morning," the older sister said. "Shoved his things in a gunny sack." She nodded to the next crib over as if to explain. "He slept in that room. He said he was leaving. Apologized for bringing us here." She shook her head. "Bastard just wasn't sorry enough to unlock us."

"How about the others?"

The younger girl started crying again, and the older one held her. "We heard Marco when he came in. Sent all his men on their way."

"Except the Twins," the younger sister said. "They stuck around long enough for Marco and Mr. Napoli to leave. They said they would follow as soon as they took care of the marshal."

"So they knew—"

"Darla?" Will said. He squatted in front of the girls. "Darla Lone Tree. My daughter. Was she—"

"Moonbeam," the younger girl said.

"What's that?"

"Moonbeam," she explained. "That's the name Charlie said she'd have to use from now on."

"She was here." Will grabbed the older girl by the shoulder and shook her, but I shoved him aside and turned to the sisters. "Where is Darla—Moonbeam—now?"

"Charlie freed her. She was two rooms down. She was supposed to be shipped out, just like us. But Marco said that'd be dangerous. He was going to kill Moonbeam, but Charlie talked him out of it. Said she was too hot a commodity to kill outright. All the men asked for her."

"But where is she?"

"We overheard her and Charlie making plans to hide her out at some cabin Mr. Napoli never uses. Some fancy place up on Crooked Dog Gulch."

"You know where that is?" Will asked.

"Above Ten Sleep Canyon," I said. "And there's only one fancy cabin there that I know. Heard some rich guy bought it last year, but I didn't know it was Gustavo."

Will stood abruptly. "Then we better get the hell after them—"

"I got to go it alone," I told Will.

"The hell you do."

"Look: if it's the same cabin I'm thinking about, it'd be all one man could do to sneak up there." I motioned to the girls.

"And I need help here. These girls have to be returned to their homes."

Will started to interrupt, but I held up my hand. "If these girls were *your* daughters, wouldn't you want them home safe?"

Will dropped his head. "Okay. I'll get these girls home." He flicked one of the shackles encircling their legs. "Unless you got a key, one of us will have to go to town and get a hacksaw."

"I might be able to help," James said. He hung his floppy hat on a hook on the wall and took out a thin pocket knife. He looked the shackles over before selecting one of three blades. He knelt beside the younger girl, who smiled at him. James turned red and averted his eyes as he turned the lock over in his hand. "Sheriff Darcy had me in shackles about like these the last time he hauled me in for truancy."

"Why do I get the feeling you never made it to town?" I said.

James only grinned as he looked at the sister a moment before slipping the blade between the pawl and the body of the shackle. The arm pivoted open, and the girl threw her arms around James.

I winked at Will. "If you can pry her off James, take them into Sheriff Darcy's office. James can help—"

"I'm not going near the sheriff—"

"Then Will is going to have to help these two young ladies alone. Now, do you want to help out or not?"

The girl hugging James clutched his neck tighter, and he reddened again. "I'll go with Mr. Lone Tree."

"In what?" Will asked. "All my tires are shot out, and you'll need your truck if you want to make it to Ten Sleep Canyon."

"What if I told you Gustavo said you could use his new Lincoln. Since the Twins shot your car to heck."

"When did you talk with him?"

"I didn't," I said. "But I'm certain if he were here, he would agree to it."

"But he'll claim I stole it—"

"The car will be the least of Gustavo's worries when I catch up with him."

"Am I still going with Mr. Lone Tree?' James asked.

"Whenever you drag yourself away from that young lady."

James blushed, and I let him off the hook. "And as soon as you help me patch the tires on my panel that got shot out. But before you go to town, I need to follow you to your house and talk with your father."

"So, I am in trouble?"

"Not hardly," I answered. "But I'd wager he's got a saddle horse in his pasture, and a trailer to haul it he'd rent me."

"We've got a mule," James said. "One of Precious's foals before we gelded him."

"That will work," I said and turned to the women. James managed to get the other shackle unlocked, and they sat rubbing their ankles where the metal had scraped their skin raw. "As soon as you finish romancing these ladies."

"You really think you can find Darla and that coyote Charlie Grass?" Will said. " 'Cause when you do, I'd appreciate you leaving Charlie to me."

"I want some of him left to stand trial," I said and turned back to the girls. "When Marco and Gustavo lit out of here, did they have Rosie with them?"

Both women looked at each other. "No, Marshal. She came and talked to us most every day. But now that you mention it, we haven't seen her today. And she sure didn't run out of here with Gustavo."

"She might still be in the house," I said. "Will, keep these girls in here. I'm going to search the house. God knows what reception I'll get there."

I stopped at my panel, grabbed a handful of pistol rounds, and stuffed them in my pocket before I made my way across the open ground to the house as quickly as I could. When I stepped up on the porch, I paused for a moment, standing to one side of the front door, listening.

Silence.

I drew my .45 and tried the door. It swung open and hit the wall, the sound hollow in the empty entryway. I stepped inside and stood to one side of the door beside a carved walnut coat tree taller than me while my eyes adjusted to the dim interior.

In the living room next to the entryway a grandfather clock chimed, and I jumped.

I waited until I had my breathing under control from that, then began searching the house. Each room I went into had been decorated in a different color scheme: this bedroom decorated in the colors of Italy. Probably Marco's or Gustavo's. Another room was also decorated in the national colors if Italy, but this one had pictures of Frankie Love hanging on the wall, his smiling face just like I remembered him right before I shot him dead.

I had started down a long hallway when that too-familiar acidic odor of a putrefying corpse reached me. The closer to the end of the hallway I walked, the stronger the stench became. I stood outside the room where I was certain a dead body lay and took a final deep breath before throwing open the door.

I slumped against the wall and took my Stetson off. "Oh, Rosie," I said, and sat in a chair across from the bed where she lay. Blood had soaked the bedding and mattress from a deep gash encircling her throat that had all but decapitated her. The fingers of one hand touched the back of the wrist where they had been broken while she lived, and two teeth had fallen on the floor where she'd been beaten.

At the foot of the bed her suitcase lay open, clothes hastily stuffed inside. I closed my eyes, trying to imagine what had happened. She must have told Gustavo she was finally fed up with the abuse and began packing her travel bags when he came in and confronted her. More likely, it was Marco who had delivered the fatal beating, the fatal slash across her throat. I couldn't see Gustavo bloodying his hands. He'd have the Twins or his nutso son for that. And it would have been Marco who beat her before killing her. Just for fun.

I'd thought that Gustavo and his crew hadn't intended returning to the ranch. Now I was certain they were gone for good. And the only logical place Gustavo would run to would be the cabin he owned in Ten Sleep Canyon. The one he rarely used. The one that fool Charlie Grass was taking Darla to.

Chapter 26

"Why would they want Darla dead?" Will said, well away from the earshot of the girls sitting in Gustavo's Lincoln. "When she was so . . . popular with the men? Don't make any sense."

I had thought about the same thing on the drive over to the Kincaid ranch. Darla might have brought big money for the right man, if the two sisters had their facts straight. The only thing that had kept her alive was Charlie, but I doubted his protection would have lasted very long.

I sat on the running board and lit a cigarette, thinking back to Rosie and why she had decided to leave Gustavo. With her pre-death injuries, I could see Marco beating her to get her to confess to passing information along to me that was damning to the Napolis. No other explanation seemed logical—they would have pulled up stakes if they thought they were going to be arrested for the murders of the two revenuers last year. Of if they thought Rosie knew too much about their trafficking of young girls, and her leaving triggering a case of conscience. Gustavo had bought the foreclosed ranch for a song and probably had little money in the one cooker we'd found. He'd be free to start again somewhere else. But not if I could help it.

I stood when James came out of the ramshackle one-room house ahead of his father. "Jimmy Kincaid," James's father said. "Lordy, when James said a US marshal was out front, wanting to talk to me . . . Lordy, I was afeard James had gone and done something really bad this time."

I briefly explained what had happened during the last few hours, and how James had saved our bacon. "Can't hardly arrest a hero for that, now can I?"

Jimmy grinned and ruffled his son's hair. "James says you need the loan of a horse."

"Horse or mule or trained cow. Anything that'll get me along in the mountains."

"I can let you borra' Precious, but I understand you've already ridden him, and you two didn't see eye-to-eye."

"He's definitely a one-boy horse."

"Then all's I got left is Peckerhead. My mule."

After assuring Jimmy that the federal government would reimburse him the daily rate for use of his stock and the use of the horse trailer, I gave final instructions to Will and James and hitched the horse trailer to the panel truck.

I stopped right before I hit the Worland Highway to double check the trailer and mule. Or, in this case, a hinny. James was a little off—Peckerhead being the Tobiano-marked product of Precious and a female donkey Jimmy inherited when he squatted on the place two years prior. But that was all right by me. The hinny might be slower than my mule back home, but it would be even more surefooted in the back country. And certainly more surefooted than any horse I could take into the mountains. I'd need Peckerhead's trail sense if I were to approach Gustavo's cabin above Ten Sleep Canyon.

When I pulled up to the Esso Station in Ten Sleep, the same stooped old man hobbled out to gas my truck as he had days before. "Fill 'er up with oil?" he asked again, as if that was his stock question for anyone driving a Ford. He walked around my truck and scratched his head. "Looks like someone used this thing for target practice," he said and flicked pieces of broken side glass with his thumb. "Or getting their rifles sighted in for hunting season."

"I wish that's all it was," I answered.

While he waited for the bowl to fill with gasoline, he walked to the trailer and ran his hand over Peckerhead's snout. The hinny snapped at him, and the old man jerked his hand back just in time. "Not very friendly, is he?"

"Just a mite stubborn, from what I was told."

The man returned to the pump, stopped it, and turned to my truck with the gasoline container. "Anyone else come through here needing gas today?" I asked.

"Lots of folks," he answered, though I doubted lots of folks would come through a town of a hundred people on any given day.

"Okay," he said after a few moments when I didn't respond, "so we don't get many customers here, but we had a few earlier." He took his railroad cap off and ran his fingers through his sweaty, white hair. "Had one of those new Cadillacs come through. Boy, was that ever a sight—"

"Some older, white-haired guy driving?"

He shook his head. "An old timer—'bout my age—was riding shotgun. Dressed like a damned congressman or something, all fancy-like. Now the driver—he was scary. Must have been the old man's kid, as he called him 'son.' They've been through here a time or two before, and I figured they have a place up in the mountains." He frowned. "But never driving something like that Caddy."

"How long ago were they here?"

The old man put the cap on my tank and wiped gasoline off the paint. As if that would hurt the looks of the truck at this point. "They stopped for gas four, maybe five hours ago. They drove off like they knew the place."

"Anyone else with them?"

The old man broke off a corner of a plug of tobacco. He offered me a chaw, but I waved it off. "A couple hours later, two *really* scary guys stopped. Never said much. But it was just the way they looked at me. No, *through* me. Scary. Like I was some future victim of something they planned on doing. One had a rag around his neck that was caked with dried blood. He claimed his brother accidentally cut him with a scythe when they were cutting hay."

"But you didn't believe him?"

The old man laughed. "With this drought, there's not enough hay around to cut. Besides, with that new Chrysler they were driving and their fancy duds, I doubt they ever cut a stalk of grass in their lives."

"Thanks for the information," I said and handed him a dollar bill. Then another quarter for more tobacco.

I climbed into my truck, and it coughed to life.

"Don't you want to know about that other car what came by?"

I turned off the truck and got out. "What other car?"

"Some beater brown Chevy missing the hood that rolled into here before the other two. Some Indian-looking kid driving. Arguing with his girlfriend beside him."

"Arguing about what?"

"Don't hear so good." The old man tapped an ear. " 'Cept she was crying. Got him just a gallon of gasoline and kept looking around all the while as I pumped it. I figured him and his girlfriend with him were running from her pappy." He pocketed the quarter. "People still elope these days?"

"You're asking the wrong feller. What did the girl look like?"

The old man tried whistling through whatever teeth he had left. He didn't pull it off. "A real looker, she was. At least she was before she got slapped around. Few bruises on the side of her face, and I asked the kid about them. He threatened to put the boots to me if I didn't mind my own business. But I thought the old man in the Cadillac might be her daddy, as he asked about the Chevy when he pulled in."

"What did you tell them?"

"I had to tell them the Chevy come through a couple hours before," the old man answered. "What else could I say? The driver looked like he wanted an excuse to beat hell out of me."

"Any idea where they were going?"

The old man looked up the mountain. "By the looks of that old duffer, he could afford any place he wished. And that would include that fancy place up the gulch, the one that feller from New York owned once."

I thanked him and gave Peckerhead a carrot before starting my truck. As I drove off, the old man looked after the retired hearse with fifty fresh bullet holes. The truck had been used to haul dead bodies when it was owned by McColley's Funeral Home. I just hoped it wouldn't be used to haul another—mine—after I found the Napolis.

I'd been by the DuPrie cabin twice while hunting elk. The cabin sat a half mile back into the trees at the end of a long driveway you couldn't see from the road. It was a sprawling, one-story log affair one of the DuPrie clan had built before the stock market crashed in '29. And long before old man DuPrie shot himself in the head when he lost his fortune overnight.

The road climbed steadily higher, and I was grateful for the extra power of the truck. I grabbed the mixer stick and jammed it into first gear as I slowed to creep around a log that had fallen across the road. When I cleared the log, I stopped and climbed out to check tracks. At least two other vehicles had driven around the log. Vehicles with new tires. The only people who could afford new skins in this Depression were politicians and gangsters. And Wyoming didn't have many politicians.

I climbed back in after giving Peckerhead another carrot—I'd need to stay on his good side for later—and started back up the steep hill, truck and trailer kicking up rocks as the truck fought for traction on the loose gravel. I coaxed the truck along and, when I arrived at a saddle in the road that evened out, I spotted something dark staining the dirt. I'd seen that color enough times in my life to know that someone had bled heavily.

I unsnapped my holster and looked around carefully before getting out. I bent to the blood stain that had soaked into the dirt, the putrid smell making me retch, as it almost always did. I held my hand over my nose as I worked out the scene. A car had stopped—no, two cars had stopped—at that precise spot, but some time apart, if I was aging the tracks right. Whoever had made the blood spot shouldn't be alive, as spread out as that stain was on the road. One set of tracks ran over the blood-soaked gravel, but it was impossible to tell if it had done so right after the victim bled. I just couldn't tell.

I moved so that the sun was between me and the stain, and blood spots stood out in contrast to the gravel. I followed random spots leading into the trees ten yards off the road. I drew my Colt and kept my attention between the blood trail and the trees. When the wind changed, I heard faint moaning coming from further in the forest a moment before I spotted a boot sticking out from under some bushes.

Charlie Grass lay holding his side, blood seeping between his fingers, and he tried focusing on me as I holstered. I knelt beside him and eased his hand away from his side so I could pull his shirt up. "He gut-stuck me," Charlie managed to spit out. "Oh, God, Marshal, it hurts so bad."

"Who did this?"

He tapped my shirt pocket, and I shook out a cigarette. I lit it and waited until his coughing spasm died down before sticking it between his bloody lips. He coughed violently, and frothy blood splattered over my shirt front. "Marco," Charlie said at last. "He seen me walking in the middle of the road. Put a gun on me. Demanded to know where Darla was. When I didn't tell him he pulled his knife out and—" Charlie coughed again, and I held his head up so he wouldn't choke on his own blood. It really didn't matter, though. Charlie had but moments to live.

"Where is Darla?"

"I sent her away. I seen that big Caddy of Gustavo's. Coming fast up the road. I sent Darla ahead in my car."

Charlie retched with pain. The cigarette fell from his lips, but he didn't notice. "Thought I could delay them. Give her a chance to run."

"And when you didn't tell Marco where she was—"

"He cut me and dragged me off the road. It's bad. Isn't it?"

There were certain times I felt justified lying to a man. One was when his death was imminent, with nothing under God's sun to be done for him. This was one of those times. "You'll be okay. I'll get you help." I patted his shoulder. "Where did Darla drive off to?"

Charlie pointed to a high peak farther along the winding road. "Sent her in my car. There's a sheepherder's cabin a mile north of Gustavo's fancy one. Seen it this spring." He coughed, and I turned his head. Blood frothed out of his mouth, and his eyes began to glaze over. "He don't know about it. Ditch the car. Go the rest of the way on foot, I told her—"

"Why does Gustavo want her so badly?"

But Charlie didn't answer. He couldn't answer. His head dropped onto the foliage. His lifeless eyes looked past me, and I instinctively glanced back over my shoulder. But there was no one there, of course.

I picked up the rest of the cigarette and finished it as I tried to remember the cabin Charlie had sent Darla to. I'd never seen it, but Charlie said it was a mile north of Gustavo's. And I knew where that was.

I stood and arched my back. I'd drive further along the road until I came to where Darla had ditched Charlie's car. I'd pick up Darla's tracks there as she continued on foot. And Pecker-head and I would get to know one another better.

Chapter 27

Three miles farther up the mountain, Charlie's Chevy sat askew along the side of the road. I approached the car from a distance, walking around it, working closer, as I studied the tracks. The driver's side tire had blown out, and I imagined that—even if Darla knew how to patch a tire—she wouldn't have had the time. If I recalled correctly, Gustavo's cabin was another two miles along, making the sheepherder's cabin where Darla headed another mile past that. A long distance on foot for someone my age. Manageable for some youngster like Darla.

I bent to the driver's-side door and ran my hand over ridges in the dirt made by Darla's shoes. At some point she had clipped something, and one heel had a sizeable gouge out of it. I stood and eyed the direction into the trees where she had gone. I had hunted these mountains enough I could age tracks well: she had no more than two hours' head start on me.

Before I backed Peckerhead out of the trailer, I took a moment to walk up the road and look closer at the recent tire tracks. Tracks made by new tires. Maybe tracks of several cars, though it was hard to tell with the loose gravel. My best guess was that Marco and Gustavo had passed her soon after Darla ditched the car; the Twins not long after that. Did they have horses at their cabin? If they did, it wouldn't be long before they ran Darla to ground.

The first mile tracking Darla went slowly. She must have

suspected people might follow her, and she was careful to hide her sign. She picked her way carefully around deadfalls, over rocks she could have stepped around and made impressions in the earth; walked along a trickling stream until she found a place where she could cross and leave little sign.

A half mile farther along, fatigue set in. Darla began stumbling, failing to pick her way around trees, leaving tracks that were easy to follow. I stopped Peckerhead long enough to snatch a piece of torn gingham dress from a juniper bush. I had stuffed it in my pocket when other tracks caught my eye. I dismounted, and Peckerhead grunted, as if he actually liked me riding him. Three horses had ridden over Darla's footprints. They came from where I remembered the DuPrie cabin overlooked an expansive meadow a half mile from it. I led the hinny as I backtracked a hundred yards, learning something about the men who followed Darla. Two horses rode over trees and rocks, rather than around them. A cigarette butt had been discarded haphazardly, as if the rider didn't think anyone could follow. Sloppy. Were those the Twins?

It was the third rider who concerned me. He rode around bushes with jaggers that would gouge horse and rider. Rode around a deadfall from some recent wind storm, careful not to leave any more sign than necessary. Marco? Gustavo would certainly have raised the crazy bastard in the ways of the affluent. Which included the finest riding lessons in Chicago the gangster could afford. And this one knew how to ride without disturbing anything more than necessary.

I climbed back up on Peckerhead and slipped a piece of carrot out of my pocket again. I checked my rifle and kept it ready. I had the feeling I'd need Peckerhead and the rifle sooner than I'd have liked.

Even though it was summer, snow capped the peaks and drove

the temperature twenty degrees cooler than it was at the Esso Station in Ten Sleep. When I pulled my coat from behind the saddle and slipped it on, I almost missed the drop of blood. Peckerhead smelled it and snorted. He stood with the whites of his eyes looking wildly, but he remained still while I dismounted and bent to it. A piece of torn shoe lay some yards from the blood where Darla had ripped her foot or a toe on a sharp rock.

And her stride suffered with her injury. Fatigue had ground her to a halt, no doubt aided by the drop in temperature, and she had sat on a fallen tree. For how long, I could not tell, but longer than she should have according to the amount of blood under the log.

And the hoofprints I'd spotted before pursued her as she trudged higher up the mountain toward the sheepherder's cabin, hoof prints that rode over the blood spot left by her.

I mounted Peckerhead and continued through the trees. A quarter mile through the forest, it suddenly gave way to a flat, grassy meadow bigger than a city block. Snow had piled up on the east side where it had blown unimpeded across the field. But there *was* grass, and there should have been elk or deer grazing at this time of day. But none were.

I stepped off the hinny and tied him to a tree. I squatted and examined the tracks. Darla had stumbled straight across that clearing, disregarding any attempt at secrecy. If she'd tried to avoid anyone following her before, she had thrown all caution out the window as she stumbled on. Whoever spotted her tracks might by now have caught up with her. She might already be in the clutches of the Twins and Marco, for their hoofprints showed them riding straight across that field.

The hairs stood up on my neck, and Peckerhead snorted as if thinking just what I was: I dreaded riding across that clearing and imagined the hinny did as well. I could ride around the meadow, keeping to the cover of the trees, and pick up her tracks on the other side. But that would take twice as long. And Darla might not have time.

I mounted Peckerhead and fed him my last carrot as I patted his neck. "I don't like it either, pard'ner," I said, as we left the safety of the forest and started across the field. I was scouring the trees on the other side of the meadow when Peckerhead stopped. I nudged his flanks, but he refused to go farther. Mules—and hinnies—often stopped dead, refusing to move when they sensed danger near. Folks thought they were just stubborn or stupid. But owning them for as long as I had, I'd learned they were smarter than a horse. And I'd grown to respect their judgment.

I leaned down and talked in his ear. "Let's just do this, pard'ner," I said. "I don't like it either, but we gotta' go." He finally started slowly across the field, and I slipped the safety off my rifle. I rode bent over, spotting Darla's tracks—and the tracks of the three horses—across the meadow. When I was within fifty yards of the safety of the trees on the other side, I breathed easier.

Until Darla's tracks disappeared. "Shit!" I said to myself as I realized the riders had split up. One rode back toward Gustavo's cabin. The other two made for the tree line. Too late I spotted sun glinting off something shiny in the trees, and the first round ricocheted off the cantle of the old McClellan saddle. Peckerhead humped up, and I threw myself to the ground as the next bullet nicked his rump. He brayed and bounded for the trees as more shots came my way. Someone must have told the Twins shotguns were useless past lobbing range, and they both carried Winchesters as they levered rounds from the cover of the forest.

Out in the open, I scrambled for any cover, and I crawled to a slight depression in the ground as I watched the trees. The Twins pinned me down from the safety of a stand of lodgepole pines, ducking from around cover, firing and laughing.

One of the Twins poked his head around a tree, and I sent a shot his way. He ducked back, and I waited until the other Twin showed himself beside a spruce, and I fired. Like his brother-cousin, he fell back behind the tree, and I took the lull to break and run across the meadow in the direction I'd come, away from the Twins. Back to the safety of the trees I dove as bullets impacted dirt and branches above my head. The Twins didn't shoot rifles any better than they shot shotguns.

I low-crawled behind the trees as the Twins kept pumping rounds where I'd disappeared a moment ago. When I was twenty yards deeper into the forest so that I was sure trees would mask my movement, I half-stood and made my way around the outside of the clearing. When I had moved a hundred yards around the perimeter, I arrived, shaking, at their flanks and had a clear view of them. Yosef rested his rifle against the side of a tree as he fired steadily, while Rafael thumbed fresh cartridges into his Winchester.

Peckerhead ambled back onto the meadow, ignoring the bullets piercing the air. He dropped his head and grazed casually, and I hoped no stray bullets found him. The Twins momentarily stopped shooting as they stared at the mule. I ducked back farther in the trees and started working my way round toward their backside as they resumed their steady firing that masked my movement.

When I was within thirty yards of them, I peeked through the trees just as they stopped shooting. "Where the hell did he go?" Rafael said.

"I think I hit him," Yosef said. "I saw him go down."

"Must have," Rafael said. "He ain't shot back."

"That's 'cause he's got the drop on you two fools."

Yosef spun around, and I shouldered my rifle. "Don't even think about it."

Rafael stared wide-eyed at my rifle pointed at him, and a look passed between them—the same look I'd picked up that first day at Gustavo's—and I *knew* they were dead men. Yosef dove for the ground, spinning around, bringing his rifle to bear on me, while Rafael dove in the other direction, shooting from the hip. I shot him first, taking him high chest, and operated the bolt as quickly as I could, swinging wide to line up on Yosef. But I wasn't quick enough. The surviving Twin shot from the ground, and his bullet tore through my forearm muscle and struck the receiver of my rifle, snapping the bolt handle off.

I dropped the rifle as hot, piercing pain shot through me. Time seemed to slow then, as if I were watching a picture show that had slowed down. Yosef stared at his dead cousin and screamed.

But I didn't hear it.

Yosef struggled to lever another round into his Winchester, but it looked as if he were taking his damned sweet time doing so. I looked down at my shattered rifle, and all I thought about was drawing the Colt on my hip.

But my arm didn't operate right. I couldn't grip the pistol with my injured arm, and I rushed him just as he closed the loading lever and brought the gun to his shoulder. I flung my two hundred forty pounds of ranch-boy into him. He flew backwards, falling to the meadow, and lost the rifle somewhere a half-dozen yards away from where he landed.

I rushed him as he sprung up from the ground and clawed at a large knife on his belt, but I crashed a fist into his face. Again. And again. Blood splattered my cheek, but Yosef seemed not to feel it as he drove a knee into my groin.

I groaned and rolled away as Yosef's blade cleared the sheath, and he lunged at me.

I jerked back, the blade missing me by a hair's breadth, and he landed on top of me. He pinned my good arm with his weight, as he cocked his knife with the other.

He plunged his knife at my head, but I jerked aside. The blade buried itself into the dirt just as I freed my good hand. I hit him flush on the chin, and his eyes rolled in his head for the briefest moment. I grabbed his hand holding the knife and twisted the arm. Yosef brought his knee up once again, but I was ready and blocked it with my leg as I rolled over, straddling him.

I fell atop his knife hand, and the blade went deep into his chest, instant frothy blood spurting from his mouth. His disbelieving eyes looked a final time into mine, and I ripped the blade upward, disemboweling him.

I rolled off him and lay on the ground, sucking in air through lungs that felt as if they would implode any moment. The icy temperature already had begun cooling the sweat dripping from my head and face and down my neck, and I wiped it dry with my bandana.

I struggled to my knees and knelt beside Yosef. I wiped blood off his blade on his shirt and used the knife to cut strips off his shirt, wrapping my arm tightly. The bullet had nicked a bone, but not broken it. I was more worried about blood loss, so I wrapped another piece around my arm and tied it tight.

I fished into Yosef's suit pocket and came away with a handful of rifle rounds that I pocketed. I struggled to stand and walked to where Yosef's rifle lay. The Winchester still had one round in the magazine, and I topped it off. I left my own rifle—damaged beyond what I could fix right now—and approached Peckerhead, still grazing like it was just another day for him.

He didn't even look at me or acknowledge my presence, the haughty SOB. I used more of Yosef's shirt to dab the blood from Peckerhead's rump, and he only looked at me as if he thought I had a carrot.

I spoke to him softly before grabbing the saddle horn with

my left hand and swinging atop the saddle. Desperation set in, and I began cutting sign, looking for Darla and Marco. I needed to find Darla before Marco killed her. If he hadn't already.

CHAPTER 28

A half-mile past the trees, I reined Peckerhead up short when I spotted Gustavo's Cadillac and Lincoln parked at his cabin. I would have liked to say that Darla had out-thought her pursuers and made it safely to the sheepherder's cabin. But she hadn't, and now she was probably held inside the large log home shielded by spruce and pine on three sides.

Beside the cars a blue roan stood saddled, tied to the hitching rail in front of the covered porch spanning the length of the cabin. It looked like those Norman Rockwell paintings on the cover of the *Saturday Evening Post.* Except what was going on inside the cabin was anything but idyllic, I was certain. What I feared I'd find once I made entry into the cabin sent chills up my spine. As if the cold hadn't done that all ready.

I grabbed another strip of Yosef's torn shirt and made another wrap around my arm. The blood had soaked through the other wraps. I'd prayed the cold would have stopped it. I was wrong, and after I burst into the cabin, the wound would open up even more.

I squatted behind a thick stand of pine and watched the house. The cold had nearly frozen the sweat under my shirt, and I pulled my coat tighter around me. It had little effect. Once a man chilled, it took some miracle to thaw him at this altitude. I didn't have time to sit around and wait for that miracle.

I checked my Colt, now hanging from my left side where I

could get to it, and opened the action of the Winchester. A fat round sat in the chamber, three more in the magazine. God help me if I needed more than that. God help me if Marco or Gustavo had brought a Tommy gun with him.

I waited behind cover of the trees for another half hour and had seen no movement inside. But I knew folks were in the cabin, warming themselves in front of a roaring fire, if the smoke billowing out of the chimney was any indicator.

It was time to make my move, and I used the tree to help me stand. My muscles ached from the fight with Yosef, and I felt older than I had in many years. But I knew what I had to do.

I had left the safety of the trees and started for the cabin when the sharp, distinct sound of a gun being cocked behind me stopped me in my tracks.

"I wouldn't turn around just now." Dan Dan's gravelly voice made the hair on my neck stand at attention, and I knew he had the drop on me—stupid, like a tenderfoot. "Why don't you just lay that rifle on the ground and step away from it. And that .45 of yours while you're at it."

I did so. Slowly. Even without knowing where he was, I knew Dan Dan was savvy enough to challenge me from a position of cover.

"Now you can turn around," he said after I stepped away from my guns.

Dan Dan emerged from the trees pointing a large caliber revolver at me. "Not that I don't trust you"—he grinned—"but raise those arms."

I raised my left arm and nodded to the right one. "One of the Twins nailed me with a bullet. That's as high as I can lift it."

"I'm surprised they hit anything with those Winchesters," Dan Dan said. He backed away and sat on a log. "They never could hit a bull in the ass. Their specialty was . . . close work, shall we say." He carefully reached inside his shirt and grabbed a plug of tobacco. He was ten yards away, but the big Smith and Wesson would tear me a new one at this distance before I took a couple of steps. "I found those two boobs shot to hell back down the mountain a ways. I heard the shooting but got there too late, even if I'd wanted to help them."

"If?" I asked and slowly brought my hands down.

Dan Dan shrugged. "All I was paid to do was to track Darla after that crazy-ass Marco cut hell out of her boyfriend. Gustavo didn't pay me to get involved in a shooting war."

"I thought it odd that the Twins and Marco were able to track Darla," I said. "Yours was the third horse—that roan tied to the hitching rail—not Marco's?"

"You're good," he said, his breath coming as faint smoke in the cold. "Marco wasn't along for the party—he stayed with his daddy to make sure the old man had some protection. Just in case." He spat a string of juice and wiped his mouth with the sleeve of his sheepskin coat. "Just me and those two fools. About the time we come onto the girl wandering around like Moses in the wilderness, I saw you picking your way up the mountain on that goofy mule—"

"Hinny," I corrected.

Dan Dan smiled. "Whatever you rode on, I spotted you. I took Darla to the old man's cabin over there and left the Twins to set up a welcome committee."

"You're as guilty as they are in trying to kill me—"

"They were supposed to wing you at the most," Dan Dan said. "Bring you in alive to talk to Gustavo and Marco. Find out who you told about them. They've had their belly full of you poking around. They figured the least they could do for you causing them to leave everything is . . . make sure you pay as long as you might last."

"And what of Darla Lone Tree?"

The muzzle of Dan Dan's pistol drooped slightly, and I

thought about rushing him. But for just a moment. In my younger days I wouldn't have been able to make it in time with a normal man covering me with a gun. Dan Dan was familiar with weapons—Dan Dan wasn't normal. "I have no knowledge of their plans for the girl. They didn't tell me, and I don't even want to know."

"Why Darla?" I asked, moving closer. "What the hell did she do to Gustavo?"

"She got greedy," he answered. He saw me inching closer, and his revolver came up to center on my chest. "She was at Axle Denny's the day Marco came back there. The chicken-shit little bastard couldn't do his own fighting. He had to bring the Twins with him on that . . . special kind of visit."

"His last visit to Axle's?"

"The Twins said . . . I can talk bad about them, now that they're dead?"

"We both can talk bad about them," I said.

"All right then." He chuckled. "I admit I hated Axle. I didn't lose one minute of sleep when I heard Marco and the Twins drove there. And Darla figured neither would anyone else. Darla could have gone to that idiot, Milo Darcy, but he wouldn't have believed her. And if he did, he wouldn't have done anything about it, being close to the old man and all. And no one would care a whit if the Twins and Marco killed Axle. He wasn't exactly popular, except for his liquor customers.

"Now trafficking young girls is another matter. Darla saw what Gustavo was doing and threatened to go to the highest level with that pearl of information." Dan Dan ran his finger around the inside of his cheek and pried out the tobacco. "What she got was a trip to the cribs, and visits from more men in a week than she'd had in her lifetime."

I reached inside my coat, and Dan Dan pointed his revolver at my head. When I came away with my pack of Chesterfields, he lowered his muzzle. "Why not sell Darla like he did the rest of the girls? Or better yet, kill her?"

"Charlie Grass," Dan Dan answered. "Charlie promised he'd keep Darla under wraps."

"By shackling her to a bedpost and giving her to whatever man had the price?"

Dan Dan shrugged.

"And those . . . plain girls, like Wanda Bent?"

"She was one of those he couldn't sell. Men want lookers. Which she wasn't. Marco was afraid she'd rat on them for keeping her friend Darla. So when two of Gustavo's associates took a liking to her for some reason, it was like a gift. But it was that psycho son of a bitch from Detroit who came to the ranch that probably killed her. I spotted him as a sick bastard right off."

I snubbed my butt out with my boot and eased Yosef's bloody knife from my back pocket. The thought of rushing Dan Dan armed with only a knife was frightening. But I'd reach him before I collapsed and would plunge the knife into him right before I died. "Then I don't feel a bit sorry for killing those thugs," I said, though I didn't feel any remorse about it at the time. Or since.

"And Gustavo didn't much, either," he laughed. "After all, they couldn't take their new Chrysler or Lincoln with them to the grave. The old man got a couple free cars he gave to the Twins. Toss your pack of smokes over here."

I tossed my cigarettes to Dan Dan. When he bent to pick it up, I concealed the blade alongside my leg and moved ever so much closer. "But Marco was madder 'n hell you killed them." He lit a smoke and tossed back the pack. "Almost as mad as when you killed Frankie Love."

"Marco paid him to kill me."

"I told Ol' Gus you'd figure it out. Frankie was one of those killers who would off anyone, even if he *wasn't* paid. But Marco slipped him some greenbacks to kill you."

"And see how that turned out for him." I painfully bent and pocketed the rest of the pack of Chesterfields with my shot hand, figuring how many steps I'd make before he shot me the first time. My weight alone would propel me the rest of the way to him, and I'd slice his throat before I collapsed. I'd seen men in the war shot bad and dead on their feet, shooting, running, sending grenades in the direction of the Germans. They were men dead on their feet for their last few moments until blood caught up with them, and they didn't even realize it. Barring a shot in the head or heart, I'd make Dan Dan pay for what he was about to do.

But I needed to know about Charlie before I was worm food. "Did Charlie have some . . . epiphany? Uncuffing Darla and fleeing up the mountain?"

"Charlie knew Darla had worn out her welcome. And her usefulness. Gustavo ordered Charlie to take her out into the woods somewhere and kill her. Except he saved her instead." Dan Dan tipped his hat. "Ain't true love grand?"

"Did you tell him that right before he died?"

Dan Dan blew smoke rings upward that the wind took away in the direction of the cabin.

"What now?" I asked.

Dan Dan frowned and aimed his revolver at my head. I could sprint as best I could and hope the surprise factor would allow me time to reach him.

I had shifted my weight to my back foot and taken another breath, when . . .

Dan Dan lowered his muzzle, still aimed in my direction. "Gustavo pays me. *Very well,* for all things pertaining to keeping the ranch safe from people like you. But"—he stood from the log—"he doesn't pay be enough to murder a federal marshal. Even if it would be so sweet to see you bleed out on the ground."

I motioned to the gun. "Then what's your plan?"

"My plan is . . ." he said, bending and grabbing my guns. I cringed when Dan Dan blew dirt off my beloved Colt and stuck it in his waistband. He holstered his revolver as he checked the condition of the Winchester before pointing it in my direction. "I'm not going to kill you."

"Then what—"

"You have a dilemma." He smiled. "Do you go back down the mountain to find a gun somewhere and return, only to find out Darla's just been killed? Or do you do something foolish and rush right in there to save her and get your sorry ass ventilated? By the time you do either, I'll be so far up the mountain no one will dare come after me until the snow melts this spring."

"They're armed with God-knows-what firepower. How am I supposed to go against them?"

Dan Dan shrugged. "That's your problem. Any US marshal worth his salt ought to be able to figure something out. If you want to save that girl in there."

"I recall you had a daughter once."

Dan Dan took a step closer and raised the Winchester. "I ought to blow a hole in you right now."

Dan Dan had been married once to an Indian woman from the Crow Agency. Their one offspring—a girl who died at eleven months—had been found dead in a hot car in August. The mother had never surfaced, and it was speculated she lit out for California with a passing drummer. I'd always figured Dan Dan had made certain she'd never let another child die. "Why the hell bring Marjorie into this?"

"Because she would have been about Darla's age by now."

"So?"

"If she were being held by some Chicago thugs, wouldn't you want her saved?"

He paused just long enough that I pressed my point. "Give me one of my guns so I can at least have a fighting chance to save Darla."

Dan Dan's trigger finger relaxed, and he grabbed my Colt from his waistband. He dropped the magazine and tossed it into the dirt in front of me. "Never had much use for automatics anyway," he said as he pocketed the magazine full of rounds.

"One round?" I said. "You expect me to go against them with one round of ammunition?"

"It's the cards you were dealt today," Dan Dan said and motioned with the rifle. "Toss that knife over here, too." He smiled. "Wouldn't want you to have too much of an advantage."

I tossed Yosef's knife to Dan Dan before I picked up my Colt and blew dust off it. He never made a move as I snapped the gun up and leveled it at his head.

"Make it a good one," Dan Dan said. " 'Cause as soon as you drill me, Marco and his old man will know you're here. And if Darla's not dead already, she will be soon's they hear that .45."

Dan Dan knew what I'd do, and he turned and headed up the mountain.

"As soon as I take care of the Napolis, I'm coming for you," I called after him.

"I'm not worried," Dan Dan said over his shoulder. "As good as they're armed, you'll be lucky to fire that one round."

"I'm coming for you," I said as he disappeared into the trees.

Chapter 29

It's hard to tell just when the sun sets here in the mountains; it just comes on sudden-like. One minute I could see the cabin and cars and horse tied to the hitching rail clearly. The next minute, it seemed, all was dark. And with the setting of the sun, the cold came. In the Big Horns, the temperature could drop thirty degrees with sunset. Even in the summer. Cold enough that I cupped my hand to my mouth and breathed warm air onto it. It had begun to stiffen from the fight with the Twins. I'd need the hand and fingers in passable shape. Especially because it was my off hand.

I fought to recall what James and Milo and Lucille had said about Gustavo and remembered he was a horse lover. Lucille said Gustavo had not brought any horses with him when he bought his ranch, and I could see why—he wanted a quick getaway. If things went sour for him, he didn't want to be encumbered by anything as troublesome as horses.

But Gustavo had kept horses here at his remote cabin, probably getting away every so often to ride, times when no one knew he was here. Safe from people like competitors. And US marshals. As I looked at the cabin, I knew a true horse lover would never leave a horse saddled and tied to a hitching rail for very long.

I crouched behind the trees and watched, the chill seeping deep into my hands, and I longed for my gloves that were in my bag hanging off Peckerhead's saddle. But Dan Dan had led the hinny away and put the hat to his rump. The last I saw him, Peckerhead was running hell bent back down the mountain.

And the more I thought about what Gustavo would do, the more I suspected he'd figure the Twins got lost in the woods at night after bushwhacking me. The thought might never cross his mind that his professional killers were bested by a hick marshal. He'd figure they would start a fire to warm themselves and would return to the cabin once the sun rose.

And Gustavo would eventually send Marco out to put the horse in the barn across from the house.

Darla's life might depend on Marco coming out of the house and entering the barn, where I planned to wait for him.

I made my way toward the barn and slipped inside. When my eyes adjusted to the darker interior, I looked about. There were four stalls, presumably for horses, though it was hard to tell with this crazy bunch. The barn door opened inward, and I saw there was enough room that I could hide beside the first stall when Marco came in leading the horse. He would be within a few feet of me as he passed. I had the one round Dan Dan left in my Colt, but I couldn't waste it on Marco, nor could I alert Gustavo that I was at the cabin by shooting Marco. I'd have to wing it and take him out with my fists. I smiled at that last thought.

I spotted several bales of alfalfa outside one stall and moved them closer to the door, creating a choke point. Marco would have to come leading the horse close to me now. I sat on my haunches to one side of the door, blowing into my hands. Within the hour, my wait was rewarded.

I heard Marco cursing long before I heard him untie the roan and lead him toward the barn.

I crouched and covered my mouth with my hand to mask my breath.

Marco swung the barn door wide, still cursing the Twins for

not making it back after their job. He paused long enough inside the barn door to light a lantern hanging by a nail on a wall before continuing, leading the roan. When he had just cleared the door, I lashed out with a straight left that caught him on the side of the head. He fell to the barn floor and rolled over onto his back.

I bent to him and grabbed at him with my one good hand when he rolled away. When he came up on his feet beside the next stall over, a stiletto blade reflected the flickering light of the kerosene lamp.

I drew my Colt and thumbed the safety off. "Drop it or you got another hole in your head."

He grinned. "I see you got no magazine in that gun of yours. Lose it?" he asked, circling me, shuffling the blade between hands like a border shuffle with pistols.

"I got one in the chamber. That's all I need at this distance."

"You don't dare shoot me," he said, flicking the blade out but not getting close enough that I could deal another blow. "You got that one shot, and you don't want to waste it on me." He passed the knife from hand to hand. "My old man thought you might track us to the cabin." He exaggerated a tipping of his porkpie hat. "But he didn't figure you'd best the Twins. I bet they were a handful."

"They weren't so tough after all," I said, keeping my injured arm away from him, hoping he wouldn't see the damage. He'd have no qualms about knifing a one-armed man.

He moved in and flicked out the knife, the blade slicing my forearm just deep enough that it severed muscle right below where the bullet had passed. I took a step toward him, but he leapt back, far enough to give me time to throw my coat off and wrap it around my injured arm. I had just enough coordination in that arm to raise it the next time he made an attack. "The Twins were amateurs," I said. "Like you. They couldn't take pain so good."

"That so?" he said and lunged. His knife cut my coat, and I lashed out with a jab that skidded off his cheek. He jerked back but kept his balance and circled. "Who bought all those girls you abducted?" I asked, matching his movement.

"We abducted no one," Marco said, flicking the blade but missing me, and he quickly drew back out of striking range. "Those girls came to us on their own. Wanting jobs. Only after we got a look at then did we figure out which ones would bring the big bucks—"

I stepped quickly while he was gabbing. He slashed, but it caught my coat, and I swung a roundhouse that caught him on the chin. He dropped his knife, and I kicked it away. When he struggled to get up, I wrapped my hand around his shirt front and hauled him to his feet. "Who killed Rosie?"

Marco shook his head to clear it, and he laughed. "I did. She was feeding you a little too much information. She screamed when I snapped her hand back like a twig—"

I hoisted him high with my one good arm, the blood rage rising inside me. I took a deep breath to calm myself. I needed him alive to tell about the aftermath of this little adventure.

I set him down on the barn floor, and his foot lashed out. His blow meant for my groin caught me on the inside of the thigh, and I set myself before putting all my weight behind a blow that landed flush on his temple. He slumped and staggered a step forward before toppling over. Blood and grey matter leaked from his crushed skull, and I leaned back against the stall.

I took a moment to put the roan into one of the empty stalls before bending to Marco. I searched him, but he had no gun on him. I was back to only one bullet to go against Gustavo, who was inside the cabin and armed with whatever firepower he could lay his hands on.

I blew the lantern out and picked up Marco's knife from the

floor. I blew straw off it before tucking it in my belt at the back. Now I was a US marshal with one knife, one bullet, and one good arm.

And that's all I had at that moment.

Chapter 30

I was grateful for the darkness masking my approach to the cabin, with only a lantern swaying from a hook beside the door. I made my way around back, expecting to gain entry there, but discovered the cabin had been designed with the sole door being out front.

I cautiously worked my way back around to the front of the cabin and stood at one corner, trying to figure the best way to get inside. But with only the one door, my options were limited.

I tested my weight against the four steps leading up to the porch. The cabin had been built solidly by craftsmen, and no creaking of the boards gave my presence away.

I duck-walked, and my knees popping made more noise than the boards as I inched toward a bay window to one side of the massive door. I raised up just enough that I could peer inside. Gustavo paced the floor in front of a girl I recognized from the photo her aunt had given me—Darla Lone Tree. She sat in an occasional chair, her head on her chest, breathing heavily. I thought at first she had passed out, but soon she lifted her head and glared at Gustavo as she gestured with her hands.

She wasn't shackled to the chair.

I thought Gustavo and Marco had gotten sloppy by not securing her, when I saw her swollen ankle already turning brown. A swollen ankle. Perhaps broken on the trail as she made her way to the sheepherder's cabin she would never see. Her chance of making a break for it went right down the outhouse—Darla couldn't run if her life depended on it. Which it might in the next few minutes.

My attention turned to Gustavo. He wore a thick, knitted sweater and pleated worsted-wool trousers. Still living the life of a *patron,* I thought to myself. Dressed like nothing in his world was amiss. His thugs had taken out the only lawman on his trail, and Marco would soon be coming back from the barn where they planned to do God-knew-what to Darla. Except Marco would never be coming to see his father again, and this lawman was far from finished. A little cut up and partially disabled, but not done in yet. It reminded me of the time I'd got my foot caught riding saddle bronc as a kid and broke it coming off after the eight seconds. By the time my name was called for the bull event, I'd wrapped my foot tight enough to compete. I just sucked up the pain and went on. I'd have to do the same thing now. Suck my injuries up, and hope to catch a lucky break when Gustavo was distracted.

While he yelled at Darla, I wrapped my hand around the door and carefully tested it. Unlocked. When the cursing inside stopped abruptly, I backed away, ready for Gustavo to come through the door. But after a silence of a few moments, he started hollering at her again, and I looked around the side of the window.

I drew my Colt. When the time came, I had better make it good.

It came a few moments later. Gustavo set his wine glass on the fireplace mantel and grabbed a poker. When he began stirring the coals, I turned the knob and burst through the door.

For an old man, Gustavo moved surprisingly quickly. He dropped the poker and spun around, instantly bending behind Darla. He produced a gun from somewhere—perhaps the folds of his sweater—and pressed the revolver to her head. His other arm encircled her neck, holding her fast.

"Drop it," I commanded, but I knew it was a hollow threat.

Gustavo smiled, and his thick Italian accent returned. "I would say the same to you. This is what you cowboys call a Mexican standoff, no? Now, Marshal, drop *your* gun."

When I hesitated, he cocked the gun.

"Kill the son of a bitch," Darla sputtered.

Gustavo's grip tightened on her neck, and her face contorted from lack of air. "Is that any way for a young lady to talk?" He nodded to my gun. "I will kill her unless you toss that gun over here. Besides"—he grinned again—"I see you have no magazine in your pistol. That means you have one shot, if that. For all I know, the gun is empty."

"I have help on their way—"

"Ever play poker, Marshal? Because you're not worth a darn at bluffing."

I extended my arm and took aim at his head. "Only thing that's keeping her alive right now is the possibility that I'll kill you with this."

He jerked his gun away and fired a round into the wall beside Darla's head. She screamed, and her hand covered her ear, just as Gustavo jammed the gun against her head again. "Unlike you, I have five more bullets. The next one goes right into her brain."

I had run out of options. If I killed Gustavo, the reflex action of his trigger finger might fire his gun, killing Darla. Unless I merely wounded him, at which point he'd kill her anyway before training his gun on me.

"Marshal!"

I laid my gun on the floor.

"Kick it over here."

I did as Gustavo ordered. He kept his gun on me as he picked up my Colt. With one hand, he opened the slide and jacked the round in the chamber to the floor. Smooth. Like he was familiar with all sorts of weapons. But then, he was a gangster. "You *did* have a round in there, Marshal. No matter." He gestured with his gun. "The couch."

I sat on a spotted white and black cowhide divan and laid my bad arm on the arm of the couch made from cow horn. When I leaned back, the hilt of Marco's knife jabbed me. As if to remind me that I *did* have another weapon at hand.

Gustavo moved away from Darla. He scooted a chair closer to me and sat backwards with his arms resting over the seat back. "I assume because you are here and Marco is not, that he will not be coming back." He motioned to my arm. "But it looks like he made a fight of it."

I looked at the blood-soaked wrapping and shrugged. "Actually, one of the Twins shot me. Marco tried making a fight of it, but it never quite worked out for him there in the barn."

"I never could teach that boy any common sense." Gustavo shook his head. "Now the Twins were different. They could *always* take care of themselves."

"But not this time," I said.

Gustavo gave me a weird grin that caused me to shudder at the thought of such a cold bastard having the drop on me. "I wish Marco were here to hear that. I bet him a dollar the Twins were not lost in the woods like he thought they were. I bet him you had taken them out. He would have handed me over a dollar for losing the bet, were he here. No matter." He cocked his revolver again. "Enough of the small talk. Time to wrap up this little party—"

"Let the marshal go," Darla pleaded.

Gustavo backhanded her, and his fist caught her flush on her mouth. She screamed as she fell from her chair. She massaged her swollen leg and stifled a cry.

And she landed atop my empty gun.

"I might just kill you a little slower." Gustavo sat back on his chair and glanced sideways at Darla, rolling around the floor, nurturing her ankle. "Just for the Twins and for that idiot son of mine."

"You're the one who sent a boy out to take care of a man—"

"I'm not upset about Marco." Gustavo waved the air with his pistol. "He was a damned fool. But the Twins—they were more like my own boys than Marco ever was." The stately old man's attitude had changed dramatically from when I first talked with him at the Napoli ranch. He was, after all, just another gangster. "But how did you get the drop on Dan Dan? He was—how you say it—a savvy woodsman?"

"Actually, I didn't," I said, dropping my bleeding arm beside me, closer to Marco's knife. "He let me go. Figured the gig was up with you, and his . . . services wouldn't be needed any longer. He didn't want to be a part of your slavery ring anymore."

"So that's what you think we were doing—running a slavery ring?" He glanced down at Darla squirming on the floor, holding her ankle, and kicked her foot. She screamed, and he laughed.

I dropped my hand back closer to the knife. "What would you call keeping young girls against their will? Selling them to men to take them away to work in brothels, or whatever their fate is?"

Gustavo motioned to Darla on the floor rubbing her ankle. "These girls came to me to make money. Word got out I had jobs for them. Many girls came expecting a job."

"But we didn't think you'd send us away," Darla said. She moved off the gun and scooted closer to me. "Or figure you were pimping us out."

"I didn't start out doing that," Gustavo said. "I originally wanted to just keep some girls—"

"For your own use?" I said, gathering my legs beneath me.

Gustavo nodded. "I adore women. Especially . . . girls who

need some guidance. But some friends got wind that I kept a few and . . . well, I had to help my friends out. It sort of snowballed from there, so to speak."

"For a healthy fee, I'd wager."

Gustavo grinned. "I am a businessman, after all." He looked down at Darla. "But you were a special case." He moved the muzzle of the gun between me and Darla in a lazy figure eight. "We weren't all bad, Marshal. Occasionally we encouraged some of our girls to pursue other . . . careers."

"Like Emily at Sheriff Darcy's office," I said, my hand clutching the knife handle. "Seems like you let her go quite easily."

"She, too, was different. Milo took an interest in her, and I let her go with him."

"So she could report back to you every time I was on my way to pay you a visit?"

Gustavo shook his head. "I haven't talked with Emily for many months." He pointed his gun at Darla. "She never got greedy like this one."

Darla spat at Gustavo, and it hit his shoulder, but he seemed not to notice. "Greedy? If you would have paid me, I would have kept my mouth shut, and Charlie and me would have been in another state."

Gustavo frowned. "This one thought she could extract money from me."

"Because she saw the Twins murder Axle Denny?" I asked as I eased closer to the edge of the couch.

"Darla was there when Marco and the Twins paid Axle a visit. They were just supposed to rough him up a little. Talk him into getting into a different line of work."

"But Axle didn't cooperate?"

Gustavo shook his head. "They got . . . carried away in talking with him and hung him." Gustavo stood and looked down at me. "This one could have jeopardized the Twins and my son if she went to the authorities. And she would jeopardize me if she told anyone about what went on in the barn." He cocked the gun and pointed it at my head. "Now tell me who you told about me?"

Out of the corner of my good eye I saw Darla look around the floor, and her hand fell on the round that Gustavo had shucked out of my Colt. "I have a deputy who knows all about your little operation—"

"The Twins intended visiting her as soon as we got this Darla Lone Tree business behind us." He grinned. "Now I will have to talk to her myself. Deputy Red Hat, is it?"

Darla palmed the .45 case, and she rubbed her ankle, inching closer to my gun a few feet behind her.

"Now, Marshal!" He fired a round that whizzed past my ear. "Who did you tell besides Deputy Red Hat?"

Darla brought the gun to her side away from Gustavo. I saw she worked out how the gun loaded and slowly brought the slide back. I moved slightly closer to the edge of the couch, distracting Gustavo, as she inserted the fat round into the chamber. Now all she had to do was drop the slide and fire.

"Enough!" Gustavo said, cocking the gun. "I will find out myself. Goodbye, Marshal."

Darla let the Colt's slide drop, chambering the round.

Gustavo snapped his head around and looked down the muzzle of my gun.

Darla fired.

The bullet whizzed past Gustavo and into a picture frame hanging on the wall behind him.

He turned his gun on her.

I sprang from the couch, drawing Marco's knife.

Gustavo saw me too late and snapped a shot as I thrust my knife at him. The bullet nicked my ear, and I flung myself atop him, missing with the knife, slicing his leg. He brought his gun around when I head-butted him. His nose broke, splattering blood over me, and I wrenched the revolver from his hand.

He clutched his leg as he writhed on the floor, and I saw Marco's knife had cut him high on the inside thigh.

"Hold still," I commanded and motioned to Darla. "My hand doesn't work so good. Come here and cut his trouser leg open."

"You're not going to help him . . ."

"Darla!" I yelled. "Do it!"

She crawled over to where Gustavo had sat with his back against the couch, bleeding from his nose. But when she ripped his trouser leg away, I saw his nose bleed was a minor thing. Blood spurted out of his sliced femoral artery and had begun pooling on the floor. "Help me, Marshal," Gustavo said, reaching for a monogrammed handkerchief that cost what I made in a week. His face had already paled from the blood loss, and he handed me the hankie with one shaking hand, the other holding his leg.

"Nothing I can do for you," I said. "You got two minutes, tops."

Gustavo began crying.

"Is there anything you want me to know? Anyone you want me to tell how you died?"

"Remee," Gustavo managed to sputter as his head bobbed on his chest. "My brother Remee. Chicago. Never went into my business—" Gustavo coughed, and he shuddered violently before his head dropped, lifeless, on his chest.

Darla nudged him with the hand. "He really dead?"

I nodded and eased his body onto the floor.

Darla began crying, and she slumped against me. "He was going to kill us, wasn't he?"

I draped my arm around her shaking shoulders and stroked her head. Much as I would do with my own daughter, if she were in this spot in her life.

She drew away from me, and a concerned look entered her reddened eyes as she touched my arm. "We'll get you home, as soon as we get that arm wrapped enough to stop the bleeding."

I nodded to her leg. "You got your own problems to worry about."

She nodded. "It will be hard riding one of Gustavo's horses down the mountain."

"Riding? We're going to take that fancy Caddy of his."

"Isn't that stealing?"

I looked at Gustavo. "It is, but I doubt that he'll ever report it."

CHAPTER 31

I sat next to Maris before Yancy got a chance to slide into the booth beside her. We were at Mom's Diner for business, and the last thing I needed was for them to get frisky and distract one another. They could do that later if they wished.

Will Lone Tree sat next to his sister, who looked none too happy with her brother. "I said, tell them," Josephine ordered. When Will remained with his head down staring at his coffee cup, Josephine slapped him on the side of the head. "Tell them."

"All right." Will rubbed his ear. He nearly filled the booth, but he shrank down like a little kid at his sister's commands. "I apologize," he said, almost a whisper.

"Go on," Josephine ordered.

"I apologize." He looked at Yancy. "To all of you."

I looked at Maris, who looked at Yancy. I guess we were all in and didn't hear right. "For what?" I asked.

Will kept quiet until Josephine cocked her slapping hand. "Okay," he said. "I apologize for mistrusting you all. If I had let you do your jobs, maybe Darla would not be in the hospital right now."

I had driven Darla to the hospital in Worland when we'd come down from the mountain in Gustavo's Cadillac. The doctors had admitted her—for her broken ankle, and to treat the beating Marco had dealt her. After the doc had sewn my arm up where the bullet had passed through the muscle, I sat with Darla in her room. When Will arrived, I left them to work things out while I paid a visit to the Washakie County sheriff's office to report Gustavo and the other dead bodies in and around the DuPrie cabin. "Those croakers are gangsters?" Sheriff Bucky Jones asked.

When I gave him the headline version, he just shrugged. "Then I'll have a good day cleaning trash off the mountain today."

"When Darla gets out of the hospital," Josephine said, "I think she and her father will have a long talk about their relationship."

"I have been smothering her," Will admitted. "She needs to get out in the world. Be her own person. I was so worried she would not be able to accept life as an Indian in a white man's world—"

"Understood," I said. But did I really? I wasn't an Indian. I hadn't lived Will's life. But I had been an alcoholic who'd hidden my addiction and my feelings about life from everyone who mattered in my life.

Lucille emerged from the kitchen, balancing a tray with biscuits and bowls of stew—the special of the day—and sat a bowl in front of each of us. She set the platter of biscuits in the middle of the table along with butter. *Real butter,* not some concoction made out of donkey milk and lard.

I looked askance at the bowl, and noticed Yancy and Maris both watched my lead. I dipped my spoon into the stew and found an abundance of meat—tender meat surrounded by vegetables. "This is actually good," I said, and Maris and Yancy began eating. It was so thick, I almost had to eat it with a fork. "I knew the law of averages said you'd eventually get it right."

Lucille snubbed her cigarillo out on the floor and pulled a chair up to the booth. "Young Kincaid came back. I grabbed a broom and was about to beat him for stealing them chickens the other day when he apologized."

"James? That's a positive step."

Lucille nodded and stabbed a piece of meat in Yancy's bowl with a fork. "James said he did wrong, and he dropped off a front quarter of beef." She set Yancy's fork down. "That now resides in them bowls."

I recalled the two cows I saw at the Kincaid place. When I stopped to thank Jimmy for lending me Peckerhead, who I'd found grazing halfway down the mountain after I'd killed Gustavo, two scrawny cows hung their heads over the empty feed trough. None would have been this tender. I immediately thought about the rustling call Milo got yesterday. "Where'd James get beef?"

"He said that gangster—that Napoli feller—wouldn't be needing his cows. James figured someone might as well get some use out of them."

"His dad bring James into town?"

Maris nudged me. "I seen James when he drove in to Thermopolis. Driving some Plymouth."

"That was reported taken from Delmonico's this morning," Yancy added. "And found out back of Mom's. Like someone had abandoned it."

"But don't you dare tell Sheriff Darcy," Lucille said. "He'd put that boy away for sure. Be a shame, too, him with some new filly." Lucille described the girl who'd stopped by the diner when James dropped the beef off. She sounded just like the younger woman we'd found in Gustavo's barn.

"Then you'll be serving food this good for some time?" Maris said.

"Do not bet on it," Will said.

Josephine elbowed Will in the ribs. "That any way to talk to Lucille?"

"Well, it is true," Will said. "Lucille does not want to serve good food. It just might bring customers in." He grinned at her.

"Is that not right?"

Lucille stuck another cigarillo between her red-plastered lips. "I can't lie. Delmonico's does a landslide business compared to me."

"Tell them why," Will pressed as he polished off his second biscuit and eyed the plate for another. "The real reason."

"All right," Lucille said. "I own Delmonico's building. Bought it when the owner walked away from it after the crash. Monte Delmonico thought he could open a booming diner there." She smiled sheepishly. "And he does one hell of a business."

"Tell them the rest," Will chided.

"Besides collecting rent every month," Lucille said at last, "I get a substantial cut of his business."

I finally saw her scheme. "So, the more he makes—"

"The more I make," Lucille said. "And I can sit back and relax." She glared at me. "Until folks come in expecting a meal."

Yancy motioned to his empty stew bowl. "It's not that you're a poor cook—"

"It's just that I'm a lazy cook," Lucille finished.

She pulled up a chair missing the back and sat close to Will. I got the impression she had dibs on the man. Even if he was twenty years younger than she was. "I still don't know how the Napolis could have gotten away with abducting women these past couple years," she said. "You'd have thought folks would be asking about their girls when they never came back home."

"Not everyone has a loving family to look after them," Maris said, nodding to Will and Lucille. "Lots of girls just go west. Live the adventure, like that hoity-toity banker's girl that run away couple days ago and wound up in Hollywood. The family just figures they made it big someplace and don't look for them."

"And I'd bet old Gustavo had some help," Yancy said, slurping up the last of his stew. He eyed the last biscuit, but Will stabbed it first. He grinned at Yancy, then put it on Yancy's plate. "Sheriff Darcy's secretary—Emily—used to work for old man Napoli. By what Nels says, every time he went to the ranch, they knew about it ahead of time."

"What did she say when you talked with her?" Lucille asked Maris. She had nosed her way into every other conversation we had. I should have deputized her. " 'Cause she should have known a lot of what was happening."

"I haven't been able to find her," Maris answered. She took out a Lucky Strike, and Yancy lit it for her. "She quit the sheriff's office sudden-like. Last anyone's seen her is, she was hitching a ride to Riverton where she was gonna' catch a bus someplace."

"What's wrong?" Josephine asked Will. He cradled his coffee cup in his huge hands. "Charlie Grass is what's wrong." He looked across the table at Yancy and Maris and looked sideways at me. "In the end he saved Darla. Or at least got her out of that barn before Gustavo's thugs could kill her."

"I thought Charlie was a little more than he let on," I said. "When I gave him a ride to pick up Gustavo's Caddy, the old man told him to be *very* careful. At the time, I got the gut feeling the old man wasn't telling him to be careful with the car, but careful about talking to me, no more than he said on the way to town."

Will slapped the table. Not hard, but with his pie-sized mitt, it was hard enough to rattle plates. "So that's it? With the Napoli bunch dead, that's it? What about all those girls that were reported as runaways? And the ones that just came up missing? Left home . . . They cannot all have left to seek their fame out West."

I lit a Chesterfield and offered Will the pack. He hesitated before taking one. "I have a contact in Chicago," I said. "He knew the thugs I killed in that gunfight, the ones who murdered Wanda Bent. He raided one crib house on the south side and found two girls reported missing last month. And he planned more raids this week."

I scooted out of the booth and finished my coffee.

"Where you going?" Lucille asked. "Dessert will be right up."

I finished my coffee. "That's what I'm afraid of." I headed for the door. "There's a trout stream calling my fly rod."

"You're leaving?" Will said. "With an investigation to finish?"

"Maris can wrap up what needs to be done here, and Yancy can finish the interviews on the reservation. Relax." I smiled. "These two are quite competent."

"Come back for another meal sometime," Lucille yelled after me.

"I will if it's as good as this one."

"Don't bet on it," she answered.

CHAPTER 32

When I walked into the sheriff's office, I half-expected Emily to be at her desk or swooning over Milo Darcy in his office. But then, I really wasn't looking for her anyway. The person I wanted to talk to sat at his desk when I barged into his office. Milo was kicked back, his feet up on his desk, with a telephone receiver screwed to his ear. When he saw me, he sat upright and looked wild-eyed at me crossing the room quicker than he expected. With my good hand, I snatched the telephone from him and flung it against the wall. Bakelite shatters incredibly well, as it did that morning.

"What the hell—"

I hit Milo hard on the end of the nose, and I felt the satisfying crunch of cartilage. Blood splattered over his starched white shirt, and over papers on his desk when I hit him again. He fell backwards into his chair, and it rolled hard against the wall. He spat out a broken tooth as he clawed for his pearl-handled Colt. I snatched it from him and dropped it into the trash can.

He slumped over, holding his nose, and I grabbed him by the shirt front and dragged him over beside a chair in the middle of the office. I let him fall to the floor and sat on the chair inches from his face. "If I'd seen it before—you feeding Gustavo information—I would have busted the damned phone long before now. And you."

Milo mumbled something, and I pulled his hand away from his face. "Couldn't understand you. Your hand was in the way."

Milo spat blood out of his mouth. Then a bonus—another gold tooth pinged off his deck when he spat it out.

I plucked the silk hankie from his suit pocket and handed it to him. "Pinch your nose shut, and tilt your head back long enough for the blood to stop. And tell me what you said."

"I said, what the hell you doing?"

"Didn't Sheriff Jones call you?"

Milo dropped his head. "He said the whole Napoli bunch was dead, and he wanted me to go to the ranch with him. Conduct some follow-up investigation. I heard the Napolis didn't quite make it back to Chicago."

I lit a cigarette and couldn't resist blowing smoke in his face. "Now, how'd you know that stately Ol' Gus and his boys were running from their operation?" He dropped his head, and I squeezed the sides of his cheek to look at him. "No answer? Maybe I can help—Gustavo told you. Just like you told him every time I planned another move. All along I blamed Emily for tipping him off. But in that respect, she was as pure as the driven snow."

"Emily fled," he said. "Didn't you notice she wasn't at her desk? As soon as she heard the Napolis were dead, she got scared you'd implicate her. She took off—"

"Shut up," I said. "Unless you want a broken jaw to go along with that nose of yours."

He kept quiet and held the handkerchief over his nose.

"I kicked myself in the ass for not seeing it as soon as you rushed into Axle's barn to look for him. As dangerous as you thought he was—and as a cowardly an SOB as you are—I should have picked up on that right away. You *knew* Axle was dead already because Gustavo told you. If he were still alive, there'd be no doubt he could implicate you. Knowing after the fact could get you hard time. And when you asked where Denise was hiding . . . nothing you'd have liked better than to give

Gustavo the whereabouts of a potential witness.

"Nothing to say?" I asked Milo when he remained silent. "I had a chance to have a nice visit with Gustavo at his cabin. I ran it by him about Emily tipping him off every time I was headed to his ranch, and he denied even talking with her since you hired her."

"He lied."

"No, he didn't." I dropped the cigarette butt onto his hardwood floor and scrunched it with my boot. "See, Gustavo had the drop on me. Intended to kill me any moment. He had no reason to lie to me, knowing I'd soon be dead." I kicked Milo's leg, and he yelled. "That leaves you."

"What are you going to do?"

"I've thought about that. A lot. It wouldn't do me any good to report you to the state investigators—I have no proof. Just like you'd have no proof that I busted you up just now. Now if Emily were at her desk, she could back up your statement." I stood. "Here's my suggestion—Erik Esterling will no longer have his truck-driving job subsided by Gustavo, so he'll effectively be out of a job, and he's got a family to support. I'd like to see him sitting there." I motioned to Milo's chair still against the wall behind his desk.

"But he dropped out of the race—"

"I know," I answered. "But if you announced your early retirement—as I suspect you'll do this week—the county commission will need to appoint someone to fill your . . . honest boots. And who better than the only other man interested in the job this last election."

"What will *I* do?"

I shrugged. "After you get your nose set and some emergency dental work? You could always go to your wife's ranch and tend to her horses. I understand there's a lot of manure generated from all the purebreds she raises."

I had started for the door when I heard Milo dragging himself along the floor. When I turned, he had just dipped his hand into the trash can.

I faced him and pulled my vest aside to show him my own gun. "There's nothing I'd love better right now than for you to come out of that trash can holding that hogleg of yours."

Milo withdrew his hand and sat back, bleeding, on the floor.

"That's what I thought," I said as I shut the door behind me.

I drove onto the dirt road leading to the Kincaid shanty and soon spotted a paint mustang coming my way. I stopped and climbed out while I waited for James to ride up.

"You got a smoke?"

I'd given up trying to reform the kid from his bad habits and tossed him my pack. "Lucille from Mom's Diner said you dropped off a quarter of beef at her place. That was a nice thing to do."

"It was, wasn't it?"

"It was. Especially since it was old man Gustavo's steer to begin with."

"Ask the old man to identify it."

"He's dead."

James smiled. "So I heard."

I motioned to a water bladder hanging from the pommel. "What's in there—moonshine from Napoli's still?"

James held up his hands. "I'm too young to drink," he said. "Want a nip?"

I would have if I actually thought it was just water.

"Where you off to now?" James asked.

"Back to Bison."

"Will you ever be down thisaway again?"

"Maybe for a wedding one day."

"What wedding?"

It was my turn to smile and taunt him. "The wedding to that filly from Worland you helped rescue from Napoli's barn. I heard you and she have been keeping company lately."

"Don't mean I'm going to marry her. She wants me to go back to school. And her papa thinks I can make it painting landscapes." James laughed. "Who ever heard of such a thing?" He waved his hand around the treeless span of the rundown Kinkaid spread. "I'm a free man, Marshal. I can't be held back—"

"When you supposed to see her again?"

James blushed, and I was enjoying every minute of it. "Her papa is supposed to bring her around this weekend. We plan on going for a ride." He patted Precious's neck. "Her on Peckerhead."

"Well, you take good care of Peckerhead," I said. "He took good care of me. He's doing all right then?"

James nodded and started coughing from the smoke. "That bullet wound on his rump is healing just fine."

"Then I got to make it home before nightfall," I said and climbed back into my shot-to-hell Ford panel.

"Marshal." James rode Precious over to the window. "Thanks for ridding the neighborhood of those thugs."

"My pleasure. And thanks for helping me do the ridding."

James smiled. "My pleasure."

EPILOGUE

I drove the five hours back to Bison, stretching it into six hours. I took my time to enjoy the scenery without the worry of someone shooting at me, stopping once to pick some wildflowers along the side of the road. And taking time to thank God I was still alive after these past few days. I thought back, knowing that at any time—whether it was the three thugs who murdered Wanda, or the Twins ambushing me, or my fights with Marco and Gustavo, not to mention Frankie Love—I could have been a dead man. And that was besides eating Lucille's horrible cooking.

By the time I pulled into my cabin on the forty acres up the mountain overlooking Bison, I was beat. But not so beat that I wouldn't say a kind word to my mule. Buckshot saw me and ambled across the pasture like I hadn't been gone but a few minutes. But I could tell he was glad to see me—his twitching tail always gave him away. He hung his head over the fence—sniffing the wild flowers in my hand—and I stroked his muzzle. "I had to use all the carrots for one of your cousins," I told him, but he didn't seem to mind. I ran my hand over his withers and felt the scars he'd gotten when he'd run into a farmer's corn field as a colt and took a load of buckshot.

He stayed with me but a few moments longer before turning and walking back across the field. He sensed, I'm certain, that I had another conversation waiting; the one I always had when I returned from the field.

I walked in back of the house to a white picket fence where I'd strung chicken wire to keep the rabbits out of the flowers I brought whenever I came home. I opened the gate and stepped inside the tiny compound, not sure what to think. Not sure what to say.

But then, I never did.

I closed the gate and stood a moment before laying the wildflowers reverently at Helen's grave. I squatted beside her marker—plain, with nothing more than her name and dates of birth and death. For all the pain I'd put her through, she deserved something more elaborate. But then, when she was alive, she needed nothing elaborate. Except my love, and I wasn't sure if she knew I was capable of loving through all the years of my stupor from the bottle. Perhaps, I thought, I'd get this marshaling out of my system. Get a real job that pays enough to afford a nice slab of granite, perhaps with an angel atop it. To represent what my wife certainly was.

But for now, all I could do was continue to hunt bad people and talk to my daughter now and again when I was home for a brief respite. And, sometimes, I'd find time to visit a trout stream that accepted my homemade flies. Anything that helped me stay sober. Which I somehow manage to do.

One day at a time.

ABOUT THE AUTHOR

C. M. Wendelboe entered the law enforcement profession when he was discharged from the Marines as the Vietnam War was winding down.

In the 1970s, his career included assisting federal and tribal law enforcement agencies embroiled in conflicts with American Indian movement activists in South Dakota.

He moved to Gillette, Wyoming, and found his niche, where he remained a sheriff's deputy for more than twenty-five years. In addition, he was a longtime firearms instructor at the local college and within the community.

During his thirty-eight-year career in law enforcement, he served successful stints as police chief, policy adviser, and other supervisory roles for several agencies. Yet he always has felt most proud of "working the street." He was a patrol supervisor when he retired to pursue his true vocation as a fiction writer.

The employees of Five Star Publishing hope you have enjoyed this book.

Our Five Star novels explore little-known chapters from America's history, stories told from unique perspectives that will entertain a broad range of readers.

Other Five Star books are available at your local library, bookstore, all major book distributors, and directly from Five Star/Gale.

Connect with Five Star Publishing
Visit us on Facebook:

https://www.facebook.com/FiveStarCengage

Email:
FiveStar@cengage.com

For information about titles and placing orders:
(800) 223-1244
gale.orders@cengage.com

To share your comments, write to us:
Five Star Publishing
Attn: Publisher
10 Water St., Suite 310
Waterville, ME 04901

